THE LAST ROMANTIC

THE LAST ROMANTIC

Dorothea Buské

St. Martin's Press
New York

Galley 2

F
Bus
— a

Copyright © 1979 by Dorothea Buské
All rights reserved. For information, write:
St. Martin's Press, Inc., 175 Fifth Ave., New York, N.Y. 10010.
Manufactured in the United States of America
Library of Congress Catalog Card Number: 78-3966

Library of Congress Cataloging in Publication Data

Buské, Dorothea.
  The last romantic.

  I. Title.
PZ4.B9794Las   [PS3552.U8232]   813'.5'4   78-3966
ISBN 0-312-47135-1

E. D. B.
1886–1974

and

F. C. B.
1889–1975

I

It is now twelve years since Celia came into their lives on an October afternoon in 1927, the lazy tag end of the day after the last class and the basketball practice. They were lying about on the west porch, still in gym clothes, in that angle of the school building where the sleepy afternoon sun had warmed the flagstones. Below the hill lay the broad river and the roofs of town, the white gleam of walls, between trees and hedges. There was a faint dry smell of leaf smoke and, across the valley, a breathtaking color on the mountainside. Somewhere a lawn mower cut its way through the quiet, a swathe of persistent sound running straight across the stillness.

Martha lay still, stretched out on the hard flags, their sun-stored warmth striking through her clothing, her sweater rolled under her head for a pillow. She was half-asleep with a sweet muscular weariness. Over her recumbent body the voices of the girls drifted back and forth in broken words and phrases, languid and desultory.

They were talking about the faculty-student basketball games. Bennett was ridiculing Mademoiselle's old jersey. Virginia giggled, a sound like water being poured from a bottle. Irritation fled along Martha's nerves like a hum over wire. This was the old antagonism between Bennett and Mademoiselle, carried on with the small, sharp, dishonorable weapon of ridicule.

"Half the fun of faculty games is the clothes."

A flutter of laughter arose, echoed around the porch

and flew out into the bright air. Where did the little sounds go? Martha wondered: the sharp bright fragments dancing on light, revolving in descent like bits of paper thrown up to come down . . .

The lawn mower had gone. The silence held a small neat sound of tennis balls whacking rhythmically back and forth out on the courts.

"Who's playing?" asked Virginia lazily.

Martha raised herself on one elbow. "Alicia."

The sun's horizontal rays, deepening to copper from gold, shone upon the southwest face of the building, firing the windows and the reddening ivy. The river lay in the valley, holding the expectation of evening in its clear stillness.

They heard The Taxi coming up the hill before they saw it turn into the school drive and pass from their sight to the front door. There was only one taxi in Hammondville: Mr. Sims' ancient asthmatic sedan, which he piloted to and from the railway station several times daily at a decorous twenty-five miles per hour. He was also in demand for funerals.

"Did anyone see who was inside?" wondered Virginia.

"Probably the new girl," drawled Bennett smugly.

Virginia rose immediately to the bait. "New girl? What new girl?"

"The one whose trunk was delivered yesterday while you were all in study. I went over to the Hall to get my history notes and it was being unloaded from the express truck. They put it in Jane Patten's old room, across from yours," she said to Martha.

Behind them the door opened and one of the younger girls put out her head.

"Martha MacLean. Miss Severn wants you in her office."

The head was withdrawn. The door clanged.

Said Lois quickly, "Martha, you're a sight. You can't go in to Julia like that. Take my comb. That's better; now run!"

Virginia's voice followed her, severed by the closing of the door. "Come back and tell us . . ."

[4]

The white walls and single tall east window gave Miss Severn's narrow little room an air of monastic severity. Miss Severn herself was seated at her desk, her back to the window. Her slim, cuffed wrists and blue-veined hands lay upon the blotter before her, easily, reposefully crossed, one upon the other. The top of the broad desk was exquisitely bare and neat. The appointments were few: a crystal inkwell, a silver paper knife, a leather calendar. Several letters which had been opened lay at one side, a clean pad of notepaper on the other.

Martha, apprehensively hesitating in the doorway, glanced quickly at her face. A little line between her brows, often seen, was absent. She looked up and smiled.

"Come in, Martha."

Relief weakened Martha's limbs. It wasn't bad news from home, then.

Julia Severn was, at that time, a youthful woman in her middle forties, with a certain severity of manner. Her dark eyes lightened as she smiled, momentarily dispelling the impression. Her short hair, dark at the nape, was even then whitening above her brow, as if age had touched her with a light and gentle hand.

The girls dared, privately, to call her "Julia"—a perverse form of admiration, which even Bennett uncritically shared.

Martha sensed rather than saw that she was not alone in the room.

"Martha, this is Celia Pence."

Thus, her oldest memory of Celia: Celia at sixteen, seeming taller than she was because of her slenderness, at once fragile and awkward. Seeming younger than she was because of her deceptive air of naiveté, and her clothes—a plain dark blue coat, cotton stockings, and childish square-toed shoes. Her hair was cut in a thick dust-brown bang hiding her forehead; beneath it her topaz-colored eyes looked out of her small face, unsmiling, transparent and calm.

"Celia comes to us from France, where she has lived most of her life, so although she is an American girl, much of our life here will be strange to her. You will see that she becomes acquainted with the school and the Hall, her fellow students, and her instructors." Miss Severn smiled again, fleetingly, at Martha.

Coming to the front of the desk, she placed a light hand on each girl's shoulder. "Celia, this is Martha. Martha MacLean. I commend you to each other. Mrs. Gracie is expecting you. *Allons!*" Her hands flew upward with that airy, flexible turn of the wrist which Martha was always to remember—in the wonderful way whereby a sound, a scent, a gesture is able through a long lifetime to reopen a whole lost book of living.

Together, they passed out of the darkening school into the late amber sunlight. Avoiding the group on the porch, she took Celia out by another way, across the lawns, skirting the now deserted tennis courts, to the Hall. As they went, they heard the small anonymous sound of voices in the stillness.

Celia turned a bright, quizzical look upon her. "Is this your job? Do you like doing it?"

"It's a tradition at Severn, a sort of sister thing. This is my first time." She knew why she had been chosen. Not because of any particular qualification of her own; rather because of lack among the others. Lois was too shy, Bennett too intimidating, Virginia too frivolous . . . The feeling of Miss Severn's touch upon her shoulder was an accolade. She was not quick, or clever, or challenging; but dimly she knew that she had some quality of heart or mind in which Julia believed. At fifteen, self-knowledge was fragmentary and elusive. Not knowing herself was like walking blind with hands outstretched for the touch of some familiar thing; but that is looking backward out of the knowledge which is the present.

Then, all she knew was that she wished to do what Miss Severn had commissioned, to welcome Celia Pence to this place as Alicia Whittaker had welcomed her three years before, with a steady friendliness lending courage in the midst of strangeness. But Celia was four years older than she had been; and she did not know that Celia would always carry with her her own courage, so that even when she had gone, willfully, to tread thorns where another's patience was of no avail, she bore with her a kind of glory to blind her to danger.

Walking there beside her, Martha wondered whether this girl, three years hence, would recall her first days at Severn with warm gratitude for remembered friendliness—and felt the touch of prescience. Three years! They would be gone from here then; all of them, including Alicia, whose swift balls had been flying over this court half an hour since, those back there on the porch, and she herself . . . Scattered, departed; and walking here over the short grass, in and out of these buildings on the sunlit height, accepting the beneficence of books to the hand and the worn edges of desks beneath their wrists, and the bright bronze of autumn on the hills . . . others. The unknown, unimagined faces of the usurpers crowded about her like an enemy host unseen, waiting in ambush. All at once time was not limitless and must not be heedlessly spent; that which one loves is constantly in jeopardy, and time is the thief.

She would not realize for some time that Celia's coming marked the beginning of awareness, of an emergence from careless acceptance, which has no name. Yet even on that first evening she was captive to a personality utterly unlike Bennett's aggressiveness, Virginia's avidity, or even Alicia's forthright dependability. Immediately apparent was Celia's composure, oddly at variance with her childish appearance; the way in which her calm regard rested upon Martha, giving her an identity in her own eyes. From their first hour there was no awkwardness between them—as if they had been traveling toward each other across a wide distance, hands outstretched, until their fingertips touched . . .

Bennett was right, as she so often was; Celia's trunk had been placed in the room across the hall from Martha's. Downstairs the maids were getting dinner. A light would be burning in the dark pantry; the swinging door to the dining room would creak as they passed in and out, Sylvia banging down the plates, rattling the silver, her bright yellow hair stuck behind her ears, humming and smiling to herself. Quiet and quick and plain, Elsie would be laying the napkins, placing the centerpiece, filling the glasses, the water sighing upward to the rims . . .

"I'm supposed to help you unpack," said Martha. "Do you have your trunk key?"

"Let's not," Celia replied carelessly. She crossed the room and sat on the floor under the open window. "There's a lovely smell, a warm smell, left over from the afternoon." Her clear voice became part of the evening, colorless, tranquil, pure.

Martha sat on the edge of the single bed. In the darkening room the lighter square of the window still held the crowns of trees, dark now, and of an indistinct color. The outlines of the furniture and the trunk blurred out of angularity.

Distinctly, like pebbles dropped one by one into still water, Celia's separate sentences echo in her memory. "There are no stars!" One sentence, quiet with regret, from that first evening.

There were none, but with a quick anxiety Martha wished for stars, that Celia, to whom she was already committed, might find no flaw. She saw Celia's face tipped upward to the clear gray evening light, her heavy hair fallen back upon her shoulders. The last light fell palely on the tender outline of her cheek, which curved inward at the corner of her mouth as if she were smiling, and on the immature line of her slender throat promising loveliness. She found herself wanting to go to Celia, to kneel beside her, to lift that heavy soft hair upon her hands; wanting to feel its warmth about her wrists, to relieve those slim, childishly angular shoulders of its weight.

"Julia—Miss Severn—said you had lived in France. Is your family now here, in this country, also?" The question was hesitant, stilted. She didn't want to push against the reserve which seemed to envelop Celia, but she suddenly wanted to know her, to be close to her, closer than she had ever been to any of the girls she knew.

Celia did not answer for a lengthening moment. Then, without turning her head, she said, in a voice which had somehow lost its resonance, "My father died three months ago. My mother died when I was a baby. I have a half sister in New York who is my guardian."

"I'm sorry . . ."

The house brooded in stillness. The first pale stars finally appeared.

Downstairs a gong was struck three times lightly. A door opened and closed somewhere along the hall. There was the unfinished sound of footsteps, the fragment of a whistled tune, another door closing. In the room above, a chair was pushed back, footsteps sounded over their heads.

"We have half an hour to get ready for dinner," she told Celia, moving at last. "Wear a dress—something simple—just so it isn't a blouse and skirt."

In her own room across the hall, she switched on the light and drew the shades. The narrow bed stood against one wall, her student's table against the other. The bureau was in a corner between the windows. There were three photographs in front of the mirror: one each of her mother and father, her vivaciously attractive mother looking slightly unnatural in satin, her hands palm upward in her lap. Between them was a snapshot enlargement of Austin. It was not a very good picture, but it gave her his length and his slimness, his smile against the sun.

In Glen Fells her mother and father were sitting down to dinner. By this time, Miss Severn had left her office and had gone up the hill to her neat little house. Thinking of the beautiful warm afternoon just past, and of Celia across the hall, she stood poised in wonder, savoring content, not knowing that this was perfection which she would hold and cherish, neither dreaming nor desiring any future beyond this enchanted present . . . and long remember.

The second gong sounded in the lower hall. Doors opened quickly all along the corridor; steps sounded on the stairs coming down from the top floor; voices broke out quickly in the quiet, one after the other. She put out her light and stood waiting. As they went past her door, someone asked, "What-

[9]

ever happened to Martha?" A little secret smile curved her lips. When the last heels had thudded down the stairs, she went to Celia's door.

Thirty years had passed since that gentle, learned man, Julia Severn's father, opened his School for Young Ladies. Traditions were begun then, when Julia herself was fifteen, one of the four original young ladies. Now there were over a hundred girls, day and boarding students; a dignified building; a smart catalog (which had captivated Martha's mother)—and the hovering spirit of an ardent idealist whose aspirations for youth, kept constantly before them by his dedicated daughter, were his immortality.

Here Martha had found her spiritual home, a life precisely suitable for her personal need of an uncomplicated serenity. At Severn the roar of the Twenties was a distant subdued murmur.

Severn School was not a finishing school for daughters of the wealthy. As a school its purpose was the deepening of an appreciation of life, a preparation for living designed to utilize the creative talent of the individual. Without stridency, it put forth the idea that these young women could and would avail themselves of any of several options in choosing a career. They were, almost without exception, granddaughters of a working class which sent its sons (and sometimes its daughters) to college. These sons, if they survived the Great War, had, as business men and professionals during the Twenties, achieved an upper-middle-class status which afforded them the good things in life—houses, cars, smart clothes, club memberships, domestic help, and a congenial social milieu.

When the Hall was opened, later, Severn became a boarding school. Martha came with the first of the boarders, and Bennett, who was a day student from town, moved in. Helena Gracie's story endowed her with a romantic aura and endeared her to the girls who found themselves under her roof. All the properties of her charm enhanced her influence over them: her silver-blonde hair, her quiet voice and smile, the loveliness of her profile, her early widowhood. Certain of the girls who had been household terrors at home (like Bennett) became sociable beings, consciously or unconsciously emulating her. In her presence, natural rowdiness was dampened, voluntarily, and small hostilities were concealed.

There was a time when lights blazed late in the Gracies' big house at the top of the hill and music could be heard faintly down in the town on summer nights. Hammondville families like Bennett's could remember when the Major came home from a year in France, 1917–18, with a shattered ankle and a permanent limp. They remembered his red Stutz roadster, his broad shoulders and his grin, and the winter night when lights burned until dawn in the big house; but there was no music because the Major lay dying of pneumonia. (Five years earlier, while he was overseas, his father, the Judge, had died in the same house, and then, too, the watcher was Helena Gracie.)

After the Major died, she had the house, the furniture, and the red roadster, but very little money. She also had a daughter, Lois, in the fifth grade at Severn School. That spring, from the windows of the school (if anyone noticed) a fair young woman could have been seen pacing back and forth on the flagged terrace under the trees. She paused, one day, raising her eyes to the walls where the ivy climbed, and an idea was born. Julia Severn was her friend; they had been girls together, and Helena had been one of the original four pupils of Professor Martin Severn.

Celia would never know the Hall as Martha had first known it, with its air of careless luxury, the deeply napped rugs rich and bright, the upholstered chairs and sofas unacquainted with the vigorous weariness of young bodies. All through the house colors had grown grayer, paler; the curtains were faded, and the girls identified the sheets by their neat patches. Comfort remained though elegance had fled, and the essential notes of graciousness were indestructible: the chime of the musical dinner gong, the breadth of the mahogany dining table, the carved mantels and wide fireplaces.

[11]

The upstairs study had been the Major's sleeping porch. Always, for Martha, thinking of the Hall and their years together, a memory of evenings in this room comes uppermost. The picture is static, although the life of that room was a flowing thing: a room full of windows, their black night surfaces giving back the lighted interior. There stood the big desk in the center with its large reading lamp, light shining from under the green cone of its shade on the smooth bent heads of the girls, upon the white pages of opened books, slanting across the dull lettered bindings of many books in the tall shelves flanking the doorway. The lamp spread a pool of light in a circle around the desk; the corners of the room were in shadow.

There was Alicia, who was going to study medicine. She read anatomy books as if they were novels, one knee bent up to hold the heavy book, her brow furrowed, her head thrust forward, drowned in seeking and the world vanished away. In the other corner, Lois, with her leg slung over the arm of her chair, was preoccupied with *Silas Marner*. Lois had none of her mother's prettiness; she was large and bony and freckled as her father had been. A lock of her sandy hair fell diagonally across her forehead, hiding her left eye.

The sofa was Bennett's place; she lay on her stomach, her chin in her cupped hands, her eyes moving from one to the other, not reading, momentarily immobile.

. . . Oh, sometime it must have been spring or young summer and the trees thick with leaves standing quiet in the night outside those windows; but sharply, sharply, in her mind's eye, Martha can see a car flying down the road which was not visible when there were leaves. She can see bare November branches moving in the wind, and the fitful glimmer of street lamps and scattered lights down the valley. On such a night Bennett, bored with study, flung down her book and began walking relentlessly across the room and back, seeking diversion; and Martha recalls how, within her own body, unease stirred and curled, anticipating malice.

Bennett leaned against the doorpost, her thumbs hooked

in her belt. Her narrow black eyes glimmered, a sign of her boredom, preliminary of her sarcasm. She could be witty or she could be ridiculous and revolting like a small boy, with grimaces and uncouth imitations of mannerisms which she knew were irritating. At such times they were embarrassed for her, and she enjoyed their embarrassment. She was the smallest of the girls; straight black hair framed a small pale face freckled from brow to chin. She intimidated the girls and some of her teachers. Her mother was a determined, efficient, domineering woman who had been unable to control her only child in all of her fifteen years. Her sense of failure had made her deal more severely with Bennett than she otherwise might have done. It was a relief to the entire household when the Hall opened its doors and Bennett demanded a room there. Her grandfather, to her surprise, seconded her request. He foresaw, rightly, that the benign influences of Julia Severn and Helena Gracie, coupled with a sense of independence, might benefit his granddaughter's stormy temperament.

Still, having lived all her life in an atmosphere of stress and friction, Bennett occasionally missed its excitement. This was one of those times.

Pushing out her lower lip scornfully, she threw down a challenge for Alicia. "I wonder . . . Is it a scientific mind or a morbidly curious one?"

Alicia smiled faintly but did not raise her eyes from the page.

Bennett drew down the corners of her mouth. "If there's anything exciting in those old books, you might share it with us. Selfish." A lively note of derision entered her voice. "It's either morbidity or indecency, wanting to cut people open . . ."

Celia laid down her pen and leaned back, rubbing her finger. She looked up at Bennett and her eyes were bright with impudence. She moved her shoulders lightly in the way she knew Bennett disliked because it reminded her of Celia's French background. Bennett meant to be a writer; she meant

[13]

to be famous; someday she meant to live and work among people who "did things." Until Celia came, "someday" had been enough, but Celia had already known the world she desired, and her envy was a sudden and passionate thing.

Celia said gently, "No worse, cutting people up than impaling them alive like butterflies on pins, and watching them squirm. Nor half so indecent to be morbid as to be cruel, my dear."

There was a shouting silence in the room. Within her breast Martha felt her heart stand still, quivering in the shadow of strife. At last she dared to look up. Celia was still smiling at Bennett.

Bennett was not smiling; her face, her eyes, her whole body were impassive, but she was looking at Celia with malevolent unbelief. At length she moved, shrugging her shoulders; and the gesture was an unconscious caricature.

"Idle wit," she remarked bitingly, "must have been included in the curriculum of your last school."

"All of us were not *born* clever, alas!" replied Celia softly, and picked up her pen.

She bent her head and her hand began to travel smoothly across the white paper as before. Opposite, Martha looked at the shadow of her lashes on her cheeks, and the mild even arch of her brows, knowing that nevermore would Bennett possess the old power of making her nerves vibrate with the fear of her cruelty.

In the morning, gray light lay upon the walls and ceiling; before the open window the curtains hung still. There was no wind now, only the soft, sweet, incessant sound of rain . . . rather like a spring rain if you closed your eyes and listened, not seeing the cold early light, not feeling the chill which stood in the room.

The bright golden autumn was gone. All night, somewhere, a shutter had banged, disturbing at first, then the monotonous accompaniment of dreams and the sound of the November wind, rising and falling, and the occasional slash of rain on the windows.

Alicia was in the shower, singing "Die Lorelei" in careful dignified German syllables. Bennett was in the other bath at the opposite end of the hall, drawing water so that the pipes thundered. Memory evokes the chilly mornings, clammy feel of cold carpet under bare feet thrust warm out of bed, the quick slam of doors, the urgent notes of the breakfast gong. The evocation brings with it a small pain of regret for the uncomplicated, irretrievable past.

Helena was sitting at the head of the breakfast table. Valley and mountain had vanished into the mist of rain beyond long windows overlooking the terrace. Trees were standing like shadows at the edge of the invisible. All the wet, bright, fallen leaves were scattered in a random pattern over the lawn, the drive, and the shining flagstones. Lights were burning bright on the girls' faces and their busy hands, on the neat partings of their hair, on the large glass sugar bowl in the center of the table.

Helena murmured to herself about things which must not be forgotten, scribbling on the pad beside her plate. Someone made a remark about the change in the weather. Mademoiselle, leaning above the faint warmth of her teacup, said she had shivered all night. She was always cold or hungry, stretching her long hands above the radiators, eating with downcast eyes, in quick economical mouthfuls, as if she were saving against a leaner time.

Sylvia came in with the steaming plates of cereal, carrying a large tray shoulder-high, thrusting open the swinging door with her hip.

Helena made a note. " 'Extra blankets for Mademoiselle's bed.' "

The sugar went around. Steam was snapping in the radiators. In the kitchen Sylvia laughed, a high sound quickly stifled. Helena scribbled.

". . . loose shutter . . . order coal . . . flour . . . Lois, dear," she said, raising her voice slightly, "don't go over to school without your slicker this morning."

They all wore yellow slickers. Celia's raincoat was gray, made of cloth like a man's. They looked like a gaudy flock of giant canaries with a dove in their midst as they set out.

First class of the morning that year was Letty Leonard's English II in the big room upstairs facing south; the room cheerful with light and Letty's pictures and Letty's presence. The pictures were Watts' Galahad and blinded Hope, Will Shakespeare with his chin on his ruff, pen and ink drawings of Oxford and Rheims. Late in the year had been added a delicate, pencil-drawn head of young Lindbergh, very blond, with a young mouth, the deep cleft in his chin noticeable and touching.

Martha remembers Letty at the blackboard writing review questions in a firm round hand, a moving gleam of light on the smooth crown of her golden head. A certain light blue woolen dress. A gesture of fingertips dusted lightly together. Letty, in her first year out of college, was not much older than they were. She ran away one day with a young man who worked in the mills at Bakersville and thus became a legend at Severn with her pink-shaded boudoir lamp, her blue satin nightgowns, and her tam o' shanter.

In the French room, Mademoiselle stood at the window looking out at the rain flowing down the shingles, a small river in the angle of the roof, rippling from shingle to shingle, hurrying, hurrying . . . She did not turn as they came in. There was no light burning in the narrow room. The high double windows faced northeast. There was a row of chairs against the longer wall, a table used by Mademoiselle as a desk, a bookshelf under the windows. No pictures, only a large map of France hanging in front of the blackboard.

(Martha's imagination endowed the map with magic images: land of Rouen, where young Jeanne d'Arc in an orchard under the apple trees heard voices . . . Rivers of wine flowing out into the gray salt sea, dark and smooth, breathing upon old walls and old stones of port cities with a rich fragrance.)

Mademoiselle stayed motionless at the window, staring out at the stripped trees crowning the summit of the hill, and the wet road going up, as if she did not hear the confusion they made in finding their places. In the unlighted room only her silhouette could be seen: her profile with the wispy bang curving out above her large nose, the flat little knot at the back of her head. Pale light from the window lay upon her cheek and down the front of her dress. She had a nice little figure with a high rounded bosom and a neat waist.

When it was finally quiet, she turned and walked to her desk. Without looking at them, as if they were not there, she pulled a book from the standing row with her long forefinger and opened it, holding it upon her spread hand. Her long colorless nails looked dingy against the olive green cover. She paused, raising her eyes to look at them. Her gaze blurred vaguely, as if her thought had gone beyond them. Martha saw her shoulders move as she sighed.

"Today we read," she said in French. The corners of her mouth moved slightly downward with disdain. "Page fifty-two: Lois, if you please . . ."

Lois rose, cleared her throat nervously and read haltingly for half a page.

(Celia was born in France. She had gone to school there in a convent, taught by smooth-faced Sisters who moved like shadows, swiftly and quietly, and sometimes laughed together like merry girls. She had seen chestnuts bloom in Paris, and the lilac; she knew the color of the Seine and had sat at the little round tables in sidewalk cafes, watching people stroll by and the lights also bloom softly in the Paris twilights . . .)

When Celia read in French, going on from where Lois had faltered to a stop, one saw all these things having never seen them—saw Mademoiselle stand still, attentive, and her face lose its look of weary disdain.

Martha's turn came to read. Looking up at the end of a

paragraph, she found Mademoiselle regarding her with the old expression of impersonal scorn.

There was an incident one morning in the studio. Celia had been with them for over a month.

Art classes were the high point of the week: a full hour on Mondays, Wednesdays, and Fridays. The studio was their favorite room. At the high windows, deep blue strips of curtain pulled far back framed a view of the town spilling itself down the hill and out on the floor of the valley, a pattern of streets, roofs, and spires, the clustering bungalows pushing out toward Bakersville, rails curving in from the south, smoke rising from factory chimneys, mountains converging at the end of the valley with the river twisting in its length.

Half-finished work, work just begun, oils, watercolors, charcoal sketches, and pastels stood on easels around the room. The walls were covered with finished work from floor to ceiling. The closet doors stood wide; the shelves were stacked with paper, canvas, stretchers, tubes of color, boxes of chalks, crayons and charcoal. On long shelves below the windows, pots of brushes stood bunched like spears. The clean, exciting smell of stationery lived in the room, flavored by the combined essences of oil and turpentine.

Celia was working in charcoal. The grace of her hands, small and supple, with deft strong fingers and a neat bone in each wrist, was beautiful to see. Her hair, fallen forward, hid her face.

Miss Dilling came and paused behind her chair. Her eyes narrowed critically.

"Child . . ." At the mysterious note of excitement those nearest looked up. "Was Hubert Pence a relative of yours?"

Without pausing in her work, Celia said clearly, "He was my father."

Miss Dilling caught her breath, nodded once, touched Celia's shoulder, and left her.

Later Martha heard the whispers flying, flying . . . Who was

[18]

Hubert Pence? . . . Had Miss Dilling known him? . . . Where? . . . And yet not known his daughter? Was this romance, scandal, or deception? . . . For here was Celia come into their midst, unsuspectingly accepted as a stranger, and yet not a stranger; now, suddenly, in some manner beyond their knowing, distinguished. Was Hubert Pence . . . *Who* was Hubert Pence? . . .

Bennett's mother was one of those people who read newspapers as part of their day's work, carefully and assiduously, down to the last remote item from Tangier or Tiptonville. Horty's mother, whose hope of a career on the stage had died aborning with a comfortable and secure marriage, was interested in the Arts.

A clipping came to light. And another. From the obituary column of a respected New York newspaper and the pages of a magazine devoted to gossip about the lives of famous people.

Hubert Pence was an American painter and expatriate who had died at Interlaken of a heart attack during the past summer. Considerable space was given this story because it included repetition of an older one. There was a brief résumé of his career, a necessarily casual appraisal of his work, and a list of his better-known pictures including, of course, "Nightshade" and "Smile in a Mirror," which had enjoyed the popularity which led to calendar reproductions and framed copies on sale in art stores. In fact, for an earlier generation, in what was later known as his Middle Period, he had shared in the popularity of such painters as Maxfield Parrish. Later, with the radical change in his work, he "abandoned" his public and was, in turn, quickly forgotten. For a time, however, he was *news:* his past, what there was of it . . . his marriages . . . his amorous exploits (which may have been largely the work of journalistic imagination), and his manner of living (bohemian and expatriate in the world of Cézanne and Picasso and the Steins; and, of course, later, the bittersweet postwar years of the Lost Generation, although he was too old to have been a part of it).

Like many of his artistic and literary compatriots, he had

earned his professional reputation abroad after arid years of struggle and obscurity on this side of the Atlantic. With the coming of recognition and opportunity, willfully or otherwise he had acquired another kind of reputation. As the first step, he was divorced by his wife, Lilian Reed Pence, whom he had married in their native Iowa when he was not yet twenty. In the uncontested divorce action she charged him with desertion and retained custody of their child, a daughter. It was true that Pence never again returned to the country of his birth, but it was also true that Lilian lived with him for three years in Paris before she returned to New York with their two-year-old daughter.

During the eight years which followed the divorce, Pence led a well-publicized life, climbing to maturity on the stepping-stones of his popular art and the fame of his amorous adventures. His name was coupled with the photogenic and moneyed beauties of London, Paris, and Rome at one time or another in those years; he worked hard and, it was rumored, lived and played as hard as he worked.

Then he met and married, after a "whirlwind courtship," a young English girl named Cecily Stone. The entire affair— Paris elopement, the bride's youth and beauty, the opposition of her guardians (she was an heiress, an orphan, and not of age) —furnished Sunday-supplement material for weeks. In spite of the opposition to the marriage, however, the expected annulment was never initiated. The marriage was allowed to stand.

The second Mrs. Pence was only seventeen when Celia was born in a Paris spring. A few weeks before her nineteenth birthday, young Mrs. Pence was killed in a motor accident on the Riviera. She had acquired a reputation for liking fast cars and fast companions. Innuendo had it that her husband was not the man with her when she was killed.

Hubert Pence had not married again. He entered his Third Period, during which he passed into a kind of obscurity as his new work was experimental and of little interest to his former admirers. His last years were spent in peaceful penury in Paris. The guardians had established a small trust for Cecily's daughter and the rest of his wife's estate reverted to other heirs. When this fact became known, it explained why there had been no annulment—Pence had, apparently, married for love and had no interest in his wife's wealth. So romance had been allowed to have its way.

The papers, having given much space to the background of this life now ended, would have been happy to wring one last drop of bizarre sentimentality from its conclusion, but the heart attack was genuine and the circumstances commonplace, the final curtain upon a drama which had its beginning in a small white frame house in an Iowa small town. The artist was survived only by his daughters, Lilian Reed Pence of New York City, and Celia Rosemary Pence "at school in France." The first Mrs. Pence had died in 1918 of influenza.

There were popular girls at Severn. Celia was not popular. She wore that subtle mark of difference which is sufficient in itself to nurture a veiled enmity in a feminine world, but because a girls' school is so small a world, only two relationships are possible: friendly and unfriendly. Therefore, after some time had passed, she was accepted. A stranger would not have known the difference; you must live with it in order, not to know, but to sense the nervous disparity between friendship and tolerance.

The circulation of Bennett's and Horty's clippings made no appreciable difference in their attitude toward Celia. Guileless souls like Lois and Alicia may never have seen them. The avid little group which conducted the research held its discussions in private. (After all, what good was a secret that was no secret?) But Bennett thrust the pieces of newsprint in front of Martha, her gamin face alive with mockery. Martha knew that by now her own swift, unreasoning attraction to Celia was no secret. All through her life her feelings would be transparent to others—save in one instance.

She handed back the clippings. "I don't see that this makes any difference to us—or to Celia," she said. But her heart twisted within her as she imagined herself in Celia's place: coming to a new life, possibly unaware of the wreath of scandal woven about the names and memories of both parents whose brief drama had been colored by romance and talent and an impetuous zest for living, suddenly confronted by this nauseous sensationalism.

Bennett lifted a deprecating shoulder. "Coming events cast their shadows before, perhaps. As the twig is bent, and so on, you know."

If Celia knew about the gossip she gave no indication. For a period less prolonged than intense, Martha lived in apprehension lest it confront her suddenly. Inwardly, during those days, she prayed that Celia might not taunt Bennett; knowing that Bennett felt that she now had a weapon to turn on her. Later she knew that it was possible for Celia to know and not to care; that, even then, she had passed beyond innocence, so that Martha's fear and pity were as unavailing as Bennett's malice.

This was the first of her fears for Celia, and the least. Greater ones were to follow and she was powerless to arm herself against them. Her inexperience, devotion, and the prudence blended of training and instinct could not look at Celia and fail to see a prophetic vision of disaster. In time she was forced to accept this.

There was the usual four-day recess at Thanksgiving. Martha was shocked to find that Celia was not going home for the holiday, that she would be virtually alone at the school except for the Gracies. Celia had no real home; she had only a couch in the studio-living room of her half sister's New York apartment for those awkward nights which would occur, unavoidably, between the months at school and the weeks of summer . . . Martha realized suddenly that Celia would become one of those adolescents shuttled between school and camp.

Hubert had divided his modest estate between his daughters, appointing the elder guardian of the younger. It was not a happy arrangement. Celia sketched the picture for Martha with light, acid strokes of a mature perception: "Lilian is very, very 'career woman'—highbrow lit., drama, and a string of young and not-so-young men—executives, she calls them. Marriage?" She shrugged lightly. "I'm not sure she wants it. Or maybe the ones she would consider are already married. She likes the money she makes, I think; likes to come home and kick off her shoes and be as grumpy as she pleases. Everlasting charm can be a strain, you know. She puts on her smoothness and her charm with her clothes when she goes out . . . No, I don't think she would enjoy helping some nice young man struggle up the ladder. No ties and no responsibilities—except at the office."

Celia's topaz-colored eyes held a glint of laughter.

"My father did a dreadful thing to her, but he hadn't seen her in years; she was *two* when her mother took her back to America. I wonder what he thought she'd be like." Her gaze turned absent. "He never forgot her. 'Your older sister—' He was an idealist, my father." She sighed. "So here I am, the embarrassment . . ."

"I wish you were going home with me," said Martha miserably. "I wish I'd known sooner. You have to get your guardian's permission to visit away from the school, and a letter of invitation from your hostess. Trustees' rules. To protect the school, you know. They're responsible for us from September to June."

Celia smiled. "I'll be all right. I don't mind being alone sometimes. But ask me for Christmas, instead. That's almost three weeks—a bit too long. The Gracies will feel they have to include me in everything during their holiday and that could be awkward . . ."

Now it no longer seems strange to Martha that one day Celia rebelled against rootlessness and then reverted, whatever guise her compulsion wore; not strange, only painful. In justice to Lilian Pence it should be said, perhaps, that the beginnings were older; they went back to high, bare rooms and a bohemianism which had contained all that Celia knew of home and love.

But, again, knowledge is too late.

Martha's train moved out of Hammondville with the lonely sound of gathering speed, clacking smoothly mile on mile through a rural landscape whose hilly distances were lit by November sunlight so mild it scarcely cast shadow. Her thoughts were all of Celia left behind in the school on the hill. Her sense of separation was so intense it was like a bereavement. She was experiencing for the first time the animate pain of longing. Almost from the first hours of her relationship with Celia, she began to experience new emotions—small fears, strange delights, obscure regrets—which until then had been unknown to her serene existence.

At Glen Fells Rodney, the chauffeur, met her train. The Packard slid suavely through the town. The sunlight seemed brighter there, falling on the fronts of buildings, on the parked cars lining the curbs, on the quiet tide of well-dressed shoppers moving along the sidewalks. The plate-glass windows shone opulently, displaying the new winter fashions. The graceful mannequins were posed this way and that, their hands held up in arrested grace, as if a spell had been laid upon them. Women lingered in contemplation before windows arranged to show the new boxy shapes of modern furniture. There were shops with silver and china, one with leather goods suggesting travel to far places. People were going briskly in and out of the bank on the corner, passing between the Ionic columns of the porch; the glass doors swung first in, then out, flashing light.

They turned the corner by St. Paul's Episcopal into Raynold Road, and her sense of homecoming increased. There is an irreproachable dignity in an avenue lined with tall elms. Martha loved the vista between their arching branches. The heartbreak of change and decay were real for her in a later summer when disease rusted their leaves and a small army of booted young men passed that way, marking them for execution; but that November day the gentle arcade was still unbroken and the lawns, hesitating between green summer and sere winter, were a nameless color in the clear sunlight. She saw

[24]

a gardener working, raking the gravel of a long drive; a pile of leaf-ash smoldering at the edge of the road, sending up a faint spiral of smoke; a long gleaming car parked before an entrance. They passed the Birketts'—the Walds'—old Madame de Vary's.

The road went up a little hill. She was almost home.

It was late afternoon on Friday, the day after Thanksgiving, which had been a family day with dinner just for the three of them. A fire glowed redly behind the screen, falling asunder in a soft shower of sparks at quiet intervals. She looked at the room reflected in the bellied silver side of the teapot which had been her grandmother's. There was the tiniest dent in its smoothness. She wondered how it happened to have got there; had someone dropped it?

The room was filled with people, the tinkle of thin china, an oppression of voices and laughter. The ladies were drinking tea. They wore straight slim frocks and long strands of pearls which fell into their laps as they sat. Some were wearing little hats which hugged their heads and enclosed their ears. Their brief skirts showed their legs, long and silken.

Her mother moved among the guests, neat and slender, with short smooth reddish hair just a shade brighter than her own; that changeless, vital color which in a few years other women, graying, would say was dyed.

Not difficult to remember that holiday—any holiday during those school years—for they were all similarly patterned in submission to the restless, eager spirit of her mother. Martha had been patient up to now, giving a little of herself, a little of her time, to please her mother, knowing that there would be other hours, hours of escape; but Austin was in England that year, and a strange new feeling burned within her—the rebellious, impatient, lonely desire of a new self which she was lately discovering. Her hand, lifting the silver teapot automatically above a succession of cups, felt heavy and listless.

A voice detached itself from the polite clamor. A breath of

scent enclosed her with it in a small privacy. She said, ". . . a lovely time, thank you," and felt like an actress playing a bad part. Then she said, "Lemon?" And again, "Yes, until Sunday . . ." Only until Sunday, then she would be on her way back to Celia and her other self.

Left alone for a moment, she looked for her father's erect figure standing near the fireplace in a group of men. He was easily the youngest and best-looking man in the room.

"You'll have to introduce me to your bootlegger, Doug," said one of the men, holding up his glass appreciatively.

"You'd be farther ahead if you'd let me introduce you to my broker," said her father, laughing.

With an odd detachment she listened to the laughter in the room, gusts of banter from the men mingling with ripples of mirth and vivacity from the women. The carefree enjoyment of these people was, she knew, a compliment to her parents, in whose charming house they had gathered. For their sakes she should try to adapt more graciously to this routine. It was never for long—a few hours now and then out of a life she lived pretty much according to her own desires.

How would it feel, she wondered, to be Celia—footloose and all but alone in her life? . . .

In the special peace of that postholiday Saturday, she went out of a quiet house. It was midmorning: another day of sun with a sharp little wind blowing from the east. She faced into it, crossing the wide fields to the wood a mile or so distant. An old habit turned her eyes to the Cutting place. While Austin was away his mother was visiting friends in Connecticut. Williams, the chauffeur, and Mrs. Maxwell, the little Scottish housekeeper, had been given a vacation but would be back to ready the house for Christmas and Mrs. Cutting's return. Meanwhile, the place had a lonely look borrowed from her imagination because she knew no one was there; the tranquil look of a house surrounded by the individual beauty of fine trees, elms flaring tall on their stems, heavy-crowned oaks and maples, the light gray tracery of beechwood against a gentle distance of hills and sky. Behind the house lay the old stable building with its clock tower, used as a garage and storage for garden tools. There were no horses now; when she and Austin rode, they hired mounts from the livery stables at Brookside. At the west side of the house were the gardens; beyond them the lawns rolled gently down into what she and Austin called "the valley," a shallow, grassy declivity between their adjoining properties.

The house was a large Victorian home, built by Austin's grandfather to house a large family which failed to materialize. There were only three children: Austin's father, an older brother, and a young sister who had died of diphtheria in her tenth year. The house, to which Mrs. Cutting had come as a bride in the late Nineties, had for Martha a romantic fascination from the first days of her acquaintance with it. This was the touchstone of a past which had produced Austin: polished mahogany and walnut, long windows letting in light along the floor, the high-ceilinged library, the curved and shining balustrade on the stairs, English Spode, Ruskin bound in dark leather, and Mrs. Cutting's carefully executed oil paintings— products of a slight talent and the "lessons" fashionable in her girlhood.

It seemed now, in the late Twenties, as if the Cuttings had always lived in Glen Fells. There were still a few members of the original families, like Madame de Vary, living in ornate old houses of the Victorian period, attended by servants who lived under the same roof. The "new people" (even after five years, the young MacLeans and most of their friends were still in this category) lived in large recently built stucco homes, pseudo-English Tudor and French Norman architectural fancies on spacious grounds beautifully and expensively landscaped. Their maids came in by the day and went home at night to the unfashionable part of the town which lay "under the hill."

During those five years Martha's memory of the city apartment in which she had spent the first years of her life grew fainter, until it seemed that she had never known any other home.

In an easy partnership with time, Austin Cutting, the amiable fair-haired boy who lived across the wide lawns, had made her over, transforming the prim city-bred child into a long-legged tomboy. They were vivid years, and she was becoming aware that their particular magic was now doomed to change or die. While both were in their school years, each the only child of his parents, they were to each other as the brother or sister each might have had. Now Austin was a man. He was almost seven years older than she; and life and death had combined to sweep him away, out into the deeper currents.

The brown November fields reached away to the line of the wood. Summers, she and Austin rode here. She remembered their cross-country canters, Austin passing her, turning in the saddle: "Come on, Slowpoke!" She saw again his slim figure against the sky, felt the summer wind on her cheek, her hair lifted from her temples as she leaned into it, and a little ahead, the blue challenge of a boy's jumper. He had taught her to ride, to skate, to swim. Everything she knew that was joyous and free was connected with Austin. Together, they had known days filled with a companionship that was like the dreams people have of flying: wondrous, and yet unmarvelous.

His relationship with his mother must have had the same effortless grace and freedom. For Martha, to realize this is to know the measure of her loss, at last. A broken sharing is a poignant sorrow: the more so for being an inward and indiscernible loss.

In the wood the wind hung suspended in the tops of the trees. The ground was crisply covered with leaves; her footsteps made a dusty whisper among them. She came to the Glen, a deep ravine with a stream running in its depth, so far down that the sound of it was almost lost before it reached the top. She clambered down the steep, tree-studded bank. At the bottom was a place of stillness and water music, foam-flecked pools between the rocks, and a fugitive sunlight from above.

This place knew them well. It had lovelier moods than this on drowsy summer days, when one could linger in a kind of waking dream, companioned by the soft, incessant sound of running water and the delicate nervous flutter of the aspens. She glanced up; they were leafless now, their slim trunks standing gray-green against the banks bedded deep in brown leaves. Here Austin had taught her to use a fly rod. Once in a while there was a diminutive trout to throw back into the pool.

She sat upon a stone and was possessed of a longing for the companionship which was missing from this holiday. Austin had been away five months. He must soon come home. There was comfort in that.

But things would be different, she thought, crumbling a leaf between her fingers. A year ago, beneath the staggering, unexpected blow of his father's death, she had seen his gaiety sobered, his boyishness put away, as they said, overnight. He had been close to his father. A tragic loss at twenty-one. And there was the family business, in which it had been assumed that he would someday take his place. Founded many years before by Mrs. Cutting's father, Michael Fairlies, for the manufacture of a single mechanical device, it had since been expanded to include the development of countless automatic switches and valves for a hundred different purposes. Joining the firm originally as its inventive genius, Austin's father eventually became its principal administrator when Mrs. Cutting's father died and her brother returned to England to manage the London office.

James Cutting's death at fifty-one was a shock to his business associates as well as to his wife and son. For Austin it meant a much earlier assumption of responsibility than he had anticipated. He was a senior shortly to be graduated with an engineering degree from a small college in upstate New York. Ironically, he had chosen this college because of its excellent music department, because music was his avocation. With no pretensions to genius, or intention of becoming professional, he was an accomplished pianist. At the time of his father's death, there had been a still unresolved question in his mind as to his future.

This he confided to Martha before he left for England after graduation in June. "The business was always there, waiting—but it seemed more of an insurance than a responsibility, and so many other doors were open . . ." They were sitting on the top step of the side porch. He was silent for a moment, his gaze fixed on the far line of the wood. "There was to have been plenty of time. Funny, there's never as much time as we think. Grandfather was relatively young when *he* died. Dad was *young* —fifty isn't old nowadays, although a hundred years ago fifty was considered a great old age."

In England he was, he wrote in one of his short, infrequent letters, "learning as much as I can as fast as I can" under his uncle's tutelage. There was to be a reorganization at Fairlies and Cutting just after the first of the year, he wrote; his mother and he would be included in the new board of directors, and at that time he would know in what specific capacity his older associates planned to use his abilities and new knowledge. He had a presentiment that he would end up in management. "I don't believe I'll mind. What I have learned here has been extremely interesting—exciting, even. Working with people seems more lively than working with facts."

If Austin was to be home in time for that meeting at the first of the year, it was possible that he could be home for Christmas. Martha became aware again of the November day, the sound of the stream in the Glen, of her solitude. Only a month to Christmas. Sharply, with a stab in her whole physical being, she missed him.

She was, on the whole, satisfied with her life, although recently she had been touched by a fleeting wish to have a purpose, a direction—like Celia, who was going to be a painter, or Bennett a writer and Alicia a doctor. Thinking of Celia, she resolved soon to bring her here, welding together the parts of her joy to make it whole. If Celia had no home or family, she would share with her all that she owned . . . Even then, she was no longer completely Austin's, for now there was Celia. She belonged to both, but Celia, unbidden, had taken the greater part. Afterward, long afterward, she knew that this was like Celia: to possess unquestioningly. Thus far, she had not been touched by the anguish of Celia's rejections. She knew only the delicate joy of their intimacy, the sweet pleasure of living with her grace.

December shrieked past the corners of the Hall at night, moving the stiff shadows of branches on the shade in a fantastic ceaseless ballet. The river froze. They skated on the broad curve below Cemetery Park and came up the hill in the sunset when the pines stood black against the pale green and lavender of the wintry west. The ground was rutted now, the dead grass crisp. Ice crept up the window panes in the twilight. They hurried between the Hall and the school in the mornings, leaving a trail of dark footprints across the frosty lawn; and Bennett, secure in her room at the Hall, made gleeful, unpitying remarks as the day students who walked up from town arrived with reddened noses and numbed fingers.

In the printing room the mimeograph spewed forth its closely lettered pages. The *Sentinel* was going to press. Across the hall in the studio, Martha and Celia were hand-blocking the covers; the smell of printing ink mingled with the vapor of alcohol. Through the open doors came the sound of the machine—clickety-clack—clickety-clack . . . Later years saw professionally smart *Sentinels* arriving in bundles from the printers, with glossy paper, clear photographs, and stiff cloth covers. The classes which sponsored them were justifiably proud, but they never knew the harmony of those busy hours spent in putting the magazine together.

The sound of the machine ceased and Horty, stretching her arms above her head, appeared in the doorway. Tall, incredibly thin, with dank, gleaming blonde hair and a vividly rouged mouth, she was her own prototype of the John Held girl.

[31]

"Tea, anybody?"

They drank it sitting on tables, on the window sills, holding their cups with inky fingers, nibbling saltines. Their faces were impartially smudged. Bennett was a witch in a yellow smock, her hair all black elf locks from running impatient fingers through it; but a strangely peaceful Bennett, her energy diverted to the work in hand, not even roused to vehemence when someone, inevitably, introduced the subject of companionate marriage. This was a recurrent and favorite topic of discussion. Typically, there were vocal pros and cons. The idea embodied in Judge Lindsay's formula was antipathetical for some because it ruled out the one-boy-one-girl-one-love-forever ideal of romantic love. The question was, however, would it work? Would it result in more lasting relationships, lead to better marriages, bring down the divorce rate (one for every six marriages in 1928)? Or would it encourage "migratory love"—a year here, six months there? . . . And, of course, the tragedy would be the children. Oh, there weren't supposed to be any children, but "the best laid plans," notwithstanding, there would be children in some cases.

They enjoyed these discussions. It made them feel important and capable of being serious. Politics was boring; anyway, the war was long gone, the Kellogg-Briand Pact (to which they had all affixed their signatures) was a fact; at least there would never be another war. It was true that the United States was not a member of the League of Nations, but then "we" never went out of our way to look for trouble. Sex and love and marriage were good solid subjects with which to be concerned; all the choices lay before them; these subjects would touch all their lives . . . The war, which they were too young to remember, had changed many aspects of women's lives. Old patterns had been broken; there were decisions to be made.

They had music appreciation with Trude Haas in those years. Thus they were always richer than those who came after them. Trude spoke so little that it is doubtful whether anyone can remember anything she said. She passed, some years ago, to her reward; and if there is any particular reward for those who have enriched the souls of others with beauty, it is hers.

To enter that large room and see her broad, bright-cheeked, smiling face was an ascent into light. If anxiety pressed upon them—and how even was the tenor of their ways in that remote interval!—here tension could be forgotten. Trude expected nothing of them. They sometimes felt that she had forgotten them, or that they had strayed in as eavesdroppers upon her intense, enraptured absorption with her music.

At the piano she played capably, spreading her strong square hands over the keys, nodding her large head with its mass of white hair. Perhaps she remembered to tell them what it was she played, and then she would turn her face for a moment in their direction with a blue stare which made them feel that she did not even see them. Sometimes she forgot; sometimes they would ask; often, under the spell of her enchantment, they did not.

No one knew her whole story. At the time of Celia's coming, her age might have been seventy-five or eighty-five. The active part of her life, at any rate, was behind her, and it had been a long love affair with music which took her to all the capitals of the world, before crowned heads, in an era when all was pomp and glitter and drama and glory and honor. This came to them by hearsay; Trude never reminisced. But these were the scenes she may have been living again as she played, half-closing her eyes, allowing her heavy, now aged body to sway on the bench, her phrasing accented with still-graceful gestures of her large hands in a theatricality which was passing out of style.

Years later, Martha knew why Julia Severn had felt privileged to have her, and why she had impressed the girls with this sense of privilege. Trude's classes were not aimed at formal excellence. There were no quizzes or examinations; all that was required of them was that they sit, for two hours each week, and *listen.* Old Trude steeped them in music, giving them what Julia called "a background for the heart." No girl who sat in that room can ever hear Chopin or Liszt, Bach or Handel, without seeing again those square hands rising and falling, that massive head deeply nodding; and feeling, again, as they almost unwillingly felt it then, the response to a deeper, more significant emotion than was customary for them—a poignancy alien to their station and their years, later identified as *Weltschmerz*.

Perhaps only Martha remembers hearing Grieg, and Celia with her chin propped upon her hand, rapt. (Ah, Celia! Do you, somewhere, remember "Ich liebe dich"?) . . . Love, like the tide, comes in almost imperceptibly, quietly lapping at the shallows and becoming still when it has become deep.

Plans had been made for Christmas. Celia was to accompany Martha to Glen Fells. The invitation had been formally given by her mother and wheels set in motion for approval of the visit as soon as Thanksgiving week was over. Permission had come from Lilian Pence.

"Relieved to be rid of me," said Celia happily, as they gave each other a quick hug of mutual congratulation.

Two days before they were to go home they woke to find a world transformed: a beauty as old as time and forever new. Dazzled, they called to each other from room to room as they dressed. Martha and Celia, descending the stairs arm in arm, found Bennett on the landing, leaning against the window sill. On her face was a white reflection of the snow, all her freckles standing forth distinctly, her black eyes narrowed against the glare. The roofs below the hill were neatly capped, the hills and valley blurred by snow still falling in fine, slow flakes, as if the storm, having hastened in the night, was now spent with weariness. Twig and branch and wire were drawn in white against a gray density.

"Beautiful and white and virginal!" said Bennett without turning, in a soft, deliberate, caressing tone. "And soon, too soon, it will be a dirty gray, like Mademoiselle's face!"

A slight sound made them look up. Mademoiselle stood on the stair above them, motionless as a stone.

"I simply cannot understand," said Martha as they walked across the lawns to the school, "why Bennett has to be so deliberately cruel. Except for that, I don't *really* dislike her."

"You haven't it in you to dislike anyone, Martha." It was the most direct thing Celia had ever said to her. Martha felt the flush of pleasure which warmed her cheeks in spite of the chilly air. "Some people spend their lives 'getting even.' I think Bennett is one of them."

A minute later Celia stood still. "Listen, Martha. I can't come with you to Glen Fells for Christmas. Lilian has rescinded her permission. She's—if you can imagine this—taking me to a 'house party' on Long Island. I can't begin to understand *why.*"

Martha was speechless with disappointment.

Celia began to walk again, her hands in her pockets, staring at the ground in front of her. "I'm to have new clothes— evening dresses. I understand that these people are wealthy, and that there will be 'other young people' among those present, all home from their fashionable schools. By the way, Severn isn't fashionable, is it?" Glancing at Martha, she saw her eyes. "I'm sorry, Martha. I wasn't consulted—and I'd give anything to know what Lilian is up to . . ."

Martha's heart gave a quick lurch. "You don't suppose your sister is planning to transfer you away from Severn to one of those other schools, do you? That she is—"

"Using me to gain a social advantage? With some rich widower who has six children, perhaps?" Celia's face hardened with an expression Martha had never seen. "Don't worry about it. It will never happen, I can assure you."

Throughout the years of their life together, Martha was to encounter, now and then, that edge of steel beneath the velvet of Celia's casual grace of living. And, each time, it was as frightening, somehow, as it was reassuring . . .

As in other years, the MacLeans drove up to Severn for the

Christmas Play, taking Martha back with them to Glen Fells for the holidays. They were only a small part of that throng of people gathered together in the darkened gym to see the lovely old Christmas pageantry complete with shepherds, Magi, Madonna and Child. For a little while there was silence and calm under the high ceiling, a candescent interval for many people, young and no longer young. When the lights went up after the final curtain, the gym, the halls, and the first-floor classrooms filled with people collecting in groups to talk, to renew acquaintance, or to congratulate the players, who came from behind the scenes still wearing their makeup, a little loath to return at once to the commonplace. Threading her way through the crowd, Martha looked vainly for Celia, harboring a sad little suspicion that her disappearance was intentional. Satisfied that she was nowhere on the first floor, she started up the east stairway. She could not leave without saying good-bye. As for wishing Celia a merry Christmas . . . With a growing sense of unease, she thought of Celia's increasing reserve during the preceding week, a withdrawal upon which she had hesitated to trespass, made suddenly aware of the unmarked spaces in their knowledge of each other. Celia had not spoken again of the house party, and Lilian Pence was not at the pageant. Presumably, Celia would be on the train for New York in the morning. But Martha could not leave for Glen Fells without speaking to her.

The classrooms on the second floor were empty; most were dark, the light from the corridor raying inward upon their emptiness. The remote hum of gaiety from below followed her anxious, hurrying footsteps.

Memory will hold forever a picture of Celia in a red dress, leaning over the laurel-trimmed bannister on the stair landing to watch the laughing crowd of parents, girls, and guests in the hall below. The landing was in darkness, so that the only light shone upward into Celia's grave face framed by her hanging hair, on her bright dress and her hands laid before her, breast-high, among the varnished leaves.

Martha came upon her suddenly from above as she was starting down the west stairway.

In an instant she saw—and wished that she had not seen, that even now she could retrace her steps so that Celia might never know that she had seen. Then Celia turned. The light shone only on the side of her face now, and on her sleeve; her eyes were veiled in shadow. Her expression thus hidden, she looked, this once, wholly young. In this long moment her assurance and her challenge were drowned; in their place were an unbearable wistfulness, a short red dress, and a fall of soft light hair.

"I've been looking for you," Martha said, going down to her, adding brightly, "There's a frightful crowd downstairs." As if Celia had withdrawn to escape the crush and clamor; as if it were not unusual to hide away in the empty solitude of the upper floor. "I wanted to have you meet Mother and Dad before we leave . . ." she chattered on.

Celia took her arm in a swift, tense grasp. "Don't, *don't* be like that! Must you . . . *always* . . . ?"

Martha stood still, hurt, breathless, astounded; and while she strove for words, Celia's hand dropped. She made a small sound with a break in it, almost a laugh.

"Oh, Martie . . ."

They went down. The crowd had thinned a little and someone had left a door open; a keen little breeze was ruffling the furs and silken skirts of those remaining. Nothing had happened, after all; all that remained of the moment was a fallen echo for the future to reiterate: Must you . . . always?

A week before Christmas there was still no word from Austin. Even his mother did not know for certain whether he would return in time for the holiday.

Cousin Rob had been invited to spend Christmas with the MacLeans. He was the red-haired stepson of her mother's cousin, Louise Farr. That year he was a junior at Yale. There was no sense in spending all that time to go home to Chicago, her mother said, especially as no one was there. His mother was spending the winter in California and there were only servants in the house. He would come to Glen Fells, instead, and brighten things up a little. "For us," said Martha's mother, meaning, for Martha who is getting older now and should begin to enjoy a little masculine companionship. Austin did not count; he was merely the boy next door, a part of the scenery. There was nothing in the association to put Martha on her mettle, socially.

Martha viewed her mother's maneuvering with the sometimes alarming perspicacity of the innocent and young. She knew that she considered herself one of the fortunate ones: she had a beautiful home and a successful husband, and the ideal family for her time and station—one daughter rapidly developing from an interesting little girl into a charming young girl, with intelligence and rather nice looks, whom it would be fun to launch socially, an achievement to marry well. All this was apparent in her mother's smiles and approving pat when she was dressed for some minor sally into the benevolent social climate of Glen Fells.

Hope of Austin's return dwindled with the days that intervened before Christmas, and Martha welcomed the diversion of Rob's company with a kind of amicable exasperation. He trimmed the tree, hung holly wreaths, and rushed through the house like an energetic cyclone. He whistled cheerfully outside her door in the morning as she turned over, pulled the covers over her head, and sought that sweet second sleep reserved for vacations. He hung a sprig of mistletoe in the living room doorway.

For days she had started when the phone or the doorbell rang; by Christmas Eve she was resigned and heavy-hearted. The scents and glitter of a lavish pre-Depression suburban Christmas were all through the house. The doorbell chimed again and again as deliveries arrived. Her mother was entertaining at dinner and at tea several times during the week between Christmas and New Year's Day; there was to be a tea dance at the club one afternoon, the ball on New Year's Eve, open house Christmas afternoon, and again on New Year's Day . . . And, of course, church services, especially midnight candlelight services at St. Paul's, which Martha loved.

When the bell pealed for the hundredth time around four o'clock on Christmas Eve, Martha went unsuspectingly to answer and there was Austin, wearing an English coat belted at the middle, hatless, his fair hair shining under the hall light. Smiling.

"Surprise!"

"Oh! I thought you weren't *coming* . . ."

As lately as a year ago, she would have flung herself upon him in the sheer exuberance of her surprise and relief. Now she stood, hesitant with a new constraint.

"Well, I just had to get here. They held a train, and a boat —I even swam part way—I certainly did: all those ships have pools, silly! Anyway, who ever heard of staying away from home at Christmas? . . . Hey, let's have a look! You've been growing up while I was gone, from tomboy to 'drawing room miss.' I won't know how to behave with you, Miss MacLean!"

No matter where you were, you came home for Christmas, of course. Oh, here was Austin, smiling, surrounded, shaking hands, her own heart filled with wordless joy. To her great consternation, tears stood in her eyes at his remembered raillery. She knew that Austin saw them, for, quickly, he threw his arm across her shoulders and drew her close in a rough brotherly hug, hiding her overflowing joy against his coat.

With Austin home, the holiday spirit advanced in tempo, acquiring a note of sweet hilarity which all Rob's antic efforts had been unable to induce.

Laughingly, she avoided the doorway where his mistletoe was hung. There had always been mistletoe in other years, the cause of much innocent merriment as her parents' friends kissed each other's husbands and wives and their own mates sat by, striving to be magnanimously amused, for, just occasionally, the sport masked a serious attraction.

Martha had not made up her mind about this kissing business as yet. Beneath the gay perversity with which she outwitted Rob that year lingered a disturbing sense of alarm which caused her heart to beat faster and her cheeks to burn at the thought of being caught off guard; a feeling so extraordinarily mysterious that she could not account for it; a feeling born, possibly, in the instant when she had stood, close-held, against Austin's new coat on Christmas Eve. Inexplicable, because she was no stranger to such physical contact; because of the countless times Austin had held her, shaken her, and teased her with playful roughness; because of their mad chases through the house, over the lawns, around trees until, cornered, she would wrestle in silent mirth.

She remembered her small square hands grasping his slim strong ones, their brown wrists crossed, muscles tensed; moments of breathless striving, and Austin's quick movement rendering her powerless . . . *"Now* will you be good!" And she was pinioned, laughing, beneath the triumphant glee in his blue eyes. Each time his additional strength gave him the victory. Yet each time she strove with greater determination.

In the afternoon of the last day of the old year, Rob took unfair advantage of her. Snatching the mistletoe from its place in the doorway, he held it above her head as she sat pouring out at the tea table. There were a number of people there—the Birketts, the Reverend Mr. Fales, Mrs. Cutting, Austin, Millicent Wald . . . The teapot careened in her hand as she dodged, but Rob's lips brushed the corner of her mouth. For a long moment she sat, not daring to look up, wanting to rub the damp spot with the back of her hand, feeling as if she had been branded, feeling confused and almost angry. Sight and sound alike had been drowned in her confusion, but presently she heard again the tinkle of spoons and her mother's voice cross the room in ordinary conversation. She glanced up and found Austin regarding her quietly. As her eyes met his, he moved his head deprecatingly.

[40]

"Enough, Martha," he said, gently. "No; there's not the slightest use . . ."

"Austin!"

With his outrageousness the world fell back into place.

New Year's Day. They went skating that afternoon at Long Lake. They took Millicent with them for Rob; she was tiny but they knew that her energy and hardihood would be more than a match for his. In their bulky raccoon furs, they filled the rumble seat of Austin's roadster.

In front beside him, she felt secluded and content. The wintry countryside flickered peacefully by the little square of window in the side curtain. Austin drove, according to his habit, with one hand ungloved: it was the first time she noticed this.

"It feels good to be behind the wheel of this little bus again," he said, smiling sidewise at her.

It was one of those colorless winter days, like an artist's study carefully done in gray and black and white. The sky was unbroken and dull, with a faint open glare, as if it had been removed. Long Lake was smoothly frozen. A little snow remained, in patches, along the shores, and higher up among the dark trees the shuttered and deserted cottages stared bleakly out. The unexpectant stillness of the cold air diminished and sharpened the sound of voices, the solitary hiss and ring of steel on ice.

The Log House was open; they had supper there, afterward, and Martha can still recall the swift, quivering onslaught of a new joy, making the little orange-shaded lamps dance with the flames in the fireplace at the end of the room. When it went, she heard the others talking, saw the door open and close as people came or went, saw the dark patches made by melting snow on the threshold, the white apron of the waitress, the warm gleam of light on china . . . But when she looked at Austin her heart flew up again like a bird startled out of cover, and these things lost their stability.

[41]

They had skated all the afternoon until the brief wintry twilight closed in and even the dull sheen of a sunless day had faded from the ice. When at last they decided to go in, the lake was almost deserted. Up at the Log House friendly light shone in the windows. The sound of a starting motor tore across the brittle quiet.

Martha sat at the end of the dock while Austin went up the slope to the parked car for her shoes. Rob and Millicent were still out on the ice, two small black figures darting ceaselessly like waterbugs. Using her fingers as Austin had taught her summers ago, Martha whistled sharply. From the hills a small, pierced echo came back.

Austin came down again just as Millicent came flying toward the dock, cut a circle, throwing an arc of ice crystals. Her small dark face was vivid.

"Don't wait for us if you don't want to. We're racing to the Point, just once more! I can hardly *bear* to stop . . ."

Austin looked after them, and a quizzical half-smile narrowed the corners of his eyes. "Want to wait for them?"

She pulled at her laces. "Guess not. Wait till I get these off."

"Allow *me.*" He was down on one knee. She watched him as he unlaced her skating shoes, slipped them off, and put on her oxfords, his slim fingers making neat bows. With a new intentness she studied his unconscious face: the modeling of brow and temple, the slight acquilinity of his slender Cutting nose, the tapering of cheek and chin, the look of his mother in his lowered eyelids.

In the midst of her regard he looked up.

"Tired?"

She shook her head.

"Hungry?"

"Sort of."

He smiled. "Cold?"

"Oh, no!"

"Cross your heart?" He took her left hand in his, held it,

[42]

looked at it for a lengthening moment, then lifted it and laid its palm against his cheek. Only an instant which memory recaptures within its frame of after and before, then he laid it down beside her right one in her lap.

She was not young enough to ask what this meant; too young to know without asking. There was only time for a fleet glance before the others were upon them; a glimpse of something beautiful and bewildering abiding in his eyes and about his mouth—a look she would have given half her life to behold once more when late she came to understanding.

Each spring sees the same purpling on the wall of Lookout Mountain, the same gathering cloud of green in the trees, the same lengthening hours of sun on their trunks. And each spring morning, time without end, will hold sounds made small by distance, of garden tools and nesting birds and a light wind like music moving up the valley. Each year the air softens, the sun grows kind, and the eager green shows upon the sloping fields; but only one spring knew a new waking and a sharp discovery.

That spring she was sixteen.

In April she was at home for a brief week of spring recess. With efficient haste she was supplied with a wardrobe to carry her through the last day of school in June. There was a routine semi-annual visit to the dentist; and, under her mother's critical eye, the hairdresser trimmed and thinned her chestnut hair, so that she went about for unaccustomed days feeling smooth and shorn behind the ears.

There was a Saturday afternoon when she walked with Austin in the woods, finding the first violets beneath sodden leaves, and standing still to listen to the sweet fervor of a whistling catbird. With the endearing fickleness of April, there was a soft stillness one moment and a cool wind remembering the taste of snow in the next, and a delft-blue sky beyond the lightly patterned tops of aspens in the Glen. Austin sitting on his heels beside the stream to crumble wet sand and hold cold pebbles in his fingers was long a talismanic memory.

[43]

There was nothing more; but to feel one's heart turn and wake within one, to be so innocent that joy is complete in simply loving—who dares to say that this will come again?

Spring had passed its waking when she returned to school. Hammondville was leafy, the wide winter vistas narrowed and enclosed. Girls sauntered in the streets. They went in couples, in threes, met each other at the turnings and on the hill. At the Pharmacy they gathered to sip nectar through straws or to buy powder puffs, filling the long mirrored room with their diverse femininity and their laughter, unsubtle as broken glass.

At school, windows stood open; Letty yawned behind her fingers and looked out, absently dreaming. Mademoiselle became harassed at their inattention. At the Hall, Ruth Kane played on the grand piano downstairs with unprecise vigor, emotional music unlike her methodical practicing, abruptly stopped as they came in, and thrust herself out of the room, head down, her cheeks wet with tears.

Martha wandered with Celia over the hill, and together they leaned from the windows in the twilight, their conversations quietly haunted by the youth of Juliet and the gentleness of Elaine. These were blueprints drawn in the cobwebs of dawn, later to be scorched by the heat of passion, torn to shreds by the wind of circumstance and, perhaps, scorned whole by sophistry. But now, still, they were of Severn; by truth or by illusion, the pattern of Julia's chaste hope for them cast a long shadow athwart the future. Their intimacy became a whole thing: where each gives, not an equal amount, but only as much as he is able, and neither marks an inequality. Thus they disclosed themselves to each other; and if Martha's picture was incomplete and Celia's animate, that was the measure of their difference. Celia spoke of her mother, whom she had never known, and of her father, whose bohemian life she had shared between terms at school and whom, as a consequence, she had known intimately. She spoke of schools and discipline, and holidays, and people. Always, of people: schoolmates from several countries, the Sisters, of men with beards and monocles,

[44]

men in shabby clothes, men eager and morose who came to her father's studio in Paris or Rome. Even, she spoke of Lilian Pence, of the life she had made for herself—an artificial creation—and permitted herself to wonder if this were all Lilian would ever ask of life, life which was so rich, so varied, so full of promise.

Out of the sparkling stream of Celia's confidences her life emerged, vivid, varied, unconventional, and lonely at times. She had walked obediently in decorously paired processions, her very footsteps measured by the swift stride of attendant nuns, beside the walls and under the archways of little French towns. Under a darkened skylight in a garret room yellow with light and dim with smoke, she had perched upon a stool, listening to men talk about the work of men's minds until daylight fell palely into the room, quenching the single naked bulb.

Beside the sharp outlines of these pictures, Martha could find few words to portray her ordered childhood and the sustaining friendship of Austin.

Upon the future they touched lightly; because at sixteen two years seems a long time, and for two years more Severn would own them and they each other. So, although one was ambitious and the other had found love, suddenly, like a bright coin gleaming in the path before her feet, confidently they left the unknown hidden in the hand of fate, never doubting that the design was plain and of their desiring.

Celia wanted to paint. She knew that she would always want to paint; it was as natural to her life as sleep. Training her eye, she trained Martha's as well. Years later, driving or walking, Martha would note, automatically, the way a shadow fell across a wall, the shape of clouds along the horizon, and remember Celia interrupting a sentence to draw her attention to things like these. The day had not come which was to see Celia's gift corrupted, this passion subservient to a greater, and Celia unmindful and uncaring.

Without her, spring would have passed, an unseeing dream. But Celia sharpened her perceptions and colored the days, making them unforgettable, blended forever two loves into a single whole. Later, from the whirlpool of too many emotions, Martha tried to reach back and recapture the clarity of that peace. Love, that spring, was a happiness without beginning or end, impersonal as sunlight, neither expecting nor imagining anything beyond this tranquil felicity.

Not once did she say to herself: I love Austin—does he love me? She merely thought of him, seeing him as he had looked sitting on a bench against the sunny wall of the stable, wearing an old sweater and painting a flower box with neat motions of his hands; or in his study, chin in hand, listening to Beethoven. Or she remembered the sun on his hair and his smile and the way the little lamps in the Log House shone like twin candles in his eyes that night in January . . .

Because life is long there will be other evenings with trees soft against a sky softly starred, and windows open into the dark. But they cannot ever know, exactly, a peace that was largely innocence.

Coming back again in September they had, in a sense, to begin again. The encounter which drew Martha so eagerly to Severn at the end of the summer was with a different Celia. Not the Celia of a year before, but a Celia lightly changed by the last quick step of emergence from girlhood.

Strange: those who knew her will never think of her without the accompanying thought of beauty, yet she was not beautiful. But even in the hours when grief and illness mirrored their ravages in her face, she had beauty—an indefinable beauty of gesture. When she first came to Severn, hers was a natural charm: childish, innocent, and assured; but when she came back that following autumn, what was natural had become careful. She had discarded (or had Lilian?) the plain white blouses, the heavy skirts, the square-toed shoes. Instead, she began to wear those plain little nunlike dresses, so distinctively her own. There was a light gray one with long slim sleeves, collared in white. Her soft, heavy hair, grown long since the spring, had been softly waved, parted above her brow, and coiled flat at the nape in Grecian simplicity. Touching her mouth with color accented the delicate prominence of cheekbone, the slight angularity of her jaw. But only her inimitable distinction could make graceful the hesitancy of her walk in those insubstantial slender-heeled kid slippers.

That year Helena gave them the northwest corner room with the bay window and twin beds which they shared for the remainder of their time at Severn. It was one of the best rooms in the house, and they were happy with its comfort, the change of scene, and their new proximity. They went to work eagerly to collect enough objects to give it their special character. Celia had no family pictures; her father had had no contact with his wife's family after her death and she had not been photographed while she lived with him, and although he had used Cecily as a model, all the pictures had been sold. Nor were any photographs of Hubert Pence available. Celia had, however, three watercolors and a pen-and-ink sketch bearing her father's signature. The watercolors were small, luminous with still water and a golden light the color of Celia's eyes when she smiled; the sketch was of Celia herself as she looked when she was ten, long fair hair framing a round childish face and the unchildish candor of her gaze.

There was a wide table in the room. This they used as a desk, sitting opposite each other in the friendliness of lamplight. (That lamp was one of the things which they bought at the secondhand store: it had a red glass base and an eccentric yellow shade which they draped with a silk tie.)

Celia had a habit of sitting, as she studied, with her long hair down over her shoulders, her elbows on the table and her hands clasped behind her neck under her hair.

The sharing of a bedroom can be the ultimate test of love and forbearance. Martha was an early riser, desperate for sleep in the evening. Celia, on the contrary, loved to dawdle at bedtime: she could easily spend an hour or two walking back and forth with her leisured graceful step, hanging things away in the closet, humming lightly in happy absorption, or sitting before the mirror polishing her nails or brushing out her hair with long, caressing strokes. She had a habit of mending after everything else was done, a stitch here and a stitch there, a broken strap or the tiny hole in the toe of her stocking which she fought ceaselessly in exchange for the aestheticism of high heels.

The change in her was not entirely visible and exterior. Much of it was beneath the surface, so that the very air about her seemed to vibrate with a demure mockery.

There was an evening when, as she sat brushing her hair, Martha lay with her hand under her cheek, idly watching. Suddenly a thought stood in her mind, stark, alone, and unbidden: Someday a man will watch her doing that, loving her for it, and for all the rest . . . Instantly, she was shocked, as if someone else had spoken.

Confidences flowered easily in the darkness between the two beds. The story of Celia's first proposal was to Martha at once pathetic and amusing, after the fashion of youthful experiences in which triumph bears a little sting of cruelty. He was a member of Lilian's coterie, twenty-three, sandy-haired, haggard and earnest. Whatever she may have done to him then, Celia mocked him gently in retrospect: his freckled hands, his desperation, his hair growing a little long on his neck. She had refused him, but whether gently or carelessly she did not say. He had vowed, with the despair that does not recognize defeat, never to forget her.

It is entirely possible that he did not.

Martha was faintly disturbed by her mockery; she had never thought of Celia as callous.

Something happened that year which had nothing to do with them. It was an occurrence unrelated to them except, of course, in its immediate effect of astonishment. Nevertheless, the memory of certain things, by force of their special incongruity, may follow one to crossroads unvisioned.

Mademoiselle, that lone and unattractive woman, suddenly, in the middle of the first semester, produced a husband.

They were not forewarned, for they could not imagine that the sleek sedan which drove up to the Hall one sunny October afternoon was the shadow cast by that particular event. That Mademoiselle had given her last class a study hour instead of a recitation period was not remarkable; she was often ill and retired to her room to lie down. Their curiosity was stirred, however, when, from the school windows, they saw her come out to the waiting car dressed in her black and wearing the wide hat which she wore to church. As the car turned down the hill they observed that the driver was a man and that she sat with him in the front seat, but their wildest speculations yielded nothing more startling than the probability that he was a lawyer and that she was about to inherit money.

Her wedding day was a month later, a cold brown November day. She breakfasted with them that morning, taciturn as usual. Attempting, afterward, to find signs they had missed, they traced backward the hours, the minutes, discovering nothing. After breakfast she disappeared and Julia took their French classes. She was absent at luncheon. When they came back to the Hall at four o'clock the black sedan stood on the drive and the stranger stood in the reception hall.

Virginia missed the climax, to her everlasting regret. She and Lois had lingered at the school. But Celia, Martha, and Bennett entered the hall as Mademoiselle came down the stairs. She hesitated for an instant as she saw them, her hand catching at the bannister in a small, frightened motion; and for the last time her eyes encountered Bennett's, angry and afraid.

She wore a new coat, black, with a fine fur drawn close about her white face. Under it they saw the gleam of blue silk as she stepped off the lowest step. She hesitated and stood still, irresolution and fear and the unaccustomed weapon of pride delivering her to confusion, as if she had stepped into ambush. Then she lifted her chin, swept them with the old blind glance of scorn they knew so well, and gave her vindication:

"Girls . . . I have ze opportunity to say good-bye . . . to

present my . . . 'usband, M'sieu 'arry Martin." (She pronounced it in French, Mar-tann.)

The man smiled and bowed. He may have been fifty-eight or sixty, probably twenty-five years her senior. A man of average height, overweight, with a sallow indoor look. His clothes were good, but he did not achieve a well-dressed look. Lank iron-gray hair lay flattened to his head, ridged by the mark of the hat which he held in his hand.

Only Bennett found her tongue. "Congratulations." Her tone was, for once, magnanimous but there was too much between her and Mademoiselle to be bridged by the surprised cordiality of such a moment. A faint dull color sprang out on Mademoiselle's cheekbones. Her husband put his hand under her arm, still smiling, bowed again, let his glance rest for an instant on Celia, and opened the door.

Helena Gracie told them at dinner that Mademoiselle had been married that morning and was sailing for France at midnight.

The news was like a flung stone in the pool of their amazement. The ripples widened into the fascination of debate: Could a woman of Mademoiselle's age actually *love* a man? Or be loved? The man . . . could you? . . . my *dear*, could I? . . . No. It must be a marriage of convenience. Was the marriage of convenience justified? They took Mademoiselle to pieces and ground the pieces fine between the hard stones of their pitiless idealism and their unblemished hopes.

Virginia said, incredulously, *"Mrs. Harry Martin!"* trying to fix the commonplace, sedate name on Mademoiselle's image, so exotic to them now, by contrast.

In conclusion: "He looked like a gangster to me," remarked Bennett dreamily. "But Mademoiselle certainly doesn't look like my idea of a gun moll!" She laughed suddenly and raucously. "Can you imagine them in bed together?"

Julia took their French classes for a few days, and within a week a woman came to take Mademoiselle's place. Madame was small and plump, modishly dressed and coiffed. She had reddish fair hair and bright blue eyes and a quick, dimpling smile. But the first time Bennett spoke out of turn, she sent her out of the room to stand in the corridor. She treated them all as if they were ten years old instead of seventeen and shamed them with references to the manners and brilliance of her former pupils. Before the end of the year Madame was more actively unpopular than "poor Mademoiselle" had ever been and, occasionally, she came back like a pale unhappy ghost to haunt their conversations.

Swiftly, it was Christmas again and this year Celia came to Glen Fells for the holidays. Rob was there again. A widening ripple of gaiety had been set in motion. The Celia who had hung over the stair railing, her face a mirror of loneliness, was only a year in the past, but Martha, watching her during that holiday, found the memory unreal as any dream. They went without pausing from one festivity to another: from the Mac-Leans' to the Birketts', the Walds', the Owens'. Mrs. Cutting gave them a supper party after the play at the Little Theatre. There was the Christmas Dance at the club, and a ball on New Year's Eve which lasted through breakfast.

They used the word "sensation" that year; it was Celia's. She wore an evening dress of scarlet taffeta and with it a look of growing on a stem. The dress had a low waistline and a bouffant skirt which dipped in the back, a ridiculous and difficult style, but Celia wore it with an infinite grace.

She danced with Austin, and with Carroll Owen 3rd, who, like Austin, had been born in Glen Fells in his grandfather's house; and again with Austin.

Rob, bringing Martha a glass of punch, stood looking at them. "She makes you think of Marie Antoinette," he said. "Plenty of heads will be lost because of her."

Martha was obscurely annoyed by the clumsy witticism, and by an underlying note of something that was not admiration in Rob's dry tones.

One afternoon, for the want of anything better to do, they went to the movies. These were the six who, of all the country

[51]

club crowd, had drifted together in a small exciting circle of compatibility. Austin, Carroll Owen (whose people lived on their investment of inherited money), Millicent Wald (whose grandfather was a banker and whose father was a concert violinist), Rob and Celia, the outsiders, and Martha.

Afterward, they went down the street to Ferrara's and lined up in a scrambled, casual manner at the soda fountain. With only a couple of hours to dinner, they ordered banana splits and fudge sundaes; except Celia, who took sarsaparilla as always, provoking the usual comments. For she was straight and slim as a reed, her bones so lightly covered that one seemed to see their polished sheen through her flesh.

Austin, enjoying an afternoon stolen from the office, sat at Martha's left; then Rob, Millicent, and Celia, and at the end, Carroll. Looking into the long mirror on the wall behind the fountain, she could see them all.

Carroll leaned a little toward Celia, something he said meant for her ear alone. She looked down, turning the bottle slowly in her fingers; the straw wobbled. Her face wore a secret, musing look, as if a smile were hidden beneath her lashes or tucked away in the corners of her mouth. She was wearing a brown beret slanted over one eyebrow and a brown suede jacket; and in brown she looked frail and dreaming, like a leaf in autumn.

Martha's glance shifted in the mirror and crossed that of Austin, fixed on the tableau at the opposite end of the counter. Something in that grave, still look should have told her then: but seeing, her mind turned involuntarily aside, as her feet would have avoided a root or a stone in the path to the Glen.

Alicia's voice broke on the last words of her valedictory. Bending her head hastily, she sat down.

Trude struck a deep chord on the piano and the school rose in a body. The morning sun shone in through tall windows at the southern end of the room and lay in bars of gold over the festive and solemn gathering as the girls sang, for the first time in public after months of intensive rehearsal, Trude's composition. Simple music, reverent as a hymn and nostalgic as time. They sing it every year at Severn, still, and the deep dying echo of the last stanza has lost none of its emotional quality through repetition. Trude is no longer there, but as long as there is Commencement at Severn the valedictory will be followed by her song, evoking the calm specter of her white head behind the upraised black wing of the piano.

> But the tender grace of a day that is dead
> Will never . . . will never
> Come back to me.

The last note hangs quivering in a golden silence, that tenuous silence which is broken only by the first words of Julia's address, brief, as always, definitely personal, concerned primarily with the graduating class. Not with politics or science, in rounded sentences which went floating out over their heads into the pure air of June and were forever lost; but with themselves, as individuals, in a warm simplicity which they were able to grasp and carry with them into the strangeness of new lives away from Severn, her deft touch calling forth their strength and their frailty in a bestowal of personality and a priceless integration of identity.

Alicia's commencement is strangely clearer in memory than their own, hers and Celia's, for that was a shadowy blending of immediacy—attainment and incredible finality, the light piercing grief of farewell, flowers, heat, beloved melody imprisoned in the throat by difficult unshed tears, and a weariness woven of gratitude and regret, at the end . . .

The presentation of diplomas comes at the end of Julia's address.

"Alicia Josephine Whittaker."

Alicia's despised middle name; but it was her grandmother's and she would not have it omitted from her diploma because the old lady was present, having been assisted into the auditorium with two canes and her son's arm. There she sat, those dark brows beetling with a fierce pride as Alicia rose and came forward, solid, dark, and forbidding in white silk, vividly foreshadowing her internship. (They did not wear gowns at Severn.)

"Hortense Salisbury Giles."

Horty rose and crossed the platform, her walk studied and graceful. "Our dramatic Hortense," Julia had called her. Her hair was smooth and gleaming, the curled ends like golden shells against the unfaltering color in her cheeks.

"Muriel Elizabeth Turner."

"Ellen Jane Madison."

"Rose Eaton Haig."

The bars of sunlight had shifted so that the forward half of the room lay in a cool brightness. It had grown very warm; white flags of paper moved languidly over the gathering as the guests fanned themselves with their programs. The ferns curled gently at the edges, the flowers gave off the heavy scent which is their swan song; the iris had a bruised look, the roses hung heavily upon their stems.

At the piano Trude sat waiting.

Julia stepped back, the last diploma given, the last word spoken, the last hand gently relinquished. She was truly beautiful, small and erect in her black gown, with the mortarboard set at a neat angle above her fine eyes, the tassel swinging against her white cheek as she turned her head. She turned now and nodded to Trude.

The deep chord. Its echo struck deeply, always, somewhere in one's inmost soul . . . Then they were on their feet, singing. A soaring melody. Alicia's head was bent, her hands quiet on the white scroll with the falling silver ribbons.

> Upon your hill in Hammondville,
> O Severn beautiful!
> Our hearts will yearn till we return . . .

The flowers were brought in. The girls stood, their arms laden, their skirts banked with tall-handled baskets. The people rose and separated. The crowd flowed brokenly to the front of the room to besiege the graduates.

Fragments remain:

Horty, her arms filled with roses of all colors, laughing excitedly, her chin lifted, her vivid mouth wide, as she was later to receive the adulation of her audiences, missing only the outflung hand.

Alicia, fast-locked in her grandmother's embrace, tears on both their dark-browed faces, the white head and the black one close above a bouquet of golden snapdragons.

Julia, surrounded by people . . .

Trude had stopped playing; there was a babel of voices and laughter in the room. It was cooler, someone had opened the big doors to the porch. Young men—brothers—were carrying flowers out to the waiting cars.

"Ye gods!" cried Horty blithely, coming up the stairs. "Tell me how I'm gonna dance tonight, somebody!"

"Take a cold shower . . ." This must have been the last time they heard Alicia say that.

"Or think of something pleasant and relax," added Bennett, mildly sarcastic. "Cheer up, Horty, there's a full moon and it's a long night. You'll rise to the occasion!"

"It had better be a long night!" remarked someone else in dire accents. "Danny Saxton's 'orkester' is charging eight-four cold dollars to play for us."

"I hope those boys will be a little careful about flasks tonight," worried Lois. She felt her position to be ambiguous because of her connection with school authority.

"I feel a little sad," remarked Virginia in a small voice.

"Oh, forget yourself and have a little fun!" advised Bennett. "All that ails you is the tender touch of today's ceremony on your devastated sensibilities. Next year it will be our turn

—save your tears for the final farewell to dear old Severn!"

" 'I don't care—if I don't get home—till the milkman comes!' " sang Horty in her loud, clear, unmusical voice. "Oh, gurruls, did you see my roses? I sent them home with Mama. *Mais oui,* as Madame says, they have stems four feet long! And my butter-and-egg man, wait until you see *him!* He is filthy rich, goes to Yale, and he lawves me dear-rly. But his hands are like little white cheeses and he's upholstered in pink above his collar . . ."

An enchantment lay upon Severn that night, one not of moonlight merely, although the lawns were bright as day and fringed with shadow; although, below the hill, roofs and river were silvered with light and Cemetery Park, crested with pines, lay like a black battlemented island in the night. No; this was the intangible, elusive transformation of spirit, so that, moving in its spell, they walked over the lawns, in and out of shadow, with the drifting queenly gait of evening, in the diaphanous magic of tulle and chiffon and mousseline de soie. As if each of them, for a night, owned a separate self which flowered briefly in a strange serenity, they danced, changed partners, and looked at each other in passing, their glances dark, esoteric, and mysterious.

Doors stood open upon the blue and silver cavern of the gym; music came out to them; cigarette ends glowed suddenly in the shadows like ardent fireflies, and the quick sound of laughter held low brought a sweet exciting joy to the listener's throat.

Leaning against a stone pillar on the porch, Martha saw the face of Ted Marsh clearly and briefly as a match flared: the swift flicker of a glance, a smile, a glittering instability.

There was a moment when she stood imprisoned against the pillar between his arms: a moment prolonged and crystallized in time, holding cold thought at variance with enchantment. Now I shall know, she told herself, the mystery in a kiss. As clearly as she had seen it in the flaring light of the match, she saw his face, indelibly captured upon the retina of her mind; and was able, in a space of time that might have been measured by the stroke of a pendulum or the beat of a wing, to examine it and find behind the disarming, tilted smile a faint, indolent mockery. In this interval of anonymity and moonlight, everything was divorced from reality and tomorrow. As close and intimate as the darkness, as tangible as his sleeve brushing her bare shoulder was the knowledge of her choice: the real or the unreal?

She turned her face aside.

"Oh." In the tight sardonic syllable she heard Bennett's echo. He stepped back into the light.

Still moving deliberately and gracefully with that queenly gait, she walked before him into the dance, the tulle of her skirt drifting a little backward, soft against her arm. Inside the door, she turned, went into his arms, and was once more aware of the music. For all knowledge there is a price. She had renounced knowledge because it bore a price she would not pay, but renunciation brought with it the discovery of a new power.

Ted bent his head. "Do you always lead men on this way?"

She smiled demurely. "You'd get conceited if you had your own way every time . . ." They were handing each other a line and they both knew it; the implications were important. She was not a stick or a prude, but a wise woman; he was all but irresistible.

He bent his head lower, whispering: "Next time? . . ."

She looked into his face with an expression almost gay. In her heart was a sudden tremendous happiness. However she would have willed, the touch of Ted Marsh's mouth would have been able to supplant and usurp, to color and change her secret memory of Long Lake which, this long time, had been the treasure of her solitude. By the small effort of choice she had kept it inviolate. Her heart quickened. There would be kisses for her mouth. There was time. She could wait. She let her thoughts fill with memories of Austin. The music wove in and out of her dream . . .

The dance was over; with it, the year had come to an end. The cars driving away into the night, the yellow windows at the Hall which darkened one by one, the packed trunks standing ready, growing vague in the dimming light: these were the inconsequentials of anticlimax.

The moon dropped lower behind the wooded horizon; shadow rose in the deep bowl of summer night abandoned, finally, to that stillness which comes before the spreading miracle of the pale new dawn. In the stillness, before the small questing voice of the first waking bird, Celia sighed and spoke.

"A year from tonight it will be our turn . . . But a year is such an *endless* time!" There was a desperate note of impatience in her low voice.

As if thunder muttered in the distance or the sky had turned livid in an instant, Martha's heart faltered and plunged. The enchantment of this night was only a veil for its portentous finality; the year, which Celia would have swept aside, a respite, slight and precious, from change. A little wind made a cool sound among the leaves. Celia was silent so long that it seemed she slept. Then she said, distinctly and dispassionately,

"Ted Marsh kissed me tonight."

Lightly stunned, Martha sought the connection between this and what had gone before, knowing that it existed.

"Does he mean anything to you?" she asked; coldly, because of love and the nameless trepidation deep within her.

"No." Martha seemed to see the smile which accompanied the quick, scornful syllable. "It's so exactly like you to ask that, Martie. Couldn't you think of any other reason? . . ."

Out of another silence she spoke again, but her voice had changed, warmed and colored with an intense eagerness. "Life is so short, Martie! You're eighteen, twenty, thirty; and then you're old a long time. I wish I were Horty tomorrow, and free —ready for the things that are going to happen to me!" She moved restlessly. "Oh, how can I make you understand, Martie? Living means to be alive, to experience, to feel—even to suffer. Or to burn with confidence to your fingertips, so that *anything* seems possible! Everything, Martie, is going to happen to us within the next ten years. I can hardly *bear* to waste another whole year—I want to begin to *live!*"

She had thought that within the integrity of their relationship, she understood. But the security of her world was reeling on its foundations, shaken by a passion she could not understand. The parting of ways, which she dreaded, was not a year distant; it was suddenly upon them, no less frightening because it was unseen.

"How can I make you understand?" Celia asked despairingly. She could not. Martha had no understanding, only love; and fear of so desperate a philosophy of haste. Who could understand the whirlwind and its centripetal compulsion who had not seen the chaos at its heart? Or feel terror inherent in the flight of time who saw time as a long garden reaching gently into infinity?

That summer, instead of going to New England for their vacation, the MacLeans took a cottage at Long Lake; because in that year of blessed memory business was booming and Wall Street was hectic, and it was necessary for Martha's father to keep in close touch. The cottage was on the steep West Shore where the road runs along the water's edge close to the narrow beach. There was a high porch jutting out into the very treetops; the ground fell rapidly away beneath it. They had to cross the road to swim, climbing the hill and a formidable right-angled wooden stairs to return, but the West Shore at that time was still thickly wooded and far quieter than the more populous East Shore; and the high screened porch in the trees was ideal for sleeping.

Celia came in July. She got off the train at Long Lake station one sunny morning, wearing brown linen and white gloves and a panama with streamers. Martha met her with the station wagon. That was the summer she first got her license to drive. For the first time they kissed, going into each other's arms with a spontaneous, womanly affection, and Martha noticed the skin lightly freckled under Celia's eyes, the silky gleam of her lashes in the sun.

Austin's mother was in Torrington visiting her sister during July and August. They saw him every weekend, and when he had his vacation in August, Martha's mother took pity on him and invited him to spend it at the lake. He accepted with an eagerness significant only later. So the summer passed, gloriously, fused of water and sun and wind and the joy of companionship. Oh, Celia *was* beautiful that summer: she was slim and brown and lovely, her tiny freckles piquant, her hair tawny with sun, her lips curved in laughter to remember against heartbreak.

The first of September the MacLeans returned to Glen Fells to reopen their house; but almost three weeks remained before the beginning of the new term at Severn and the girls were loath to leave their sleeping porch and the bright mornings. The maples, yellowing along the shores, made patches of false sunlight; the air was clearer, the sky deeper, the days golden with a still warmth.

"Very well," said her mother, at last, "two weeks more. That will give me a week to get you ready for school. There are eggs and jam, I won't stop the milk, and tomorrow evening I'll send Austin up with groceries. You may feed him, but send him home and lock yourselves up early."

At five o'clock they began to watch for Austin's car. The table in the living room was laid for supper: yellow linen and red candles, and that set of yellow pottery which always looked so cheerful although the cups gave the coffee a bilious tinge.

At ten minutes to six the car stopped at the foot of the path. Celia sprang up.

"I'd better go down and help with the things . . ." She was wearing a green dress. The material had a dull silvery sheen, and all the rest of her was gold: hair, face, and arms . . . and her eyes were brilliant with an undefined eagerness.

Martha agreed. "I'll start the coffee."

From the living room she heard the slam of the screen door, the quick sound of Celia's heels on the wooden stair, and had a passing thought for her safety, remembering how she flew down the steep path, heedless of the roots which crossed it. She started the coffee, brought in the pitcher of batter from the kitchen, plugged in the waffle iron, and lighted the candles.

Austin and Celia were a long time but she thought nothing of it: the path was so steep that it took a good wind and a flying start to come up swiftly, and they were burdened, of course, with packages and conversation. But when the indicator on the waffle iron showed the proper baking temperature and they still had not come, she went to the door. All that she could see from the high porch was the glimmer of lake and sky through the leaves unless she went to the railing and looked down.

She had taken but one soundless step on the straw matting when she heard Austin's voice, roughened, vibrant, and unforgettable:

"Celia. Celia . . . *darling!*"

Her hand flew to her throat. Frantic, she turned and fled inside, snatching up the first thing that came to her hand as she heard the sound of their mingled footsteps on the wooden stairs. To her dying day, she thought, she would remember the color of strawberry jam with candlelight shining through the jar and associate with it a delicate, bitter anguish.

Looking up as they came in, she thought, Nothing, nothing will ever hurt, after this.

Batter hissed on the griddle, a reflection of the afterglow stained the eastern sky, the staccato sound of a motorboat faded across the evening, a breeze made a little whispering in the trees and bent the candle flames: these things she can recall, and a strange feeling of insubstantiality, as if she were suffering from fever.

Lying, at last, in the blessed privacy of darkness, she fixed her eyes upon the pattern of leaves and stars against the sky. Too late, she knew what she wanted: the explicitness of her knowing was in itself a pain too exquisite to be borne. She wanted those things which would be Celia's. Inexorably, with her own peculiar and honest courage, she leaned upon the sword-point of her pain, enumerating them: Austin's love, his lips and his hands, his gentle gaiety, all the years of his life, and his children. A part of her strange revelatory grief was the full-born imagination of fair-haired, clear-eyed children whom she mourned now as if they had lived and died.

She was seventeen.

At twenty-seven, and thirty-seven, and eighty-seven, she thought, one will ask oneself how the heart, so frail and untested, could withstand the tidal sweep of anguish which never again can be quite as full nor half as bitter.

Sometime in the night while it was still dark, she wakened, finding Celia's body lying inertly against her as if flung there by a wave, in the complete abandon of sleep. Celia's hair was loose on her shoulder, and in sleep Martha had laid a protecting arm over her: beneath her wrist she could feel the light, even rhythm of Celia's heartbeat.

Recalled to her by the lightness and fragility of Celia's body, the memory of old fears for her came back. Tenderness welled gratefully in her heart, relieving the aridity of shock.

Now Celia would be forever safe. Austin would take care of her.

Celia wore Austin's love proudly, like a tiara, all through that last year. Inexplicably, instead of setting her apart, Austin's ring on her finger drew the girls closer. Their interest was frankly proprietary. Austin belonged to all of them now. They made excuses to speak of him casually and frequently. Anyone finding a letter for Celia on the hall table would bring it upstairs as a matter of course, scaling it in at the door as she went by.

"Letter from Austin!"

And Celia shared with them—innocently, perhaps, or in delicate revenge—the peculiar delight of being engaged. She told them what Austin had planned for the Thanksgiving weekend; where they would go, what they would see, the clothes she would wear . . . On half-holidays Austin came out to Hammondville and took her to dinner, arriving at the Hall around five o'clock. Half-holidays meant an afternoon free of classes and an evening free of prep for the rest of them; but for Celia, beloved and betrothed, it meant descending the stairs, going out of the door, driving down the hill out of their sight, dining in some place with little lamps on the tables and Austin across from her, and returning at nine o'clock to the envy, the conjecture, the interest behind their clouded gaze.

They helped her to dress, thrusting their finest handkerchiefs, their silver compacts, their Christmas stockings and suede bags upon her; as if, when she returned the borrowed articles, they might speak and tell the subtle secret of those evenings beyond the owner's horizon.

No matter what they were doing when Austin's car drove up on the gravel at nine, it was suspended until Celia came upstairs and into the room. Sometimes they were in the upstairs study; or they were gathered in groups in the bedrooms, their doors open into the hall, reading, mending, manicuring . . . The sound of the front door closing came up the stairs into the silence held to receive it; then the pause, and the sound of Celia's footsteps ascending. They all listened, motionless, scarcely breathing: with a strange consent they did not look at each other, refrained from spying upon the bright, blank, listening look each wore.

A few days later, someone going by would scale a letter in at the door: "Letter from Austin." And Celia would slit the envelope with her nail file, and read quickly with the little smile hidden at the corners of her mouth and her hair down over her shoulders.

She told them what Austin *said*. It had snowed Friday in New York, the streets were full of slush, but in Glen Fells the February sun was precursory of spring. He had tickets to see Eva le Gallienne on the twenty-third. Did she know that three of her father's paintings were to be shown at the Frazier Gallery in an exhibition of Modern American Art during the second week of March?

They knew what Austin *said;* only Martha knew what Austin *wrote* in those faithful weekly letters. Celia read them to her; such is the mercilessness of friendship. There was nothing in them that might not have been read aloud in Assembly. Yet she died a small death with each of them, for they *were* Austin, from the short, factual phrasing to the shape of his handwriting on the page.

The precious year melted away little by little, like an icicle shortening in the sun. For Martha, what had been the acuminate pain of discovery dulled with the passing of the irretrievable hours. In the shadow of their invincible diminution, she performed each familiar task with a careful pleasure, cherished each word and gesture which was part of the beloved whole: and gave herself little time for personal griefs, as if she had said: I know you are there, your hour will come.

Celia, too, was content. The restlessness which had shaken her the night of Horty's and Alicia's commencement was gone, her tranquility was a clear mirror: its depths held nothing but the reflection of her felicity and the elusive hint of a smile behind lowered eyelids. And, as always, the vivid clarity of her mood destroyed for Martha the delusive memory of a mood that was past.

Toward spring they began to talk of the wedding. It was to be in the summer after Commencement. Martha tried not to let her thought go beyond the wedding. She willed herself—not always successfully—not to think of Celia and Austin alone together. The plans for the honeymoon were complete; Austin was going to England that summer for the firm and they would be able to stay abroad until the first of September. But Celia was undecided about the wedding. She toyed with ideas, dreaming and smiling through her lashes, playing with the hidden bright things in her imagination.

"I might just go away . . . meet Austin in England and be married there, with gardenias, in a registry office, and only sunlight in the street afterward. It would be so alone."

Martha saw the sunlight and aloneness. She would be safe at Wellesley when they came home in the fall.

They were walking on the hill behind the school. The road ends up there. There was only a crooked path, muddy with March, going up to the summit, and a light growth of slim trees, birch and poplar, and young oaks flying the russet flags of another autumn. The wind was northwest and met them as they came out overlooking the farther valley. Celia stood very straight in the wind, her dress and coat blown back, her chin lifted. Her coat billowed away behind her, her slim body was outlined beneath her thin dress, her face wore an eager, ethereal look . . .

Martha's throat tightened with love. Again she thought, Celia is going to be safe, safe and cared for.

Celia was gazing out over the farther valley. She clasped her hands in front of her in a sudden, passionate gesture. "Look," she said, "it's all beginning to live again; see the grayish-purple color of the trees in the swamp even though there is no sign of leaves yet . . ."

They turned and walked along the hill; the wind made a thin music in the trees, and Celia's heels left a small, sharp imprint in the brown turf.

"Of course . . . a wedding. White satin . . . I suppose I owe it to Austin to be a little unforgettable that day."

She wore, unforgettably, white satin.

Again there was Commencement on a hot June morning metallic with sunlight. Martha remembers looking down into the bright gaze of that happy and beautiful assemblage, thinking, It is all the same as the years before; none of this is exclusively ours; all of it was only folded away a year ago to be used a little while by us today: the breathless room, the ferns curling in the heat, programs moving languidly, the blue iris and the white iris, the profusion of roses and peonies . . . The Old Girls filling four rows straight across the room: matrons, career girls, nurses, brides, and spinsters, all wearing the same chin-up smile and remembering the intervening years, months, days, since this day was lent, briefly, to them. The undergrads rustling and whispering together at the back of the platform . . .

A year ago she had seen Alicia's difficult tears. Now her own hands were cold, her heart impatient for the end. For where was the virtue in prolonging an unprivate grief? This slow sundering with its panoply of music and flowers?

Thus she was unprepared for that luminous instant warm with the serenity of Julia Severn's smile and the touch of her hand.

"Martha Mary MacLean." Was there an especial affection in her quiet regard? Martha's heart moved within her, realizing that this was a final moment, a demarcation between past and present, a catalyst. Before this I was, she thought; after this I am going to be . . . what, who? She had a sense of being lost and in search of her identity.

" 'They also serve—who only stand and wait,' " said Julia, then, with her beautiful distinctive enunciation.

Now Martha can take her look and find therein the prophetic, tender knowledge it contained. But then she was aware only of her intense emotion and turned away, holding the treasure of a divining love close to her inarticulate heart.

"Celia Rosemary Pence."

Celia crossed the platform in a moment taut and lengthening with interest. There was probably no one present who did not know that the daughter of Hubert Pence was being graduated that morning. Hammondville had had time to discover art in the last few years.

The moment was worthy of their expectation. Julia let her words fall, grave but sparkling, into the bright cup of their eagerness.

"We shall watch your star ascending."

A light breath, scarcely a sigh, passed over the room. Celia returned to her place, her cheek pale and cool, her hands, bearing the coveted scroll with silver ribbons, still; but her eyes were suddenly and darkly brilliant, almost unseeing. Thus, with a phrase, Julia rekindled the hot impatient flame of ambition which burned so briefly and intensely, wrought destruction, and perished in it.

Moving aloofly through the dispersing crowd, Martha saw Lilian Pence, a tall, red-haired woman with a bony face, plain, but superbly poised. The contours of that face had a less subtle modeling than Celia's, but they were unmistakably like. That pronounced structure came to them from Hubert Pence: never having seen him, one could still have recognized him from the remote resemblance between the half sisters. He had had red hair. The newspapers always mentioned this.

Celia's dusty fairness and her eyes—their color and the sweet languid shape of their lids—must be something of her English mother. Amid the laughter and the flowers it was strange to reflect that all that was mortal of Cecily Pence had returned to earth, vanishing with a quiet sad finality, that there was no one now living to recall and cherish a single gesture.

Midway of the evening comes that charming and traditional climax of the Commencement Dance, the Senior Waltz. As they stood poised, in that instant before the music began, Martha wished she could disappear; the floor seemed so vast and they so few, the room ringed with watching eyes. But there was, after all, no terror that she had imagined. Only the dip and sway; the incomparable lilt of music nevermore so persuasively gay and tender; Rob's arm, secure and sustaining; a remote and unimportant circle of dim faces and pale dresses; a low sheen of light along the polished floor.

And the beautiful bright pain of the two-edged blade that was her love, as she saw, over Rob's shoulder, Celia and Austin waltzing. A glance gave her as complete a vision of beauty as her heart could hold: Austin, smiling a little, with Celia young, quiescent, and enchanted in his arms, Mrs. Cutting's gift of pearls at her throat, a long, soft twist of hair heavy at her nape, and the white, unerring grace of slender-heeled slippers measuring his steps.

[67]

Martha's heart brimmed with the artist's peculiar pride and regret, as if she had created their perfection and their love out of something within her, and, the work being complete, she must now relinquish it to the purpose for which it had been conceived.

At four twenty-five o'clock in the afternoon of the third Wednesday in June, Nineteen Hundred and Twenty-Nine, at St. Paul's Episcopal Church, Glen Fells, New Jersey, Celia Pence was married to Austin Cutting. It was not a large wedding, nor an elaborate one, but all the metropolitan papers gave it generous columns, lavish with biographical data, made prominent by a full-length portait-photo of Celia in her wedding gown wearing a wistful look she had not worn. And, of course, there were headlines: Artist's Daughter and Young Industrialist Wed in Suburban Ceremony.

At three-thirty the oval mirror in Martha's room held her perfect image. An old tableau, the bride surrounded by her maids.

Virginia said breathlessly: "Celia, remember you *promised* to throw your bouquet straight at me!"

And Bennett drawled, "Well, I suppose this is the traditional moment when 'till death do us part' sounds like a colossal long time and the bride does a bit of soul-searching to find out whether she's 'sure.' "

Martha cannot remember that Bennett ever spoke without producing that small faltering silence at the end of her words. She succeeded then as always, but in the pause Celia looked into her own eyes in the mirror and said, smiling, "There is no death, when you are sure."

At four o'clock the organist played a single sweet stealthy note, added another, melted into a chord, pianissimo, then allowed the torrent of joyous melody to pour forth, rise rapidly, and fill the church.

Celia came down the aisle alone. She had not wanted anyone to give her away. Her clear amber eyes held a little sadness,

[68]

but also pride. She did not say, but Martha knew that she was thinking, This is my life, *I* shall do the giving.

At first it seemed a tremendously long aisle; her white figure wavered in Martha's sight. Then she was halfway, near enough so that one saw the heart-shaped neckline of her gown move lightly with her breath and a gleam of light slide along the toe of her slipper as she put out her foot. In another instant they would be able to see the fern of her bouquet quivering. ("Your flowers will give you away," said Bennett, who knew everything.)

But Celia's flowers were as steady as the long look she gave Austin.

At four-twenty-five, Celia put back her veil and Austin, turning, bent his head and touched her lips.

As if they had come to life, Martha's flowers shuddered on her arm.

II

Martha did not, after all, go to Wellesley that autumn. Her mother sat lightly on the arm of a chair, reasonable and relentless, while she stood opposite, fighting desperately with logic, stubbornness, and finally those involuntary brief tears which shamed her and effected what proved to be a useless compromise.

"No doubt Miss Severn has led you to believe, in an excess of enthusiasm, that 'the world is full of a number of things.' It isn't; for a woman there are only two, marriage or a career. Notice that I say *or.* A few exceptional women manage both, and not always successfully. Most of us do the best we can with one. You may take it from me that all the things one needs to know to make life pleasant and satisfying are not in books. If you had *any* particular talent, literary, artistic, even, like Millicent, a proficiency in languages, I'd gladly let you bury yourself for four years at a women's college . . ."

Her mother was unerring in her judgment. At Severn she had been a capable student, but only because her mind was methodical and retentive, not brilliant. It was the serenity, not the excitement, of scholarship which satisfied her, but, released from study, she found that satisfaction easily elsewhere, in the strong sound of wind at night, in the endless sound of running water, in walking, and in merely being alone.

In a manner half-realized, then, Wellesley was the symbol and guarantee of her serenity. The four perfect years just past could not be repeated, but they could be followed by four others of the same pattern. "Bury yourself," her mother said, with an inflection of scorn. It was the sum of her desire, nevertheless. Buried at Wellesley she would be safe from the complications of grief and fear. There was the fear of sudden change, the breaking of a loved and familiar pattern, fear of the day that would bring Celia and Austin home next door; the fear that her love for Celia, still intact and enabling her, apart from all else, to be deeply grateful for Celia's happiness, would not endure the test of living daily within sight of that happiness; and finally, the fear that her love for Austin would betray itself so that people, and Celia, and Austin himself would see how her life had cracked clear across, and show pity. More than anything else she had a fear of pity; the pity that would violate her integrity more deeply than its cause. Already, she saw herself walking on and on, without purpose, never still, but trying to escape the being still that was nothing.

Abruptly, she said, "I'll probably never marry, anyhow."

"Oh, don't be so positive," replied her mother lightly. "Against your better judgment you *may* fall in love. Even Celia —career notwithstanding—"

In an instant, out of a sharp weariness, came those dangerous tears, flowing down her still face as if they did not belong to her. If she persevered she would betray herself.

"Oh, all right," she said.

Her mother made a vague, startled gesture. "My dear, I only want you to be happy, to have a good time. Try it my way, first, and then, if you still feel the same next year . . ."

Scarcely anyone felt the same that next year.

Martha remembers, across the eventful, intervening years, the September day they came home, warm and stilly golden after an incredibly hot and humid Jersey August, with the first faint challenge of a yellow leaf here and there, the lawns deceptively smooth and green, all the gardens rioting with color; but it is impossible to recall the sharp flavor of the agitation she carried with her across "the valley" to the Cutting house, simply because there is no longer any danger as bright, or joy as piercing, or cause so valiant as those we knew before the years rolled over our heads. The wide, cool hall had a serene look behind the netting of the double screen doors, and she can still see Mrs. Cutting coming toward her over the gray-green carpet, that bright look of anticipation overlaying the quietude of her familiar smile.

"Come in, Martha; I've just finished the flowers. The ship was due to dock at ten, but the customs will take some time." Her eyebrows moved a little, like Austin's, because she was amused. "Celia is bringing four trunks."

Isabella Cutting was then in her fifty-eighth year; the only really beautiful woman Martha ever knew. Her own mother had the ageless charm of a natural vivacity; Julia Severn's personality was irradiated by a crisp vigor and a clear intellect; but in Austin's mother one saw a harmonious blending of physical beauty and a sparkling intelligence precisely balanced. Someone—a woman—once said of her that she had the imperturbable facade of a Chinese: a phrase that could be repeated because it was disarmed of malice by its accuracy.

She was of middle height, a woman with the dignity and composure that have long been a forgotten feminine fashion. She moved deliberately, always; perhaps more so in later years by reason of her failing health. Her light brown hair was heavily threaded with silver even when Martha first knew her, the roses and snow of an exquisite English complexion faded to a clear pallor faintly shadowed beneath her eyes; but as long as she lived, her eyes were that lovely color, the gray of stone with the clarity of water. And her brows could move delicately in demure amusement.

They went in together to look at the festive luncheon table laid with four places. From the dining room they went out onto the porch, the wide old-fashioned elbowed porch with the tall fan-backed wicker chairs and the hand-woven India matting where, on so many summer evenings, she and Austin had eaten homemade strawberry ice cream, hiding their sighs of repletion within the dusk. But even this was swept away by the relentless scythe of change: the cook left, her successor was somehow less gifted, the old hand freezer, salt-stained bucket, dasher, and all, was relegated to the cellar, the new automatic refrigerator produced frozen desserts not even remotely related to those heaping ambrosial pink dishes; and the advancing years brought longings too sharp and strange to be satisfied by the tart goodness of fresh fruit hidden in frozen cream.

Mrs. Cutting's hands, always serenely occupied, were busy with a design of butterflies embroidered in bright silken thread on a length of white linen. As if involuntarily, her eyes kept turning to the drive entrance. When the telephone rang thinly through the house she rose unhurriedly and went in to answer. Yet the fact that she went herself instead of waiting for Mrs. Maxwell betrayed the sharpness of her expectation.

For Martha, having enjoyed that rare sincerity, the friendship of a young girl with an older woman, all the little signs a stranger might have missed fell neatly together in a readable design, conveying the knowledge that this homecoming was not for herself alone fraught with a delicate peril. In this house Mrs. Cutting had been mistress for more than thirty years—it was inconceivable that this should be changed: here was her place and these her possessions. Still, Celia must be accorded whatever dignity and privilege were due her as a wife. In no way must she be made to feel subservient, unnecessary. There was a delicate balance to be struck. Isabella Cutting would not be satisfied unless it were struck, for hers was a meticulous generation.

Martha, on the other hand, could not visualize Celia in that household as other than, perhaps, a guest; yet she was coming, she was almost here, this was to be *her* home from this day forth. All her knowledge of Celia would yield her nothing but the fear that some careless touch would send such a delicate domestic structure crashing in ruins, for Celia had had no experience of domesticity in her varied life.

Nor was Mrs. Cutting's only problem one of domestic

[76]

nicety. On this day, certain hitherto unlimited prerogatives and responsibilities became invalid. For her, too, the pattern was changed. Still a mother, with a mother's experienced heart and peculiar wisdom, she was gently but conclusively relegated. It might still be her concern, but her son's happiness was now officially another's privilege.

In a few minutes she came out of the house and picked up her work.

"That was Austin. They've landed but everything took much longer than they'd expected and they're lunching in New York before driving out. So you and I will go in just as soon as Mrs. Maxwell is ready for us." Her voice was calm, but the glow had faded from her face.

The two extra places had been removed. They sat down at opposite sides of the mahogany table.

In the last few minutes before they came, Martha had an interval of panic. What was she doing here, a stranger lurking on the edge of a family reunion? Old family friend. A flicker of mockery in the darkness of her doubt. Mrs. Cutting. Austin. Celia. She tried to invoke some blessed, homely memory for her reassurance: the recollection of some simple thing done with mutual pleasure, but all that came was a deep vibration against the inner ear of her mind—Austin's voice, urgent and low: "Celia. Celia . . . *darling!*" Quickly, she caught at the things she had shared with Celia: the room at the Hall, their long walks, Celia passing the sugar bowl at breakfast, absently, her eyes intent on the rapid review of a chapter in some textbook.

She remembered, but it was futile; for Celia had stepped calmly out of that life and all their sharing was past. She had now nothing more to share with Celia—for what was left except racketing around town in the station wagon on sundry errands, getting the late mail, buying canapés at Merrill-Thorpes', or playing three sets of tennis a day, sometimes in the cool of morning, sometimes in the heat of afternoon; or going to the Saturday night dances at the club, moving about like an automaton in the arms of some boy, any boy, tendering over and over the same thin coinage of wisecracks, getting it, giving it, passing it on without scrutiny?

And, of course, there was sex. The Victorian era was long gone—this was the age of the automobile and close dancing. One was sophisticated, naturally; one might know quite well where the line was drawn, but the trick was not to let your co-player know exactly where you had drawn it, or even that there *was* a line. According to prevailing custom, you implied that the hunting was happy but the quarry elusive . . .

By this time she had learned what it felt like to be kissed. (If only they were a little less clumsy!) She had known the touch of a boy's hand on her knee just where her short skirt ended; she could be adroit and bantering and, at the same time, set her teeth and exclaim silently: "You fool!" without being quite sure in the tension of the moment to whom she referred. It all came under the chapter her mother had called "having fun."

Some of her contemporaries, she found, were simply content with exhaustive discussions. These were simpler to deal with, although less exciting: you had only to lean your head against the back of the car seat (this showed your profile to good advantage) and make appropriate murmurs of agreement when the discussion became profound or there were pauses. The girls tagged their escorts "paw" or "jaw" to mark the distinction. Of course, after a few sessions of "jaw" the sense of old friends and confidants could very well lead abruptly to "paw" status.

The game always seemed more piquant by moonlight than it did the next morning, and there were instances where girls fell in love or got tight on repeated sips out of hip flasks and played it wild, without rules: the thought of these could be depressing, but this was her Age, this the world outside Severn. Its language was there to be learned, its tempo to be acquired: and what else was there?

There could be no sharing of Celia's new life.

She need never know how many times or in what accents Austin had said, "Celia, darling," this summer. In the deep

English countryside; on a balcony in Venice, with the flicker of sunbright water glancing upward on Celia's face; in a Paris fiacre, rattling home along the empty boulevards; in the lighted intimacy of their small cabin at sea, rising and falling, like the breast of a loved one peacefully sleeping. No, she need never know—exactly. But the approximation of a knowledge that was Celia's and not hers would be a bar between them forever.

How often had Julia Severn rallied them with her distinctive outcry against ignoble thought and action: "Be unafraid ... be brave, be noble!" The day comes, and the fear, and there are no trumpets and no flags, only (she thought) in the wilderness of one's mind the foe and the challenge.

It all vanished—the fearful introspection—in that instant when the car drew up at the steps and Williams, jumping out, opened the rear door.

Holding Celia in a spontaneous embrace; hearing her voice cry, "Martie!" with a little catch in it; seeing her laugh, turn her head, put up her hand in a remembered gesture and pull off her hat, she felt the old shining love quicken to new life in her heart. Everything was suddenly familiar and happy and unconstrained. She looked at Austin sitting on the arm of his mother's chair, his shining fair head inclined slightly to hers, and the little pang which ran her through was an old friend.

Mrs. Cutting's face was like a lovely room in which all the lamps have been lighted.

Celia was wearing blue, a dress and a long slim coat of soft wool in a pure clear shade. Strangely, she had never before worn blue: gray, and green, and brown, some black, never blue. That day even her shoes were of navy kid, glove-thin. Half sitting, half leaning on the porch railing, swinging a slender foot, she is forever framed in the sunlight of a far autumn day, brilliant with animation and happiness.

And Martha, remembering, remembers also how assurance rose within her. All her fears for herself and for them, gone. Fate would be kind to them because they were so beautiful. For herself—ah, Julia!—she would be noble, and none would ever know!

In an instant it was clear to her why Austin had been compelled to love Celia. It was because, like his mother, she could have stepped across all the barriers of the ages.

It was a beautiful autumn, prolonged and lingering, filled with the dreaming fall of leaves and the smoke of gentle fires. Martha held it, like a treasured coin, within her hand; and like a coin, it had two faces. Those days, tranquil with the restoration of a companionship she had thought was lost, were the last of their kind which she was to enjoy. Is it only some alchemy of memory, or are those last things always fairest in their perfection?

She had forgotten that Celia's early life enabled her to settle easily and gracefully in strange places, conferring favor by accepting it. She was unprepared to find their intimacy, like Celia herself, as much at home in the Cutting house as in the Hall at Severn. All that long autumn she cherished the renewal of companionship. The telephone calling her from the breakfast table: Celia's voice, "Busy? Can you come over?" Celia meeting her, on the porch or halfway across the lawns. An afternoon when she came upon her in "the valley," her face upturned and the bright leaves falling slantwise about her still figure on an almost imperceptible vagrant wind. When Martha spoke in the stillness, she turned; surprised, but not remarking it, taking Martha's fingers easily in her own, betrayed by that waking look which told Martha that this had been one of her lone and far withdrawals.

How many times, and how lightly, had they run up the broad stairs with the curving balustrade to Celia's room? A big room with a bay facing south and thick rugs islanded on the polished floor.

Celia's and Austin's room.

The room of Austin's grandparents: his father had been born in the mahogany four-poster. The heavy star-patterned spread which covered it, crocheted by Austin's great-aunt, was sixty years old. Celia was impressed by the evidences of continuity which were all about her.

"Now I know what roots are," she told Martha. "Having and using things which belonged to you before you were born."

Together they unpacked Celia's four trunks and folded away her exquisite Parisian lingerie, hung away her dresses and evening gowns, little suits and coats. There was an afternoon frock in navy chiffon with a pink ruffle soft at the throat and wrists. She wore it often through the fall and winter at the late Sunday afternoon teas Mrs. Cutting gave that year. The ruffles fell back from the arch of her strong, slim wrist as she poured. It was a dress which might have been designed to mark the grace of her beautiful hands.

In the sedate company of Mrs. Cutting's guests, she played her role delicately with a flawless precision, as if unaware of the impact her youth and demure grace and her slight air of fame made upon their imaginations. Austin's young wife. Daughter of the house. But alone with Martha a hidden mischief escaped its careful restraints: sitting cross-legged on the floor of her room in the midst of an assortment of souvenirs, she told, laughing, of how she had brought scandal upon them their first night in London.

"Austin signed the register first and then handed the pen to me, and without thinking, I wrote my name under his. The clerk looked—oh, Martie, you've never seen anything funny until you've seen an Englishman raise his eyebrows without moving a muscle. It was a very staid hotel . . . When I looked, I found I'd written 'Celia Pence'!"

Beyond the curve of her mouth, the bland, ingenuous, remembering laughter in her eyes, it was possible to see, as in a mirror, Austin's chagrin retreating, silent, before his indulgent love.

She lost the grim feeling of having crossed a line or turned a corner away from her girlhood; and although she knew she was but making the most of the present, emotionally improvident for the future, she let the thought hide from her consciousness when it could.

The other face of the coin was the pain of a loneliness which her association with Celia had no power to assuage. After a time she recognized its character and became resigned to it, but not until she had been desperate and a little foolish.

She and Millicent had their coming-out parties at the club within a week of each other. They were not pretentious affairs as such things went, but they were well conducted in the best Glen Fells tradition. There was the ubiquitous Mr. Ross, caterer, and the same quantities of flowers, music, chicken salad, and ice cream. There was a huge crystal bowl of innocuous punch, and some surreptitious handling of flasks in the darkness of the porch.

The holidays were fast approaching. There were those, even in the complacent shelter of communities such as Glen Fells, who had known some moments of dismay in October when the collapse of the stock market inaugurated the Great Depression. However, as these startling facts had not been correlated and no capitalized title yet given to the tedious and tragic era upon which they were even then embarking, people (with the exception of an exotic few who had been "wiped out" overnight) soon settled back into their habits of comfort and pleasure. Even those who, like Martha's father, were "in the Street" were certain that things would be stable by spring.

The social calendar was crowded to its margins, meanwhile, and use of department-store charge accounts rallied handsomely. After all, the market had dipped before and recovered. Everyone had been making plenty of money for years—this was the never-to-be-forgotten "boom" of the Twenties, remember? Now was the time to get in and take advantage of the upturn when it came . . .

For most of these people the process of being economically expunged from the old familiar life would be a drawn-out, agonizing, and humiliating one.

Significantly, then, that year Martha "came out." An emergence into many realities—from girlhood to womanhood, from innocence to awareness, from singleness of heart to the knowledge of many kinds of love, from dreams to desire . . .

To mark the occasion, she wore a wide-skirted taffeta gown. Skirts were longer that year. Her mother came into the room as she finished dressing. "Darling, you're beautiful!" And then she shed those surprising tears which Martha decided were not for her but for a lost girlhood in a small Ohio town so strict that it had held neither dances, taffeta, nor corsages.

Austin danced twice with Martha during the evening, his eyes seeking Celia across the crowded floor.

That was her loneliness. A little late, Celia and Austin would stand in a doorway, her hand upon his arm, glancing over the dance floor or at the people grouped, waiting to go in to dinner. And immediately, she would feel forsaken and miserable in the midst of gaiety. Austin spoke to her, danced with her, but it was unavailing. The fault was not his. She was too young, and by inclination too honest, to know how, all at once, to mask the astounding relevance of her love with inconsequentials, and therefore found little to say to him. He was unfailingly kind, never forgetting, through all that long winter, to show her the constancy of friendship which had marked all their years together: a bitter reminder that nothing had been changed by the secret discovery of her own heart.

Her spirit rebelled against that changelessness, but in a terrible, unavailing repetition of temptations by which she was met and vanquished. Now, all the winter Sunday afternoons in the Cutting living room, all the Friday-evening dinner parties of her inclusion, have merged into a single recollection of warmth and light and polite pleasantry, with Celia demure under the homage of Austin's glance, savoring the unique experience of a patterned sociability. Candlelight and firelight and the bright light of anguish have dimmed equally with the passing years, but memory will not relinquish the perfect miniatures of a transitory peace to hold against its passing.

Again and again she returned to court the irresistible pain of that tranquility, simply because the private torment she suffered there was the alternative to an unbearable aridity.

When she was alone all the strength of her will could not banish her thought of Celia and Austin together. Because it was winter and the trees slender against the night, she was able to see the lighted windows of their room from her own. Like an importunate guest the imagination of their felicity came into her mind and would not depart.

A warm, bright autumn; a long winter, a seemingly interminable winter during which events repeated themselves and experiences newly lived appeared to re-echo in the memory from a former time; and a spring fraught with uncongenial aspects of change . . . This was the first year of Celia's marriage, and this the background of Martha's struggle to accept it.

All other efforts were vain and humiliating. Around the New Year she noticed that Carroll Owen was giving her a mild rush. It was more convenient than gratifying: she was going to everything, moving incessantly against her inclination, in the stream of social activity. She could not remember, afterward, at what moment or in what alien spirit of malice she breathed the embers of a fatuous admiration into flame. Swayed by alternate moods of recklessness and derision, she learned inadvertently and effectively how to play the oldest of games but, at the end, was snared by her own perverse innocence.

A month or two . . . a few brief weeks . . . Of its nature it could not have lasted longer. She hastened the climax but did not anticipate it by very much time. There had to be one; it was demanded by half hours at midnight in a car parked on the fir-shadowed drive or in the bold hard glitter of winter moonlight revealing their white faces to each other; by the studied attitudes of pensiveness and romance; by the awkward and tentative touch of hand to hand and cheek to cheek; by the lingering kisses and the whispered phrases and eloquent small sighs of a dramatic deception . . .

All at once, on a crisp cold evening toward the end of January, she could endure it all no longer. The occasion was another club dance in the procession of such affairs. The same faces revolved past her, the same orchestra was playing the same tunes popular all through the long winter, flattened into inanity by repetition. Stepping out of Carroll's arms in the middle of a dance, she heard herself say to him, "Go and dance with someone else for a while; I'm going outside." She got her wrap from the cloakroom and let herself out of the long ballroom doors to the sun deck. The clear sky was filled with sharp stars, the long breath she drew was a knife in her breast. Below the hill she saw the little roads of Glen Fells winding away into the night, their lights bright on the cold air. Pressing her hands together, she asked herself wordless questions—where?—why? —how long? She heard behind her the burst of music as Carroll came out, and felt the gentleness of his hands upon her shoulders. He stood just behind her, saying nothing, but she knew that in another minute he would turn her to face him and lift her chin with his hand.

She shivered lightly.

"Cold?" he murmured at her ear.

She stood perfectly still, unresponsive and unmoved by his kiss, listening to an echo. (Was life nothing more than a succession of echoes?)

"Let's go somewhere else—in the car," he said urgently. "I'm fed up with these affairs, aren't you?"

"Yes, let's," she assented, almost absently. Carroll was a fast but competent driver. Speed could be the answer. She saw herself in the car, out on the highway with the night streaming rapidly past, darkened buildings falling away behind them.

It started that way and with a sigh she put her head back against the seat. Carroll drove, not speaking. Tension began to leave her mind and her body. She closed her eyes, listening to the sound of the wind of motion made by the car in its passing. Speed. The release of unthought.

She was jolted abruptly out of her self-mesmerism, sliding

[85]

toward him on the leather seat as he swung off the highway into a steep uphill. At the top he made another turn into an obscure lane, a shadowy dirt road heading into a dark wood where the clear sky and its stars were lost to them. Swiftly he cut the motor and put out the lights,

Tensing again, annoyed at herself for walking so thoughtlessly into this trap (I could write the whole scenario, she thought), for encouraging an episode that was bound to end in irritation for both of them, she stayed quietly in her corner.

"Come here," he said, after a moment. There was nothing peremptory in his voice, only a kind of loneliness which matched her own, she thought. She moved left. (The strategy was, also, to keep a corner for retreat; or, in extreme emergencies, a door.)

"I don't feel like talking," she said. "Do you mind?"

"Why should I?" he asked, with his arm around her shoulders. He dropped a light kiss on her temple. On her cheek. He ran a fingertip expertly along her eyebrow, down her cheek, under her chin, using the gesture economically to tip her face upward to receive his mouth on hers. She tried to draw away.

Immediately, he became importunate, all mouth and hands and greed.

"Stop it!" she cried, incensed. His hands were everywhere; she heard the strap of her gown tear as he plunged his free hand inside her neckline. She tried to move away, back to her corner, but now his arm was around her neck, holding her with a mindless strength. She struggled, her heart beating with heavy strokes: not exactly with fear but with a fatalistic sense that what was about to happen was largely her own fault . . .

It could not have lasted more than a minute—the gasping struggle, the rearing movement, the deep groaning (she had time to think of a horse she had once seen struggling to rise from a fall). Her head was forced back; vainly she tried to avoid his mouth, turning her face from side to side. All at once she realized, with shock, that his left hand was gripping hers, that under her hand was a column of rigid muscle and warm flesh.

There was a final convulsive movement. He sobbed once. It was over. Her hand and the front of her gown were wet. Against the darkness, in her mind's eye, she saw what the spreading stain on the nile green satin would look like as she walked into the house.

He had released her. She withdrew to her corner by the door, trying to arrange the skirt of her gown so that the sticking wetness would not lie against her legs. ("Slip, too," she thought, with disgust.)

It was totally dark. Even with eyes adjusted to the darkness they were only shadows to each other. She felt rather than saw his moroseness. He sat without moving for a long time, his arms encircling the wheel. She supposed that he had managed to put himself together.

"Is your dress ruined?"

"I imagine so. Not having any previous experience, I'm guessing, of course." She regretted the sarcastic edge in her voice almost as she spoke.

"I'm s-sorry . . . Can't you have it cleaned?" She saw herself marching in to the Glen Fells cleaners with the dress over her arm. ("What is the nature of this stain, miss? We have to know to determine what agent to use—" "Oh, that's semen. Just plain ordinary semen." "Thank you, miss.")

"Why *me?*" She hoped he wouldn't say he loved her; this was not the shape of love as she divined it. She thought again of the rearing, snorting horse, the terror and the effort . . . Could Austin with Celia . . . ? (Oh, God, where was her arrant thought taking her?)

"Why me?" she asked again, more gently.

"You've been driving me crazy for months. And I think you know it," he said sullenly. "You play hard-to-get. And then you cheat . . ."

She was silent. There was some truth in what he said. Her only excuse was that because of her inexperience she had not realized where or how fast she was leading him. Yes; she was culpable. The whole pathetic, ugly, deplorable, futile mess was her responsibility. Why me? she asked, of herself, this time. Where was the idealism and the innocence, and the *pride* that had enabled her to turn away from Ted Marsh in spite of her feminine curiosity? What had happened to the Martha who was shocked and fearful of Celia's avid reaching for experience, any kind of experience? What was the reason behind this playing games in a fantasy without feeling?

She knew, now. Daring, at last, to ask she had not far to look for the answer. She was revenging herself for the loss of Wellesley. She had been tossed, kicking and screaming, into the currents of the Twenties (now suddenly become the Thirties), forced to give up the protection she had longed for. Thus, to her mother she was silently saying, This is what it's like; this is what one does to compete, to stay afloat, to score points . . . Is *this* what you wanted for me? Is this where *my* 'special talent' lies? (And lies, and lies!)

She knew better. In spite of her mother's cheerful sophistication, she was still the product of her Ohio girlhood. Bored and blasé married women whose marriages had withered, divorcées and girls without breeding and solid suburban backgrounds, and spoiled daughters of the rich who had a wild streak . . . *these* poor benighted souls might indulge in the vulgar sport of come-on; but not—no, never—Martha MacLean!

Beside her, Carroll Owen moved abruptly, starting the car.

"My father," he burst out loudly above the noise of the motor, "has gambled away all his money! I can't finish college . . . we'll have to move and I'll have to go to work. If I can find a job!"

"I'm sorry," she said. What else do you say? A million dollars, accumulated through some wise, some lucky real estate investments around the turn of the century. Lucky his grandfather was not here to see it happen. How do you get rid of *a million dollars?* Everyone was learning about economics these days; there were, it seemed, no limits to the recklessness which had carried people along to catastrophe. Like going over

Niagara, they had no idea how close they were to the brink until it was too late to turn back and they went over with a rush and a roar.

In spite of herself her lips twisted wryly in a half-smile. The analogy was as good for sex as for speculation, she thought; one search for excitement was as valid as the other. A man with a million dollars didn't gamble just for *money,* now did he?

In the Severn library on the second shelf near the north window was a row of books. They all had read them. They were encouraged to read them. They were said to contain everything they needed to know; and the weekly classes in Sex and Hygiene with the nurse, Mrs. Matlock, were intended to sum up the subject, afford them an opportunity to ask questions. Mrs. Matlock was forty, with a strong, unsupple figure packed tightly into her uniform, which creaked with starch as she moved. She was also the mother of three children. She had a heavy head of corn-yellow hair and a ruddy outdoor complexion. She was an advocate of cold showers, plain diet, and long walks. She was anti-auto and went everywhere on foot.

Physiology and the reproductive system (female) were thoroughly dealt with in all the books and in her course. "Any questions, girls?" she would ask briskly at the end of the session. Of course not. How could they ask *Mrs. Matlock* what it *felt* like . . . to what heights or depths . . . how it changed, or failed to change one . . . *What* questions?

"How could you ask *her?*" demanded Horty.

"Well, at least we know men are different," ventured Virginia.

Bennett laughed her raucous laugh. "How? I mean, how do we know? Not from her, you don't. You'd think she'd had three immaculate conceptions!"

Alicia said gently, "Read the books: they also give you the male physiology."

"All this *physiology,*" muttered Lois, blushing bright red. "What about love? Do people do it without love—deliberately

[89]

—or do they *think* they're in love, or what? And how can they be in love so often—every time they get into the back seat of a car!"

"That may be the measure of difference," said Alicia kindly. "Women tend to believe, or to tell themselves, that it's love; men sometimes, but not always . . ."

"Why?" Virginia again.

No one but Martha noticed that Celia listened silently, contributing nothing.

"Because, biologically speaking, it's an end for men, the end of pursuit; and a beginning for women. A beginning in the natural course of things—of pregnancy and nesting and all that, the job of rearing young, which all comes *afterward.* In modern society, of course, there are all kinds of variations on *that* theme. Free love, sex without marriage, nonvirgins, demivirgins, marriage without children; perhaps, even, who knows, marriages without sex!"

But they were all virgins. Even Alicia, biologically sophisticated, was a virgin. Horty admitted, with a shrug, that she played around—"a little."

The car was on the highway again.

"I want you to know," Carroll said defensively, "I never said I was in love with you. You're attractive, and I wanted you, and that's—"

"Let's forget it, shall we?" She had already reached *that* conclusion. All she had to do now was walk into the house in her ruined dress, hoping that she could lie cheerfully and convincingly if her parents were still up. Punch? Coffee, tea? Champagne! She bit back a laugh. Champagne ought to be about right.

Why lie?

To protect her mother from a wound which she, in her innocence, did not deserve. She had just recognized her mother's innocence, married young to her first love.

No one was up when she let herself into the house. A dim light burned in the hall. She went quietly up the broad stairs to her room. She removed the diamond-chip clips (her father's coming-out present) from the neckline of the nile green satin and let the dress fall to the floor. (The slip, too, darn it! Four inches of real lace at the bottom.) She stepped out of the whole business, rolled up dress and slip, and resolved to burn them in the backyard incinerator in the morning. (Well, what else— the Goodwill?)

Her mother said nothing when, after breakfast, she passed through the kitchen carrying her bundle. The cremation took a half hour. She stood with the wind of the bright, brisk winter's day blowing her hair about, poking the charred remains with a stick, busily closing another chapter of her life, letting it blow away with the smoke of the fire.

Her mother was still in the kitchen when she went in, wearing a troubled look of inquiry.

"What on earth—?"

"The dress I wore last night. Ruined. Absolutely. Somebody spilled something all over the front of it. Major excitement of a very low evening." She washed her hands at the sink, letting her gaze travel across the distance to the Cutting house four acres away. Reaching for a cup with one hand and the percolator with the other, she saw her mother's glance meet hers and then drop away. Nothing more was said. Perhaps, she thought, she had closed more than one door.

But didn't someone say that for all knowledge there is a price?

One morning in February her father was summoned to the telephone from the breakfast table. She heard those first casual syllables, a broken exclamation, his terse, rapid questions. Her mother sat straighter in her chair, waiting, her eyes darkened with apprehension.

He came back into the dining room, his face haggard. He wore that look for the next five years.

"Doug, what is it? Something has happened!"

An era ended with his reply. Not with the telephone call,

nor even with the reason for it, but in that instant when, for the first time in their life together, he spoke without consideration for her mother's feelings:

"Les Patterson committed suicide last night. They found him in his car in the garage this morning."

"Doug . . . could it have been an accident?"

He pushed back his plate suddenly. "Not under the circumstances."

She saw her mother's face change. "It's very bad, isn't it? Oh, Doug, why didn't you tell me?"

"We thought it might not be as bad as it seemed . . . But it's worse. Speculating with other people's money, putting up their securities to raise money to speculate on his own . . . Les was finally wiped out—everything—Marsden and I are hoping we can cover, but it doesn't look good . . ."

Les Patterson was one of her father's partners, another of the "golden boys" who had gone into Wall Street in the decade after the Great War, acquired the Midas touch, and gradually came to believe that there was no direction but UP!

She remembers the funeral and Les Patterson's young widow, Irene. They were younger than her parents, and childless. Fortunately. It was inconceivable that anyone as young and sanguine as Les could find reason enough in financial disaster willingly to take leave of love and life, of cold streams filled with trout, sunny golf links, and the sound of wet sails taking the wind. When she was a little older, still more inconceivable that such a young man as she remembered Les to have been—bright, intelligent—could have considered all these things important enough to steal for when times changed and his way of life was threatened.

Retrench. It was a new word and a new idea. An idea so new, in fact, after the years of easy living and thoughtless prosperity, that their first efforts were ludicrously inadequate. The laundress was first to go, but they expected no great inconvenience; Jenny, cook and maid, could work it in somehow. They would do less entertaining, of course. Actually, this was not so;

[92]

misery loves company and friends gathered to discuss the strange new expedience which had come into their ordered lives.

Rodney had to go next. After all, they really didn't need a chauffeur. They all drove now, and they would have to get rid of one of the cars. Upkeep on two was getting difficult. The station wagon was newer and more salable than the Packard, so they kept the Packard. Later, someone saw Rodney selling apples (they said) at the corner of Forty-third Street and one of the avenues, early in 1932. But that seemed doubtful; why would he move into New York?

It was not until Jenny had to go and all the order, comfort, and cleanliness of the big house devolved upon them that they actually realized the measure of those evil days. Her mother was rueful but uncomplaining. "It's helpful to have been brought up on plain living, after all," she remarked. Nevertheless, plain living in a ten-room house surrounded by three acres of lawns and shrubbery, and the contest with ingrained habits of prodigality which ranged from the use of too expensive ingredients in cooking to the thoughtless elaboration of table settings with the resultant endless dishwashing, was a rather more complex matter than plain living in a five-room Victorian cottage on the tree-shaded street of an Ohio village, circa 1910.

The bills were the worst, for there was almost no money to pay them. Then the bills became letters: stern, insistent, demanding, ugly. A good part of these stemmed from Martha's incongruous winter wardrobe, which had included eleven evening gowns. (Minus one, she thought.)

A little later, when the mail came her mother would say, "Give me those things, don't let your father see them." And sitting down at her little typewriter on which she had formerly tapped out those sparkling, witty notes and letters to a host of friends whose lives had taken them out of sight of her own, she would compose the polite, apologetic, sincere communications which gained them a few days' grace, a week's respite, a month's opportunity to accumulate, by painful economies, five dollars to pay here, or there; around the circle, then back again. By this time, so many people were delinquent, or vanished, so many accounts totally uncollectible, that it was quite possible to handle things this way and achieve a sense of order in the midst of economic chaos.

Perhaps her father would ask suddenly, "What about that bill from Hendersons'?" And her mother reply airily, "That? Oh, I took care of that *weeks* ago!" and only Martha knew exactly what her words meant. Occasionally they managed to write "final payment" in the notebook they kept for accounts. But there was always another expense, a new bill to replace an old one: furnace repairs, a tire for the car, the plumber's emergency visit. More and more people demanded cash, not knowing whether those they gave credit to would be around to pay when the month was up. They had never waited for spring so eagerly; her mother counted on her fingers the lovely months when the furnace would need no attention.

Mortgage payments came due quarterly, taxes half-yearly. Doug's salary had been cut twice, drastically. There were scarcely any commissions, and those few were small. All their cash reserves and securities had been sacrificed to cover Les Patterson's default. But, unlike so many others, Doug still had a job, still caught the eight-ten into town each morning and came back on the six-twenty each evening, so that life seemed to move in its old grooves.

Her mother bought a cookbook at Woolworth's: *Two Hundred and Fifty Ways to Cook Meat.* Most of them were recipes involving the use of hamburger. An acquaintance remarked that "when this thing is over, I never want to see ground meat or pancakes again!"

Toward spring Martha began the long search for a job. Sitting at her mother's desk, she read and answered all those unclassifiable ads which are the hope of the untrained and inexperienced job-seeker: "Wanted, young woman with pleasant voice to read to invalid," "Wanted, companion to elderly lady. Driver's license. Must like animals," or "Model, size 10, no experience, good pay." The invalids all lived at the far end of Long Island, "companions" were offered room and board but no salary, and "model" reflected a host of diverse opportunities, most of them unappealing. Not too often she gambled with real money, traveling into the city for interviews at the agencies. Once or twice, in spite of (or because of?) her inexperience, she got as far as the prospective employer's office. In an office on the top floor of a loft building where she went in answer to an ad which read: "Receptionist, small typing, answer phone, etc. No experience necessary," a hard-faced woman with dyed black hair and purple lipstick took her name and tossed her head toward the door. "Go down that hall to the room at the end and take off your clothes. Mr. Burger will be in to see you in a few minutes."

It was her last trip to the city. Countless people had put her name down and sent her home to wait for the call that never came. Instead of helping, she was spending money as fruitlessly and recklessly as if she had gambled it away in Reno.

She did something she referred to in her own mind as "settling down." The episode with Carroll Owen she considered as a kind of watershed, the point at which she decided to go back to being herself and stop being an idiot. In the busyness of hands she recovered a measure of serenity. There was plenty to do in the house and the garden. Her love of method found satisfaction in closets and drawers filled with clothing and linens kept neat by her own hands. Her heart lifted at the sight of a long line of sheets catching the wind in a snowy curve; or the gleam of a hand-rubbed Sheraton cabinet. She and her mother planted and transplanted, weeded and pruned. She rose at dawn to mow the lawns before the day got too warm for such strenuous work; and mowed again in the cool of the evening. It took almost three days to get around the extensive lawns, and then it was almost time to start over again. Her nineteenth birthday came and with it, formlessly, dreams again: somewhere, around a corner, there must be something worthy of expectation . . . Meanwhile, a writer whose work she admired wrote a magazine article about the "minor ecstasies" of living from day to day.

She saw less of Celia. There wasn't time for the careless lengthy visiting now. Sometimes Celia would drop in for tea or turn in the drive as they were gardening. "I must run," she would say, "Austin's bringing a customer for dinner. Conversation will concern switches and valves, exclusively. I *am* looking forward to it!" Or, "This is just hello. I'm meeting Austin in the city. We're dining the world's mathematical genius and his wife at Chez Louis." Martha found her light irony profoundly disturbing.

Then it was June again and they drove up to Hammondville in Celia's car for their first reunion. And Celia Cutting, possessed and lovely, became once more the target of those bright furtive glances. To Martha they said, "Celia looks marvelous, doesn't she?" They asked Celia, "How is Austin?" And, "Are you still painting?" To each other they repeated in varying accents, "Are you *doing* anything?" "What are you *doing* now?" Accomplishments and activities were aired. It wasn't quite right to be doing nothing; they had become serious, purposeful. The college girls spoke of courses like sociology and psychology, intending to put the world right. The married girls spoke of budgets and passed around snapshots of offspring. The career girls were brisk and contained.

Celia's smile was cool with amusement, but when they came at her with their questions her face assumed an expression which Martha recognized but was unable to define. It may have been sardonic, or rueful; she could not tell. Celia's emotions, unlike Bennett's, mirrored themselves lightly and fleetingly, always.

Once, soon after their return from Europe, Martha had asked to see her sketchbooks. "You must have done so much!" In the moment of utter stillness which followed her words she saw that expression pass, faint as the shadow of smoke, across Celia's face. She gave Martha an oblique glance.

"There wasn't . . . time," she said.

Bennett was home from her first year at the midwestern state university she had chosen as her college. Virginia was engaged to a penniless young lawyer, out of college a year and still without prospects. Lois had completed a business course and was a stenographer. Horty was there, theatrical and vivid in red and white, telling everyone who would listen of the walk-on bit she was going to play on Broadway in September. "He said I had *something* which comes across the footlights!" A bespectacled Alicia took Martha's hand in a strong, quiet grasp. She seemed much older than the others.

Julia spoke to them so briefly and beautifully that they forgot for a few moments their small friendly feuds in contemplation of the new decade she held before them. It would be different from the last, she promised them. From her smile they understood that she was not promising them a restoration of the great bubble which had broken, or the ways of ease which had passed and were passing. Times of crisis were times of challenge, she reminded them. They listened almost intently; they had listened to her inspirational pronouncements for years, but they were less cynical and inattentive this year than before: they wanted to believe, they needed anchors to hold. They looked at the white lock above her brow, at the gentle upright assurance of her bearing and saw Experience. Their pulses were stirred; they forgot the humiliations and petty annoyances of curtailment and thought in terms of basic values and the courage to face future change.

The lengthening shadows of late afternoon lay across the small farms and folded hills of the rural New Jersey landscape as they drove home from Hammondville. This same countryside had flickered by a train window during her first parting from Celia in a past November. Seeing in retrospect the bright predestined curve of their friendship between that day and this, Martha thought: We are committed to each other forever; nothing can change that now. Not even . . . no, not even the fact

[97]

that you, unknowingly, stole my love, and all that is left to me of that joy is seeing you possess it.

With a quick intuition (or resignation, perhaps?) she felt that there was nothing that Celia might do and she not forgive. For Celia was a creature of impulse; everything she did sprang from her deepest feelings and was completely spontaneous.

No one but Celia, on that late afternoon, with the long drive home before dinner, would have pulled off into a grassy lane to climb a round hilltop thickly starred with daisies and throw herself down in the deep grass, careless of white silk by Lanvin and the handmade hat with the deep brim which she flung away from her. She lay with her arms beneath her head, her yellow eyes half closed and dark with dreaming. A little sunset wind blew across the hilltop, bending the daisies in a myriad curtsy.

She drew a deep breath. "I'm so happy I shall never die."

And after that she told Martha about Turetsky and the studio in New York.

Martha's first thought was that Celia had told no one at Severn, in spite of their questions; she had reserved this confidence for her. Then, like distant lightning, dismay flickered at the horizon of her thought. Here was her fear, after these many months; but like so many of her fears for Celia, it wore a strange face when she encountered it. She could not have told why this announcement and the hard-held intensity of Celia's elation should have been the cause of foreboding. To have been accepted as a student by the great Turetsky was a distinction and a promise. Something of Celia's own excitement crept into her blood, mingling with her apprehension. She accepted Celia's declaration that she could do no work in the Cutting house; moreover, she understood. Out of an instinctive realization of incongruity her first doubt had taken shape that day of Celia's return from her honeymoon.

She did, however, wish that Celia had been less scathing. The repudiation seemed to carry with it a disloyalty to Austin. For Austin's life and his background *were* Austin.

"That house wars with my soul! An hour for this, a time for that. Valves and switches, engineers and mechanical geniuses, costs, overhead, assembly lines and machines—and Austin at the plant, morning, noon, and night—mentally, at least. I can't stand it, Martie, I simply must escape!"

She could not understand that background of home and family and business to which they had all contributed some part of themselves, and which the pride of achievement and pride of obligation made as creative and significant as her art was to her, or had been to her father. Only a few days ago, Austin, reading reports of unemployment across the nation, had remarked with satisfaction that, so far, Fairlies and Cutting had not let a single man go, although it meant shortening hours for some departments and accepting some contracts at cost. In an era of daily foreclosures, no one working in his company had yet lost his home.

Martha listened and was proud; it was doubtful whether Celia even heard what he said.

On a high hill in a raw March wind Celia had planned her wedding. In the deep sweet grasses of another hilltop, straight and slim as a spear, she lay planning the long slant-ceilinged room in the attic of an old house in New York's Greenwich Village: a room with a deep northeast dormer, pale green walls, and yellow curtains where, briefly, she was completely happy and the shape of all her days was determined.

If she were really unhappy and restless, this might be good for her, Martha thought. She saw Celia studying and working all day, then meeting Austin and coming out with him on the train to Glen Fells each evening.

She asked, "What does Austin say?"

Celia sat up. "I haven't told him yet," she said carelessly.

In the interval of Martha's surprised silence, she threw her a glance. Then, reaching for her hat, she said lightly,

"You would have made a much better Cutting than I, Martie!"

On a sultry morning in August, Martha had her first look at the studio, a room in which all their lives would be changed: Celia's and Austin's, her own, and even Rob's.

After dropping Austin at the plant in Jersey City, Celia drove into New York, threading competently the heavy morning traffic of trucks and drays. Although it was early, the air in the shadowed narrow streets was heavy with the leftover smells of the day before: melting asphalt, gasoline, manure, spoiled fruit, all pervasively blended with that distinctive New York odor of bay and river. A small stray shadow of critical impatience crossed Martha's mind as Celia parked the shining black roadster with its folded top in front of the old brick house and crossed the sidewalk. What was Celia doing here, in her sheer silk suit with its immaculate wide white collar and her broad-brimmed white hat? As they climbed the echoing wooden stairs through the dead air of the old house, she thought (in agreement with Austin) that Celia could have had her studio in the cool loft room of the Cutting stable. He had offered to alter it in any way she chose, to install skylights, additional windows . . . He suggested a rough balcony at the back, overlooking the fields and the line of the wood toward which they used to ride. Her lips curling with an unspoken amusement, Celia shook her head to all suggestions. "You don't understand." There are no words in all the language more effective in erecting a barrier.

At the top of the old brick house where two doors faced each other across a dark hallway, Celia took out her key and opened the door at the right upon a large bare room. In the center of the floor a nondescript collection of furniture was shoved together.

As Celia crossed to the windows, Martha looked about her: everything but the new green paint on the walls had a battered look. There was old brass and pewter, dark with tarnish; a graceful mahogany gateleg table dull with grime; a large easel and stool, scarred with the stains of another owner's paint and effort; an old walnut cabinet with paneled doors, a piece of some elegance in an earlier day before its continuing odyssey from Village secondhand shop to studio and back again.

Celia, she knew, had spent weeks prowling in dingy little shops to acquire these things, but she found their effect unbearably dreary, a reminder of struggle and futility. For herself she would have preferred new things, bright and utilitarian, as shining as the ambition which had brought Celia to this palce, unreminiscent of the cramp of circumstance and the possibility of failure—hers or another's.

From the open window, Celia called to her. "Martie, come here!" Her face was alight with eagerness.

The wide dormer windows gave on a view of sooty roofs and chimneys stretching away under the bright swimming haze of heat that hid the sky. In the distance they heard the hoot of a tug and the deeper note of a ferryboat whistle above the subdued sullen rumble of riverside traffic. And Martha, remembering again Celia's early beginnings in the attic rooms of Paris and Florence, knew why an old hunger could not be satisfied by the broad lawns and awninged porches of Glen Fells and felt guilty about her critical thoughts.

A few weeks later Celia had her housewarming, the first of many gatherings at the studio.

A corner behind folding doors held a sink and a two-burner plate on a shelf, and a small stock of Woolworth china and glass. Watching Celia's bright face as she bent over her shopping list, she wondered if, after all, she had been right; if this, at length, was the answer to a suppressed domesticity, that here, at last, was a place of her own. She had not made the slightest attempt to assume any responsibility for the household pattern at Glen Fells. Everything there rested, as it always had done, in Isabella Cutting's hands.

"Millicent and Rob—" Rob was in New York. He had been fortunate in finding a modest niche with one of the large insurance companies, promising a secure, if distant, future. "And Carroll, for you."

"Not Carroll, if you don't mind. And especially not for me."

Celia drew a swift line. "Really. I thought there were possibilities. It would be so suitable."

Martha was silent, but mutely she cried, Don't you know? Oh, don't you *know?* For this she had desperately prayed: that no one would ever know. Perhaps, in time, these careless barbs of Celia's would cease to prick her so sharply. "You would have made a much better Cutting than I . . ." "It would be so suitable." But one short year was not enough to dull memory and feeling.

"Horty's in town and I can get a couple of Lilian's young men, I think."

In the end it was a small party. Just Millicent and Rob, and Austin. Horty sent a sprawling scrawl on a heavy sheet of violet notepaper: "So sorry, Darling . . ." Quite vulgar, remarked Celia without malice; but that same vulgarity, shameless and hearty, would one day endear her to thousands. Lilian's young men failed to turn up.

"Oh, well," laughed Celia, "we'll just have to spend the evening recapturing our lost youth."

One by one they climbed the steep wooden stairs into the long room: Millicent came from her classes at Columbia, Rob from the office, and Austin, late, from the plant across the river. They ate rolls and ham, baked beans and pickles, coffee and chocolate cake from a bakery. Rob laughed as he surveyed the spread. "A schoolgirl's dream-at-midnight!"

In the long room they talked and ate, and outside the smoky saffron sky of sunset faded. Celia got up to light all her little lamps, the battered brass and pewter; and the rich, hot, city dusk deepened slowly beyond the open windows.

Their talk was sound and sweet, as sharply satisfying as an apple picked from the tree and eaten out of doors. Long afterward Martha recalled that evening and was astonished to discover how utterly vanished was its simplicity. They shook out the bright rustling fabric of their dreams that night in the light of the little lamps, and the room glowed with the warmth and color of their imaginings. There were the places Millicent wanted to see: Andorra and the Basque country, Palestine and Hungary, and the South African veldt. Rob's house in the country. Leaning back, with his hands clasped about his knee, he created it for them, with its apple orchard and rocky brook, a roaring open fire on winter evenings, and the two dogs on the hearthrug at his feet.

"Dreams?" Austin, smiling a slow smile, was saying with his glance for Celia. "Mine have all come true."

And Celia's eyes bright and blank with an inward vision of achievement, unresponsive and unseeing.

Rob touched Martha's shoulder.

"You're next, Martha. What is your private dream?"

Caught between his question and Austin's familiar quizzical regard, she stammered: "Why—to be happy, I suppose. But, after all, that's the sum of all dreams, isn't it? Each of us dreams of something or someone—I'm saying this so badly—a fulfillment, a completion, which will add up to something special . . ."

Austin smiled at her as he used to do when she was twelve. " 'Something to do, someone to love, and something to hope for.' "

"Yes, that's about it. Julia quotes that. It seems so simple, but it isn't really. Not for people like me who haven't any special gifts." She looked across the room. "For someone like Celia, who has always known what she must do, it's so much easier."

Celia looked up then. "On the contrary. It's not all that easy for artists," she said impatiently. "There's *always* frustration. Even in the moment of triumph when you've finished a piece of work, having conceived an idea, worked on it, sometimes with excitement and sometimes with tears, and, finally, there it is—it never really is as good or as true to your idea as you saw it in the beginning. The *doing* has its moments of rapture, perhaps—and then you always say, 'next time, I'll get it next time.' "

Austin leaned forward. "There has to be some definition of what we mean by happiness. It's so many things to so many people—Celia just now used two words in speaking of artistic creation: excitement and rapture. There are others: contentment, bliss, ecstasy, felicity. Not everyone is capable of, let us say, rapture. On the other hand, many people are *born* with a temperament capable of 'perfect happiness' even when forced to live within a frame of limitation—fragile health, enforced solitude, cramped economic circumstances, without ever satisfying many of their hidden desires. The *attainment* of happiness, the perspective which permits someone to achieve joy and peace in spite of the fates, that is something else. It implies an awareness, first of all, then an achievement." It was like Austin to talk of achievement, to stress emotional and mental discipline. Was he thinking of the unexpected responsibilities which had overtaken him, the paths he might have taken instead? What, after all, had been his private dream for himself? Whatever he had forsaken, in order to do his duty, was compensated for by Celia's love.

"Everything," Celia had cried in the night, "is going to happen to us in the next ten years!" For Celia it had already begun: she had found her love; very quickly, she had found love, or it had found her. Now there was Turetsky, and ahead lay achievement with its excitement and rapture, and her ascending star . . .

For Martha, it had all settled into place on the day Austin and Celia were married. With a flash of insight, she thought, the zest of life is its expectancy. It was not only that she had lost Austin; she had lost the expectation of some bright astonishment. From now on every day would be the same. A succession of days, of years, stretching out, like Millicent's vision of the African veldt, immense and unchanging. Shelterless. That was it. For her there would be no friendly winding road, no bright place, no welcoming rapture around the bend. I am lost, she thought; how will I find myself?

Classes began in September and Celia immersed herself in work and study. She and Austin drove away each morning and, for a time, returned to Glen Fells around six-thirty in the evening. Once again the storm of discontent had passed; she radiated the assurance of a full life. Her mood was gentle, uncomplicated, untouched by the delicate irony which Martha found so disturbing. Later there were evidences that she was working too hard: shadows of fatigue under her eyes, her pallor, her hands languid in her lap; but her ardor was, if that were possible, heightened. Turetsky was a hard taskmaster, a relentless critic.

"He comes and stands behind you, saying nothing. Sometimes he will stand there for fifteen minutes, absolutely silent, until a cold chill begins to creep upward along your spine, stopping your breath, numbing your fingers, paralyzing your brain. Finally, he speaks—*cruelly*—and you shrivel, feeling the whole class wince, too. Sometimes he says nothing at all, and when he has stood behind you so long that you cannot endure it any longer, you throw a desperate glance over your shoulder and find that he has moved silently away and is standing at the other side of the room. Then you know you have something! He's terrible—and marvelous!" Her laugh would be warm with elation and they would see Turetsky, tall, thin, with a shock of steel-gray hair, a narrow face lined by humor and impatience and some old sorrow, shrewd, glittering, ruthless gray-green eyes, and his beautiful white hands folded on his back.

As Celia talked a mysterious excitement would catch at Martha's heart and afterward she would go back across the lawns to the house where her father sat with the haggard face he had worn since that cold February morning when they found Les Patterson. Absently, she would notice the little vertical line deepening between her mother's brows. But during the days when her hands were busy in a release of thought, she would muse, with more of wonder than of bitterness, upon the small twist of fate which had brought to an end all the distant glitter of the formless dream she had had at Severn of a life always fair and lovely, bearing, somehow, within it an exquisite prize of love or beauty. Who am I? she wondered. Someone special, Julia would have told her. Special for whom, or for what?

The Owens' auction was held in September. Everything in the big house, and finally the house itself. The family, Carroll, his father and mother, and his mother's mother, had left with their luggage for some unannounced destination weeks earlier; ostensibly for an extended trip abroad. Martha was not the only one who doubted this. The auction came as a great shock to the community. Fear spread in widening ripples; if it could happen to the Owens, it could happen to the least of them.

In November the MacLeans listed their place for sale. "If we can sell before March, we may be able to clear a couple of thousand above the mortgage and have a small stake to start over somewhere else," said her father. "If not, I'll have to let go. The bank will take it. I can't meet the December mortgage payment and three months' grace is all they will give us."

She saw her mother give an involuntary startled glance about her. They were sitting in the long living room. It was raining in the November night, heavily and monotonously. Wood was delivered by the cord and fairly expensive, but by husbanding their supply, they were still able to have a fire on stormy nights. From time to time a heavy spatter of raindrops would hiss in the heart of the fire; at times it would flare higher, throwing light on the sheen of picture frames, polished wood, and damask drapery. One lamp burned in a far corner. There was muted dance music on the radio from half a continent away. She heard her father speak, but it was as if his words had been washed clean of the color of disaster; they conveyed no imagination of a future away from this home.

But the next day as her mother stood with her hands in the dishpan, she lifted her head and looked out into the draggled garden with its chrysanthemums beaten to earth in frowzy sheaves by the rain.

"No one has that much money now," she murmured

through lips which barely moved, and Martha was, for the first time, oppressed by the shape of things to come.

It was Austin's birthday—January 22, 1931.

It was still light when she started, going around by the road because of her evening slippers, carrying an umbrella and Austin's gift under her arm. A few days earlier Mrs. Cutting had telephoned inviting her for dinner. It had been a sunless, dun-colored day, rather chill, with a threatening sky. Toward evening it began to rain softly and the temperature began dropping. Mrs. Cutting was at the telephone when she came in. She cradled the phone, turning.

"Austin is at the station. I must send Williams down. Celia has the car and will be coming out later." That was all, but Martha sensed the disapproval underlying her restraint.

Austin came in briskly, the shoulders of his topcoat spotted with rain.

"Hello, company for dinner! And it looks as if we're dressing. Ve-ery pretty!"

It was one of the evening gowns, no longer new, but immediately she felt festive. Mrs. Cutting came into the room. He bent and kissed her cheek. "By the way, Mother, Celia called me just as I was leaving the office. She'll be here about seven-thirty."

Only an hour's difference, Martha thought. She could just as well have come out with Austin. But she did not come at seven-thirty. Nor at eight. At nine they sat down to dinner in a strained silence. The rain was freezing; the front steps, the surfaced drive, the limbs of the trees were sheathed in ice, glittering like crystal in the light from the porch. There was no telephone in the studio. Celia had refused to have one put in, asserting that it would disturb her at work.

"It probably isn't freezing in the city; it's always colder up here," said Mrs. Cutting at nine-thirty, after they had tried to keep conversation going without voicing their fears.

Austin's face was pale. His hand shook slightly as he lifted his coffee cup. "I could take the other car—"

"There's little chance that you could connect," murmured his mother.

He got to his feet and walked to the window, parted the curtain, let it fall, and turned back to them again. "They'd surely call us if—"

Martha thrust aside the imagination of Celia crushed, burned, flung violently out of the overturned roadster in the stormy night somewhere between towns or on the turnpike crossing the deserted Jersey meadows, unfound until morning—Or of a truck swinging wildly around an icy corner, smashing the black roadster like an eggshell against a brick wall or a bridge abutment. She turned from watching Austin in his ceaseless pacing and met Mrs. Cutting's quiet gaze. She looked perfectly calm until one saw her laced fingers in her lap. As Martha's eyes met hers, her look deepened with appeal.

Martha stood up. "No news is good news, Austin. Stop pacing around like a caged tiger and I'll give you your present. Then I must go home; it's getting late . . ."

He swung around hastily. "You can't go until she comes!" He dropped into a chair, however, and fumbled at the wrapping of her gift with nervous fingers. A quiet flicker of pleasure crossed his face. She had chosen a record, a group of three Beethoven sonatas.

"Many thanks, Martha."

"You don't have it, I hope. I can exchange it if you do."

"No, I don't have it. Thanks again."

She was grateful to her mother, whose scrimping had made the gift possible. The happy days of ample allowances and charge accounts were past.

"Put it on now," suggested his mother's quiet voice.

He hesitated, then crossed the hall to the study, and presently the music came out to them. It filled the room and the empty anguish of their waiting like the slow, inevitable inward sweep of the tide, as the hands of the clock crept around to ten-thirty.

It was close to midnight when they heard the car come slowly up the drive in second gear and stop near the porch. Austin sprang up and went out. An icy current of air swept into the room along the floor as he opened the outer door. Then Martha heard the sound of his voice from the porch, his words undistinguishable and brief. After a moment the heavy door closed and she heard Celia's voice in the hall, careless and a little husky, as if she were very tired.

"Some people came in and it was rather late before they went, that's all."

"Were they there when you called me at the office?"

"As a matter of fact, they were. We were having a bite of supper at that Italian place. I called from there."

And Austin's reply, sharp with incredulity: "But you must have known we'd be frantic with worry on a night like this! You might have phoned again when you couldn't make it for seven-thirty—sent someone out with a message, a few words to let us know you were delayed."

There was a brief silence.

"Are you coming down again?" he asked, in a changed voice.

"No."

"Martha's here . . ."

Martha got up and crossed the room. A quick glance showed her Isabella Cutting in her big chair, sunken and somehow diminished, her face chill with distress. She seemed unaware of Martha's going. Pausing in the living room doorway, she said, "I was just leaving. I only waited to see if you—"

Celia stood halfway up the wide stairway, facing Austin in the hall below. Both hands were laid upon the shining balustrade in an undeniably taut gesture of impatience. Light from the pendant crystal chandelier fell upon her sealskin coat, on the flame-colored silk scarf bound over her hair, and upon her white face with its bright, scornful mouth. Her eyes slid over

Martha's hesitant entrance and back again to Austin in a preoc-cupation of resentment. Her scorn unfurled itself upon the uneasy silence.

"I shall never expect you to understand that art is not a nine-to-six job, but a way of life!" she said, and turning away, disappeared with a light, measured tread up around the dark curve of the stairs.

Walking home in the perilous icy darkness, Austin drew her arm through his. She was tremblingly aware of his grasp, his shoulder firm against hers, but she was numb with an impo-tent grief as cold as the needle-sharp rain. Like an echo of its pitiless sound in the night was the silent cry of her heart: Oh, Celia, Celia . . .

She had completely forgotten that it was Austin's birthday!

She wanted to say: Don't blame her. She isn't thinking when she's like this. Celia is never cruel, it's only her terrible, impersonal concentration which sometimes makes her seem so. She realized that it would be needless to say anything of this to Austin, simply because he was the kind of person he was. And because he loved Celia, he would have said it all in his heart long ago. The pity was that nothing could assuage the dreadful hurt of that impersonality of Celia's, her way of closing the door, shutting herself in with whatever was troubling her, shut-ting you out.

Austin left her at her porch. "No, I won't come in, thanks. I must get back . . ."

She tried to close her mind against the imagination of his efforts to breach the wall of indifference Celia had just erected between them.

There was a red glow of firelight on the curtains of the living room windows, the dim light of a small bulb shining behind the fanlight over the wide door. Remembering the former brilliance of hospitably lighted windows, she thought, soon this will be gone, too. She had no idea where they would be going. Only that it would be away. Away from here, away from Austin.

She looked down at him, hesitating on the step below. His face was turned away, giving her only the austere sadness of his profile. There was a faint nimbus of light above the Cutting house and around each lamp along the road, caught and magnified by the glazed branches. After a long moment of silence, he moved abruptly and spoke, throwing off his preoccupation with an assumed cheerfulness.

"Good night, Martha. Thanks for my present. And for coming. It was good to have you. I believe I'll go back across the lawns; it's probably not as slippery as the road, and shorter."

"Take my umbrella," she urged.

He waved it aside and she stood still at the edge of the porch, watching as he went striding away over the crusted grass. Then her eyes lost him to the darkness and the rain but she heard his footsteps a while longer. When there was nothing but the sharp pricking sound of rain on the icy ground, she turned and went inside, feeling the night inimical with the tangible portents of change.

After that came March, and Grove Street.

The big red and black sign of the realtor had flaunted their distress in vain; no purchaser came by March first (nor, for that matter, for four long years afterward). In March, when earth and air were softening and the imminence of spring on Raynold Road was unbearably poignant, the MacLeans moved into a two-family house on Grove Street, three blocks east of Main. The house was in a "respectable" neighborhood. Their half had six rooms and a bath, and the rent was thirty dollars a month. It cost ten dollars a month to store that portion of their furniture which would not fit into the house, and which they lacked the fortitude to sell.

A certain measure of ingenuity was required to arrange themselves in the small rooms. Her mother, standing in the long living room on Raynold Road, said, "We'll have to choose between the piano and the sofa. That 'parlor' will not take both!" She laid her hand on the polished mahogany case of her piano. "If only it were smaller." Her spread fingers moved as if to strike a chord, then drew back in a quick gesture of renunciation.

They took the sofa, so that her father could stretch out in the evenings. The piano, the thirty-foot fringed Persian rug, and many other graceful things in the long room went into storage. So did her father's library furniture and some of the books. The books belonged to that earlier period when her parents were young and intellectual, during their college years and the first years of their marriage when they were quite poor. Then they read and kept up with the changing ideas of their changing times. A little later they became richer and less eager, and simply kept up with other people and the demands of their merry-go-round.

Now that they were once more quite poor, she saw her father take a volume from the shelves and read for an hour or so until a restlessness she felt in her own nerves drove him to his feet and to an unconscious pacing.

Her mother looked at the books. "Your father used to like to read—we'll take as many books as we can make room for," she said. What she meant (perception grew daily) was, There must be an anchor, something a man *owns,* something not merely to sit on or sleep on.

There wasn't room for much else in the little parlor but the sofa and the books. Their library had had built-in bookcases. She was surprised by her mother's construction of bricks and boards to hold the books in the narrow little room.

She made her first protest the day her mother's scissors bit into the gold damask drapery from the living room of the big house. All the windows of Grove Street were small and narrow.

"Oh, no! . . . We may go back some day!"

She had not learned, yet, that one goes on; one seldom goes back. And, if one does go back, it is to a "back" so altered that it might as well be another place as well as another time.

Her mother's hand went steadily on. "If we do, I'll be satisfied with nothing less than new draperies. Look, baby, it's a *new beginning.* From here we can go *anywhere* . . . Let me tell you about some other people who had to create new beginnings and keep going." Her hand paused and the dry rasp of the shears cutting through the heavy damask stopped.

"Your father's grandparents, the MacLeans, came here from Scotland in the mid-Fifties, just before the Civil War. (Ireland had its potato famine; Scotland and England had starvation times, too.) They were newly married, very young, and probably frightened; but the big ocean and the unknown must have seemed worth the risk. And it was a risk—scraps of the story were told to Doug when he was a child—storms blew them off course so the voyage took almost five weeks to accomplish. They nearly ran out of food and water—there was rationing to make it last—there was illness on board, and death. How tragic and fearful it must have seemed to witness a burial at sea and see the grief of those whose loved ones had been committed 'to the deep'! They came to Boston and it is thought that your great-grandfather got work in one of the textile mills. All their children were born in America, four sons and two daughters. Eventually they scattered—Vermont, Connecticut, New York, and Ohio. The son who settled in Ohio became Doug's father. He married a girl named Moira Kelley. She passed on her Irish smile and her silver teapot to your father. His parents had a village store, a general store, to begin with. The village grew to a town and your grandfather turned his store into the local drugstore, with an 'ice cream parlor' next door."

"Where you met Dad."

"As a matter of fact, we had known each other from grammar school days," her mother said, laughing, "but it wasn't until he became a 'soda jerk' in his father's store that I found out how he felt about me. Somehow, he discovered that I was crazy about maraschino cherries and began putting four or five in the *bottom* of my dish no matter what kind of sundae I ordered, instead of just one on top."

"And what did you do?"

"Haven't I told you all this before?"

"Maybe, maybe not. You probably thought I was too young." And there had been so little time in that other house, that other life, for talks like these.

"Well, I bawled him out at the first opportunity, naturally."

"You *bawled him out!* Poor Dad."

"Of course. It was embarrassing, finding all those cherries at the bottom of every sundae. And devastating. What was I supposed to do, with everyone watching: gobble them up, or nonchalantly push the dish away—and break my heart?"

There was a long silence.

"So—what happened next?"

"Use your imagination," her mother replied lightly. "Anyway, we got married a couple of years later, and came to New York. We both worked; I was a typist, later a secretary. Your father went to college nights and finally got a job in Wall Street like a lot of other bright young men. By the time you came along, I was able to give up my job, and later still we decided that you needed lawns to play on and other things that went with country living."

"What about your family?"

"My grandparents were transplanted Yankees. Real canalboat pioneers, as a matter of fact. And transplanted is the right word. Like a lot of midwestern towns ours could have been lifted right out of New England—white clapboard houses (built with lumber from grandpa's lumberyard), maple-shaded streets, front porches with swings . . . Papa was a telegrapher and Mama was pious. We always had enough of everything, to eat and to wear, but I learned, growing up, to do a lot of useful things like washing dishes and making aprons and canning tomatoes, which I considered very unexciting then but which may prove useful now. Mama believed firmly that idle hands were an invitation to the devil's work."

She wondered what her mother's real feelings were, knowing that for her father's sake she would be cheerful and positive, no matter what came.

[114]

She herself was desperately unhappy in the narrow gray house, but she busied herself during the days, holding her feelings at bay. She would allow herself to think and feel only behind her closed bedroom door. She tried to make herself tired enough to sleep immediately when she went to bed so that she would not lie awake in the dark, besieged by her homesick longing for Raynold Road. But the sleep she longed for often eluded her, hour after hour. She had never known what insomnia meant before this, or imagined the weary reiteration of lost hopes and painful nostalgia which could haunt the dragging hours.

She could not accustom herself to the sound of cars passing in the street beneath her window at night. Or the intrusion of light into her room from the near lamp on the corner. Or the sound of strange footsteps on the stairs and in the halls on the other side of the thin wall. One morning as she was drying herself after her bath, she heard a man gargling in the other bathroom and was immeasurably revolted. Most of all she minded the feeling of being closed in, as if the walls of her life were narrowing to hold her in a prison from which there was no escape.

Another springtime. On Grove Street the tops of the oaks and maples and elms whose roots lifted and cracked apart the flagstone sidewalks thickened and shut out the bright transparent sky. Grade-school children raced up and down the block; boys perilously skimming the corner on bicycles, girls coasting stiff-legged on roller skates, jolting over the uneven flags with staccato emphasis. Roadsters with open rumble seats flashed down the street filled with high-school students, loud boyish laughter and the girls' bright hair blowing in the wind . . . In the long backyard Mr. Weeks, the man who gargled, spaded his onion bed.

She escaped from Grove Street when she could. It was a long walk—across town and up the hill—but she went at least once a week, unable to abandon the places she had loved. She did not visit the Cuttings on those walks. Her mood was too solitary for that. She cut through the untended lawns of her old home, headed out across the fields, and circled back again to Raynold Road. It was the kind of private time people seek when they pray in an empty church on a weekday.

The red and black sign of the realtor had been replaced by an orange-colored one flaunting in bold letters the name of the mortgage company which had foreclosed the property. The grass grew green, then long; the lovely garden bloomed, true to its purpose as the bird which sings not for any listener; as the unwise heart loves, because it must.

She remembered her mother going around to all the windows, pulling all the shades level. They were not the first to experience this loss, this leaving; and they were not the last. But they did not, like some, leave a bitter desecration for strangers to gape at: towel hangers torn loose, chandeliers and wall sconces ripped bodily away from their wiring, mirrors and bathroom fixtures cracked by savage hammer blows—signs of a barbaric grief, a revenge upon the inanimate for the mental anguish of the exiled.

It was unthinkable that these things could have happened and were still happening in a place like Glen Fells. Some people had lived for months behind drawn shades, starting at the sound of the doorbell, dreading the bill collectors and process servers they could not face. Some had moved quietly away in the night, leaving no forwarding address. The empty houses stood surrounded by their neglected lawns, more and more of them; houses where formerly there was music and light and cars driving up in the evenings.

Martha was impressed mainly by the awful waste: those empty houses, Les Patterson's young life, his widow's love. At times her own love for Austin seemed only part of a whole wasteful era.

In May, Turetsky took two of Celia's canvases for his Students' Show, a modest studio exhibition with a very great significance, nevertheless, for the exhibitors and the avid critics.

"Roofs at Evening" was a vague, dark interior giving prominence to a large square window holding a scene which Martha recognized as the view from Celia's own dormer, bathed in a clear, still light. Standing before it in the crowded buzzing studio, she could not tell for herself if it was "good" or "bad"; but she saw a painting competently executed, and, overlaying the whole, a feeling—a color of thought—which communicated itself unmistakably to the beholder.

The second picture, "Lady and a Mirror," had a technical similarity to the first: in the woman, a graceful figure seen from the back, she recognized Mrs. Cutting; and again the dusky interior with its small edges of light on vague tables and chairs was dramatized by the large, relucent square of the mirror.

A small dark man with a graying vandyke called it "an exquisite satire" and she wondered if he weren't more impressed by the fine precise flavor of his phrase than by the painting.

That spring Doug MacLean took another cut in salary. There was an uncomfortable pinch making itself felt on Grove Street. The cost of commuting was an unavoidable item; Doug needed a new suit desperately; her mother's shoes were no longer presentable enough for street wear; and Martha, with warm weather in the offing once more, longed for two or three fresh cottons.

Once more she began to search the ads hopefully and, at the same time, hopelessly. There were more people out of work than at any time in the memory of the present generation. Yet, somewhere, there must be something she could do, something she could be paid for doing, so that she could help a little with the mounting burden of anxiety her parents carried. There was gray at her father's temples now and his walk had lost its jauntiness. She watched him coming up the street from the station each evening, aware that her mother also watched him.

She visited stores and offices in Glen Fells, and the library. People took her name. She would have enjoyed the library with its vaulted silences and the studious rustle of papers where students sat at long tables; but the library budget had been reduced so that only volunteer help was needed.

"If only there were something I could do!" A trace of bitterness crept in: You go to school for twelve years and they teach you to think nobly, act courageously, champion the right, face "reality." You are prepared to Meet Life—You are sent forth, secure in the knowledge that you will Always Come Through—do the Right Thing—Carry the Torch—You are Invincible! And then what? You end up wondering whether the gas company or the electric company is going to turn you off first; whether you can *possibly* put any more bread in the meat loaf and still call it meat; trying to remember to keep your arms at your sides so that no one will see that your dress has been darned under the arms!

"Why don't you ask Austin for a job?" suggested her mother.

"Oh, you know Austin. He'd feel he has to make a place for me for old times' sake, etcetera. And they're trying so hard not to let anyone go, some of the men have been on part-time for over a year."

"All right—ask for part-time, anything," said Helen inexorably. "Surely old times are worth something, and if one more small pittance is going to sink Fairlies and Cutting, they're already sunk!"

It was her lucky day. Austin grew mildly hilarious when she told him that Macy's had rejected her for selling gloves because she was not a college graduate, but told her that her timing was exactly right. A girl who had been with them for three years was leaving. Her father had been out of work for more than a year and had decided to go back to the family farm in Pennsylvania where there was at least enough to eat and no rent to pay. As her grandparents were getting on in years and her mother had never lived on a farm, the girl felt that she should go with her family; especially as her salary would not stretch to a place of her own after they left.

"I'll drive you down to the plant," said Austin, "and you

can talk to Cathy—Miss Cathcart. She's in charge of office personnel and has been with us since Grandfather's time, longer than any of us have been around. Don't be afraid of her, I think you will please her. Remember, you don't know anything but you're willing to learn. She likes 'em teachable, Cathy does."

Nervously, she inventoried her clothes, and although it was May and a little too warm, chose a suit. It had been an expensive suit, fortunately, and good suits stayed with you to the last thread! As a concession to the season she wore a good deal of white: inexpensive gloves, white blouse, and a rather nice bag. (Bags hung around for years and nice ones lent an air.) She found a pair of white fabric shoes at Newberrys' for a couple of dollars but discarded them at the last minute in favor of her black kid pumps, which were slightly shabby but well-polished.

Austin gave her a sidelong glance as he drove.

"You'd better tell Cathy you need the money. She'll never believe you. You look very soignée, right out of the debutantes' top drawer."

"You're just saying that to give me confidence."

"How'd you guess?"

Miss Cathcart was indeed redoubtable. She was tall and flat as an ironing board, with iron-gray hair cut mannishly and steel-rimmed pince-nez. She wore a black suit and a collar and tie, like a man's. Until she stood up and came around to the front of her desk, Martha was not sure that she had been ushered into the right office.

Miss Cathcart consulted the application in her hand.

"Hm. Miss MacLean. Twenty years old. Private-school education. No experience. Hm. Recommended by Mr. Cutting." She looked up suddenly, fixing her sharp gray-green gaze on Martha's face. *"Why* do you want to work here?"

"For experience, mainly," said Martha with more calm than she was feeling. "And for the salary—to help at home."

"I see. Can you spell?"

"Well—I was considered a very good speller at school."

Again the grim stare through the pince-nez. " 'Considered.' Aren't you sure? Never mind; just remember to be definite. Either you were or were not a good speller. You young people tend to be foggy thinkers. If you *can* spell, we'll start you on filing. Later we will teach you to run the duplicating machines . . ."

"Mimeo?" asked Martha eagerly. "I know all about that; I was on the school paper."

Cathy smiled briefly, a frosty twinkle, and made a note on the application. "Well, then, you do have some experience. That's fine. You may report at eight o'clock on Monday and your salary will be fourteen dollars." She held out her hand. "If you find the office routine congenial, you could take evening courses in typing, shorthand, and procedures. Business offers many opportunities for young women."

It had been a successful morning, not without strain. Austin took her to lunch. Trying to smile and be responsive as he talked of this and that, giving her thumbnail sketches of people she was going to meet and work with at the office, she was at the same time fighting a sudden feeling of depression. She was seeing Miss Cathcart's tall flat figure, hearing her brisk, expressionless tones: "Business offers many opportunities for young women." If she made good at Fairlies and Cutting, it was entirely possible that one day Austin's grandchildren would say, "Martie? Oh, she's a marvelous old thing—she's been around since 1932, when Grandfather was young!"

She should have been feeling elated: at last she had a job, she would be able to make a contribution. Why did she feel that she had been entrapped?

Celia had given up the car. It was too difficult to find parking in the narrow street near the studio, she said. Austin drove it instead; Celia and Martha and he rode together each day as far as Journal Square, where Celia left them to catch the tube train under the river. Running down the steps out of their sight as they pulled away from the curb into the stream of traffic, she was plunged into the rush hour. This was what she wanted.

Telling them of those trips in the crowded, swaying trains, her face lighted with eagerness. "The faces . . . the expréssions! It's like a gallery of emotions and hundreds of models to choose from . . ."

Now she seldom came home before the last train out to Glen Fells and there were times when she stayed overnight at the studio. Always, there were gatherings of people there in the evenings. Not parties, just people who dropped in. Young writers, art students, poets, musicians . . .

Celia sat on her high stool with her hands clasped about one knee, listening to the talk which surged and eddied under the low ceiling. It could be noted that she seldom made any contribution, but in her listening attitude, the tilt of her head, the repose of her face, she conveyed an impression of complete participation.

Martha and Austin did not belong, but she was pleased that they came, at first, choosing to regard it as a mark of interest, although actually Austin came to drive her home and Martha was a passenger in the car, saving train fare. And her presence was a kind of protection for Austin; he was fond, indulgent, deeply in love, proud of Celia's gifts and her grace, amused by her little autocracy in this place which she had made for herself; but Martha was afraid that someone would notice his amusement and indulgent attitude and misconstrue them. Both were out of place here amid the intensity and earnestness.

These people interested Martha. She contrasted their disillusion and their pessimism with the relative optimism of similar gatherings in Glen Fells. Among Celia's friends there was a conviction that "the system" had broken down, and mingled with a rather desperate idealism (the undeniable altruism inherent in the idea of sacrificing the individual to the ultimate benefit of the many) was a sweeping condemnation of all that was a part of the past from which this sorry present had been spawned.

In Glen Fells the survivors clung to the memory of a very

recent past, the easy prosperity, the untroubled materialistic existence they had taken for granted; and to the hope that they would awaken some bright morning to find it miraculously restored to them. They said to each other, "Things will get better, something will turn up." They bore rather patiently, even humorously, with respectable poverty and sacrifices of things so recently important to them. There was an element of gallantry; they vied with each other in describing their hardships. Meanwhile, however, there were process servers and movings away in the night, a gradual disintegration of the "society" they had known, names and faces suddenly missing, and whispers of scandal. Worst of all, they had not yet learned that they were all in the same leaky boat: they gossiped. So-and-so had lost his job, the electric company had cut off his lights ("They're burning *oil lamps,* my dear!"); the finance company had repossessed X's living-room furniture and Y's car. These things still had the power to spread ripples of interest. Did anyone stop to think it could happen tomorrow, next week, to them? There were silly affairs of silly people striving to forget the imminence of ruin. Mrs. A. was seen where she should not have been with Mr. B., who had a perfectly good wife of his own. C's son had made a hasty marriage with D's daughter— the reason was obvious—and they were going to live on the third floor of C's house. No job, of course, and everyone knew that the Cs had been living on borrowed money for a year . . .

With the people at the studio she could not help but agree: poverty was degrading. On the Lower East Side of New York its effect was brutally apparent; in the working-class sections of the larger towns they passed through, on tired Main Streets, the evidence ranged all the way from begging children and soup kitchens, where old people shuffled slowly in apathy, cup in hand, to breadlines (Florence Converse had written a moving poem on these) and apple sellers, and everywhere—on porches, and park benches, and leaning against the fronts of vacant stores—always more men than should have been abroad in the daytime: the Unemployed. It was 1932—the year of the bonus marchers, and soldiers fired upon civilians in Washington, to the shock of a nation.

For the voluble ones at the studio, Freud and Marx had the answers, but of these, now in the depressed Thirties, Marx was considered the greater. The talk was concerned with socialism ("to each according to his need; from each according to his ability"); nationalization of resources, overproduction and underconsumption as a myth ("Who wouldn't buy more if he could? If everything was produced that people needed, there would be jobs for all and money to buy what was produced"). The Russian Five-Year Plan and the sins of capital were debated fervently and noisily. They were not inhibited by Austin's presence or identity.

"Damned little hypocrite!" remarked a meager young man with a frayed collar one evening, eyeing Celia disdainfully from the opposite side of the room. "Plays at starving in a garret, with a rich husband in the background!"

After they all had gone, she would help Celia straighten the room. On one such occasion it was after one in the morning: the studio room was in disorder, its lamps nebulous in a bluish haze of smoke, shining on chairs pulled out of place; the rug was askew, the tired imprint of careless bodies left in the cushions of the divan. Seated on the end of it, Austin was turning the pages of his newspaper while he waited for them to finish washing the plates and glasses.

She rattled the dishes in the pan. It was late, she was tired, but when Celia, yawning, said, "Oh, leave the mess," she thrust a towel into her hands peremptorily. If Celia *would* have these gatherings, she might at least give a thought to the morrow; how much work would she do if confronted by a sinkful of stubborn sticky glassware?

"How much work would you do tomorrow—in this mess?" she asked impatiently.

Celia grimaced at her. "Ma petite bourgeoise!"

Austin looked up. "Don't you think all of this takes too much out of you? After all, you complained that too much was expected of you socially in Glen Fells and this was to be your escape. It seems to me that these people take up as much of your time, and more. And I suspect many of them, poor devils, come because you feed them . . ."

Celia said curtly, "I hope you don't realize how patronizing you sound."

She leaned against the shelf with a negligent weary grace and held a glass to the light, smiling. The brilliant naked bulb hanging above her on its long cord whitened her hair and the planes of her face, sharpening mercilessly the little hollows at temple, cheek, and mouth which betrayed her weariness. By an illusion of light she looked like a picture of herself at seventy. The timbre of her voice was blurred with fatigue.

"It's so wonderful to hear real conversation! In Glen Fells people talk but they do not *converse.* You know that as well as I do, Austin: they tell stories, anecdotes, and exchange bits of gossip, and talk about the prices of things—or they did when I first knew them. I suppose even they must find their style a bit cramped by all this. But I doubt if any single person in Glen Fells would *look* for a remedy much less try one if it meant giving up any of the privileges he has enjoyed."

"Your revolutionary friends would burn down the house because the roof leaks," said Austin mildly. "And I'm afraid I can't go along with them. Free enterprise and private capital have made this country what it is—"

"Exactly," interposed Celia, drily.

"For over one hundred and fifty years we have been growing. To the oppressed and the 'heavily laden' of other nations we have offered, not only spiritual and political freedom, but freedom to enjoy the fruits of labor beyond anything these same efforts could have earned for them in the countries they left behind. As for privilege, most privilege in this country is a by-product of obligation. In theory, at least, if not always in practice, we eschew hereditary privilege."

Celia smiled at him. "I notice you never say any of this to them. Why?"

"Because I have nothing to contribute that would help them to resolve the question which troubles them most: the artist in relation to his times, and his obligation or his opportunity to change the face of the world . . ."

"My father used to say, the world does not change; men must change. But you *must* believe that in changing you *can* change the world, that ever so slowly you can put right all that is wrong . . ."

"Isn't it enough to have changed one man's world?" asked Austin gently. "Come, let's go home."

A look flew between them and Martha averted her face. It was as if they had flown into each other's arms.

At other times, the talk concerned only Art. They discussed books and plays, paintings, music. They criticized success freely, and their own work without diffidence. They were ardent, impassioned, arrogant, and bombastic. Each of them was so many things, felt so many things, and expressed it all so freely that Martha was faintly embarrassed for them. Haltingly, she mentioned this to Celia.

"They seem so arrogant—"

Celia laughed. "You wouldn't understand. When they talk like that they're not even *conscious* of any listeners. They're simply blowing on the embers of their own self-confidence. And *of course* they believe that this will be the greatest novel, the most significant play, the finest painting that has been done in years! Why not? Each of them is putting his heart's blood into a creation which is, to use a cliché, his brainchild. If you don't believe with everything in you that what you are doing is worthwhile—the best!—what is the point in doing it?" Her look grew distant. "Martie—believe me, the ecstasy of artistic creation, in any form, is complete and as satisfying as the ecstasy of love. And even you, I am sure, must have heard the phrase, 'Art is a jealous mistress?' Ah, she is, she is . . ."

Sometimes Martha remembered the first evening in the studio and thought how utterly vanished was the simplicity of that time in their lives and Celia's.

They went, in June, to their second reunion at Severn.

Everything there was much the same as the year before, of course; but this year, when she saw Celia among the others, she noted a change. It was as if, in the short interval of a year, she had been hardened and sharpened for a purpose. Watching her one saw, not her impeccable frock, hat, and gloves, but that delicate, unmistakable arrogance she had defended in her associates; and thought of her, not as Mrs. Austin Cutting, but as the Celia Pence she herself had previsioned before Austin crossed her path. Her star had begun its ascent. For although she aligned herself with her new friends in sympathy, *she was not of them* any more than she was of the secretaries, nurses, and young matrons among the Severn graduates. She had no uncertainties: her inner vision of what she wanted was complete. When pressed with questions, she replied briefly; but this year her smile had no edge of disdain.

After luncheon when the girls went into separate huddles over statistics—twins in the four-year class; a nurse's cap in the fifth; a wedding, Virginia's, in their own—Celia walked along the brink of the hill with Miss Dilling, aloof in another sisterhood.

Life settled into an ordered routine. September came. The leaves turned color, then began to fall so that each morning saw a new drift of gold in the gutters, a new scattering of scarlet on the grass in the little park near the Public Library. Each morning she waited for Austin and Celia at the corner of Grove and Main. Later the drifting shower of color filled the days and fell across the slanting sun's rays as they came home at evening. The new year should commence in autumn, she thought, setting out in the cool mornings with the dew thick and silvery on the little squares of lawn; that is the time of new energy, resolution, and hope, the awakening from summer's languor.

Weekends she met Rob, quieter and steadier than in his college days, but still flashing his ready smile, wearing his bright crest of hair. As the quiet winter days succeeded the brisk autumn they fell into the habit of spending their Saturdays together in sundry small amusements: museums and art galleries, movies—color travelogs and foreign films shown in the little undistinguished playhouses of the city—window shopping along the avenues, "slumming," as Rob called it, where the sleek town cars slid in along the curb before the grilled entrances of elegant apartments. Their little meals—tea to the accompaniment of string music in Russian restaurants, late Sunday luncheons in Scandinavian restaurants (hors d'oeuvres, excellent coffee, and thin cake between heavy layers of cream); chocolate served by a round-cheeked, high-breasted blonde with braids among the carved dark wooden tables and benches of a Viennese coffeehouse in a cellar room—these discovered to them the city's intimate heart, the warm transplanting of old folkways.

Or Rob would come out to Glen Fells for the weekend, unpacking his battered pigskin bag among the femininities of her small bedroom at the back of the house, while she shared her mother's big bed.

(Those were the days when a crack of light lay along the floor under her father's door sometimes until four in the morning, as he read endlessly in a vain pursuit of sleep.)

Occasionally they accepted an invitation to the Cuttings'; and one evening as they were walking down the hill into town, Rob said:

"Haven't you noticed how Mrs. Cutting has changed? Too much."

Until that moment, Isabella's pallor and air of weariness, the evenings when she left them alone and went quietly upstairs to "read" or "write letters," had not seemed significant. But Rob's remark blunted the shock of hearing, some weeks later, that her doctor had ordered her south for the winter.

Austin left New York with his mother on the eighth of January and Martha had no way of knowing until long afterward what a storm of contention that voyage caused in the Cutting household; how Mrs. Cutting had insisted that she was able to travel alone; how Austin had tried to persuade Celia to go with her; how Celia refused, maintaining that it was his duty to go with his mother, that she herself could not leave New York, that there was no necessity for foolish hesitation on her account, that she could very well live at the studio while they were gone . . . In spite of their reiterated consideration of each other, the discussion marched along the edge of dissension, all their motives crossed and recrossed in the warp and woof of a reluctant fearfulness.

As Martha went up the hill a few dried oak leaves spun around her on the skittish April wind. The sky was piled with heavy gray-blue clouds moving steadily across the sun so that the day was brilliant with light in one instant and cold with shadow in the next. As she gained the crest the old lovely feeling of peace invaded her heart, deeper and more poignant as she surveyed the serenity of which she was no longer a part. The grass was faintly green, the gardens uncovered, here and there a man was working along the distant borders; but the arched avenue of elms was still frail in a leafless pattern against the towering sky.

She paused at the entrance to the drive at her old home, looking over the unkempt lawns at the weeds springing green and impudent in the graveled drive, at the dusty windows with their shades all drawn to the same level, giving the house a forlorn, unchanging air. It hurt to see it like that, but she discovered with a kind of surprise that the hurt was not for herself, but rather a pity for this place, now so deserted and uncherished. A year of weather had faded the orange sign to a less obtrusive color. It was several months since she had walked up here: January, to be exact, when the Cuttings, mother and son, left, and Celia moved into New York for the rest of the winter.

She had missed them, instinctively avoiding Raynold Road in its winter loneliness. Mrs. Cutting's letter, which she had received a week ago, was written in a thin, graceful hand on ship's stationery. They would be home today—Saturday.

As she came nearer she saw Austin's car on the drive at the side of the house and a torn veil of smoke over the roof which meant that a fire had been lighted in the living room. Anticipation lightened her step; in a minute or two she would see all of them again.

She will probably never lose the memory of Isabella Cutting's face as she opened the door, wearing a shattered look more terrible than tears, covered only thinly and pitiably by her instinctive composure.

A faint hope lighted her eyes for an instant when she saw Martha.

"Oh—my dear! I am so glad to see you. You may just possibly be of some help." She led the way into the living room, where the fire burned brightly. Austin was not in the room. She turned to face Martha and came directly to the point: "Austin has had a letter from Celia, it was waiting for him here. She" —in spite of her effort, her voice faltered—"I am afraid she . . . has left him."

A swift sharp pain struck Martha through the heart. "Oh, no!" she heard herself cry involuntarily. But she felt, deep within herself, an awful certainty, although for hours she would not admit it, cherishing a false hope. All her fears had pointed to something like this, was her thought: yet she refused to believe until . . .

Mrs. Cutting stood irresolute before her. "I am going to send Austin to you. Please talk to him. I can do nothing for him —nothing!" she repeated unbelievingly, moving her hands in a quick, hopeless gesture. "But you were her friend—She is so *young!*" she finished incoherently, and went out of the room.

Martha walked slowly to the end of the room and turned. The action reminded her of the February evening over a year ago when they had waited here in terror for Celia's safety and Austin had paced the length of this room again and again. So young! Celia was twenty-two; but had she ever been young as other girls are young?

With surprise she thought, And I am twenty-one; but if this is true, I shall never be young again. Unacknowledged, suspended, waiting, a formless darkness at the boundary of her thought was the special personal tragedy which would overtake her if her faint hope were false.

Austin came into the room then with a nervous, hurried step; his eyes were dark with pain and unbelief and his pallor warred hideously with the color burned into his face by the warm southern sun. He handed her a single sheet of paper.

"Read it."

She hesitated. "Are you sure you want me to?"

He nodded curtly.

Celia's letter was brief, cool, and, like her deed, incredible. Without the slightest effort of imagination she came into Martha's mind, sitting erect and aloof, her pen moving delicately across the paper in a smooth unhesitating script:

> My dear Austin—
>
> This is not an impulse. I am leaving you for both our sakes. Believe me, it is for the best. My plans are indefinite for the present. Later you may communicate with me through my lawyers concerning any necessary arrangements.
>
> I imagine you will wish to be completely free of me. I wish you nothing but happiness. Do not try to see me; there is no possibility that I will change my mind.
>
> Celia

She held the letter still and kept her eyes upon it for a long moment after she had finished reading, filled with her awareness of Austin's desperate waiting. The paper on which it was written—a very thin, pale gray, watermarked single sheet with the entwined Cs in the corner—was her own Christmas gift to Celia. The pain of inanimate objects . . . remembrance of this has a strange vitality. Years later, the odd twist of feeling which burned across her consciousness almost like guilt could still come alive.

She looked up.

"What in the name of God is going on here?" demanded Austin. "Has she said anything to you? . . ."

She could not speak. She shook her head wordlessly.

"I must see her, of course. There's no other way—"

All the unspoken anguish of his thought was plain to her; there was no question in his mind, no room for the fantastic obedience Celia thought she could exact even in the face of her incredible desertion. Martha's anger flared; but it had no vitality, springing thus in the fogged night of her pain, like a brief match. How could Celia expect Austin to accept her written words, no matter how firmly and precisely she had set them down? Did she really believe that anyone, having held love in his arms, and met its smile at morning and heard its whisper in the night, having lived to its pulse all this long time, could meet this death on paper? Didn't she know that the whole of him— sight, and hearing, all his senses and all his soul—must demand to confront and be confronted by the physical fact; if not the comfort of denial, then, at least, the sharp and flashing glance, the taut, defiant body, the clear and inescapable word uttered in a voice whose timbre would vibrate through this numbness, this nothingness of stunned amazement?

His look held desperately to hers. She saw before he spoke the questions that came crowding to his lips. "Martha—you *knew* her. What happened while we were away? Did she say anything to you? When did you last see her?"

There was only one question she could answer with any measure of helpfulness. She had last seen Celia on a Sunday afternoon six weeks before, when she stopped by the Grove Street house, rather late, on her way back to the city. She had two large suitcases in the car and explained that she had driven out to get extra clothing.

"Everything is gone," he said in an expressionless voice.

"She must also have sent her trunks from here."

He stood motionless for a lengthening moment, staring at the floor.

"I am going to look for her. Will you come with me? She may not want to talk to me—will you plead my cause?" He saw the expression on her face and amended his words swiftly, "No, not that. Only get her to listen to me, to talk to me. I can't accept this—this way!"

She could not, afterward, recall a mile of that long drive into the city, nor what they said to each other, but she remembers searching ceaselessly backward along the trail of Celia's marriage for some clue. There was no order in her searching, and her memories, her unbidden memories—some of them obscure, most of them springing to life of themselves—were confusing and led to nothing but a piercing regret and an anguished fear. Celia, proud and lovely in her bridal satin, saying gallantly, "There is no death when you are sure!" . . . Celia, home from her honeymoon, radiant . . . Celia wearing a strange, fleeting look: "There wasn't . . . time." Celia pouring tea, her hands moving among the heavy English silver; Celia in white, with bare shoulders gleaming, at Austin's business dinners; Celia standing in a doorway, her hand on the black sleeve of Austin's dinner jacket, her smile cool and proud . . . Austin, dancing the Senior Waltz, the invisible cloak of his quiet rapture enveloping them both in its beauty. Austin's face as he kissed his bride, tender, dedicated, and severe as a note in music. Celia's voice, weary and scornful: "I shall never expect you to understand—"

Out of this she could construct no picture of their life at its heart. The imaginings of their intimacy which assailed her during the first year of their marriage had died at last. She realized now that their vividness had sprung from her own heart, not from Austin's reserve or Celia's aloof and continent self-possession. Yet surface indications were not necessary: she knew that Austin loved Celia, romantically, with a single-minded devotion that was characteristic; and she knew that

[132]

Celia had loved Austin when she married him, but that, certainly, being Celia, her love was only part of the life she intended to build for herself. Of their hours together, when reticence dissolved in the proud humility of passion, neither had given the faintest clue.

Nor did she know how much significance to attach to Celia's impatience, her transitory scorn, her independence, her careless amiability. They might easily be the ripples on a stream whose depth was undreamed of.

She had seen her mother before misfortune struck, casual, teasing, gay. And she had witnessed the growth of a stability and a warmth to which her father was subject as unerringly as the tides to the moon. Undemonstrative they still were, but she sensed the subtle intensification of the emotional climate as she sat in the room with them.

. . . Just as she had sensed something dead or dying between Celia and Austin that February night of the ice storm. Celia's words and her withdrawal had nothing to do with it; these may have been the effects of fatigue and strain and an unacknowledged guilt, forgotten in the morning, had it not been for that other, the eclipse of something bright and vital, as Austin stood in the hall below, his face upturned to her disdain.

And yet, in the year and more that had passed since then, they had gone along . . . as before? She could not know, of course, if they had forgotten what she remembered . . .

They came at last to the old brick house in the Village and climbed the familiar stairs with an unfamiliar dread. It was the supper hour; there was a sound of voices and the agreeable, reassuring rattle of china behind closed doors as they went up.

Austin tapped at the studio door. There was no sound within.

She touched his arm. "Let me," she said, low; and saw in his eyes a disheartening knowledge of the probability that Celia might admit her but not him.

"Celia." She tapped again, more sharply. "Celia, it's Martha."

The silence swallowed up their waiting.

Then there was a brief sound of quick feminine footsteps. The door opposite was thrown back and a girl wearing some kind of flowered wrapper, with a mist of black hair framing a plain pixieish brown face, stood in the opening.

"There's no one there. They've gone away."

"They?" An echo in a strange voice which Martha realized was her own.

"Celia and Thierry Galland. They didn't say when they'd be back. Maybe the landlady knows where they went."

The merciful part of it was that she was new there—Austin was spared her recognition, at least.

"Thank you," Martha said in a dry little voice, and groped with her foot for the top step.

Austin spoke only once during the feverish drive through the city. "Who is this Galland?" They swerved dangerously around an indiscreet taxi and she knew the compulsion he suffered, the longing for escape which drove him to recklessness. The streets and buildings, the traffic and the incessant voice of it oppressed her as heavily as the cruelty of their discovery. A flood of longing rose in her for the open countryside and the wide darkness shortly to descend upon it, falling, also, with a blessing of anonymity, upon their feeling.

At his question, the words of a silly song that was popular when she was at school stood in her mind: I'd lie for you, I'd steal for you, To show the love I feel for you—

"I don't know," she murmured.

She did know. But it would not have helped Austin to know, then, that a dark young man with a somber hungry look who had called Celia a damned little hypocrite was named Thierry Galland.

They left New York, and the river, and Jersey City with its congestion, its cobbles, and warehouses, and the meadows where the giant fretwork of towers and bridges stood up against the clear pale rose of an evening sky, dimmed a little by the smoke of tall chimneys fading and drifting before it.

Somewhere, before they got to Glen Fells, Austin drew up alongside the road and stopped the car. Emerging from the numb quiescence which had held her all the way, she looked about her and saw that the road was unfamiliar. From the look of the country, she saw that they were near home, on one of the smaller byroads running across country. On their right a field ploughed that day, so that the furrows gave off a gleam of caked moist earth, ran a little uphill to the horizon. Farther down the road and on the other side were trees, but the field met the sky in a clean, curved line; and beneath its colorless spring clarity the turned earth was richly purple.

Beside her, his gaze fixed on the road where it vanished around a bend made secret by trees, Austin spoke and she felt the dull fall of his disillusioned words like blows in her own heart.

"I thought she was happy. I did what I could." He stopped on a note of finality, but after a moment went on again in a changed, sharper tone: "What else *could* I have done? What was my fault . . . or my omission?" His face was gray in that clear last light of day; faint lines, incongruously like the beginning of a smile, edged his mouth.

"It cannot always feel like this!" he cried suddenly, and put his head down upon his arms.

She sat motionless, filled with her incoherent, welling grief for him, so much worse than her own. Like his mother, she could do nothing . . . nothing. She looked at his bent head and her hand ached with the tenderness she dared not bestow. Until, for both of them, a little time had done its gentle work for anguish, her sympathy, so dangerously freighted with her love, would be an unforgivable intrusion.

That night her narrow room in the Grove Street house was a prison. Kneeling at the open window she saw, over the silvered gables of neighboring roofs, a young moon ride serenely down the sky and vanish; and thought of the wide lawns on

Raynold Road where she might have walked, spending the restless energy of her bitterness and grief. She felt her heart weeping within her breast—the slow, painful tears she could not shed—for her vain sacrifice and her double loss.

Oh, Austin, Austin darling! (Her silent cry had a faint, far echo. Celia. Celia . . . darling!) The moon rode, remote and lovely in a clear cold sky from which the heavy clouds of morning had sailed away. Up on Raynold Road, Austin would be wakeful this night, tortured by the fine thrust of memory and the cold hard brilliance of that last letter Celia had written. "My plans are indefinite for the present." That would conjure for him, as for her, some shore, or deck, some moon-dappled woodland and Celia, with the world shut out of bliss—but yet, at least, he need not see that other face, dark and lean, in the intensity of possession.

". . . any necessary arrangements . . . there is no possibility that I will change my mind." What a beautiful, merciless destruction of hope. Swift, sure, and austere.

It was less than four years since Martha had relinquished him to happiness that day at Long Lake, thinking, *nothing will ever hurt, after this.* Now, too, she had lost Celia—Celia who would dwell forever in her heart, her eyes dark with laughter, her figure limned in grace—whom she would never be able to forgive and was incapable of hating.

She did not see Celia again for over a year, but she heard of her from time to time as someone passed a word along to someone else. A fellow named Todd who met Rob downtown. A girl who knew Horty. The brother-in-law of a girl who had studied with Celia in Turetsky's class. Surprising, the number of people who had been, or knew people who had been, at the studio in the Village at one time or another.

Thierry Galland was one of seven children, born of French-Canadian and Irish parents in a New England mill town. He was seventeen when he left his home, where the mills had stood silent for four years, and came to New York to educate himself by means of a series of tough, unattractive jobs and a fierce, unrelenting procession of night classes. At twenty-three he had published a few articles and a story or two; and that year he met Celia Cutting.

Less than a year later, they burned their bridges; Celia, at least, forfeiting in a single gesture all claim to security—home, husband, position, future—for an idyllic springtime in the Poconos. They stayed at a farm, one of those twelve-dollar-a-week places of primitive comfort, abounding in eggs, milk, and scenery. Ostensibly, Celia painted and Galland wrote, but more probably they wandered over the high fields and through the shadowed pinewoods, and, lying in the deep sweet grasses or the forest secrecy, shared their ambitions and the wild fervor of the love which had swept them together. In July, having spent their joint savings, they returned to the Village.

Meanwhile there was an empty place at the reunion that June of 1933, but it was not the only one. Girls who lived in Chicago, Knoxville, and Des Moines were content to send telegrams of greeting to their assembled classmates in that zero hour of the Depression.

There were questions, and although she knew that, sooner or later, they would discover the truth, Martha lied shamelessly to protect Austin yet a little while. Her heart was cold against Celia but she derived a wry amusement from the thought that, had she chosen to speak, the sensation of Celia's elopement would have overshadowed Bennett's modest triumph: second prize in a midwestern story competition. They drank her health in ginger ale.

Martha raised her glass, thinking: Only three years, and we have all lived, after our fashion—Bennett has one foot on the ladder of her fabulous success; Virginia, married a year, is fast becoming a contented, somewhat dowdy little wife, and next year will be toasted as first mother of the class; Lois, formerly so gaunt and awkward, is looking smart and capable, a business-woman, after all; I have had my heart twice broken, the future seems obscure; and Celia!—Celia has flung everything to the winds for a dark young man with a bitter mouth.

In due course Austin was invited to communicate with a firm of New York lawyers in regard to the matter of Cutting vs. Cutting. Of this Martha knew nothing at the time. There was a divorce; how it was handled she learned a long time afterward from, surprisingly, Celia herself. Through her lawyers Celia had directed Austin to bring suit for divorce through a mistaken or obscure gallantry. What she had characteristically overlooked was the fact that the only grounds for divorce in New Jersey were adultery or desertion. The first was out of the question. (Martha could imagine the horror with which Austin would have rejected that alternative.) Desertion required a period of two years' separation.

Legalities did not trouble Celia; she was already living with Galland (or he with her, at the studio). It was Austin who was concerned about her status. He sent her a check large enough to finance a trip to Reno (for two) and a curt, ironic note: "Suggest Nevada honeymoon."

It could have been the last thing he did for Celia, but it was not to be.

During this time it would have been easier for Martha to give up going to the Cuttings. She was afraid that she brought with her the living remembrance of things best forgotten; and she took away with her the disturbing picture of a shattered serenity. But she could not desert them; to do so would have been to admit the existence of a catastrophe they all tried to ignore.

She saw Mrs. Cutting valiantly upholding the gentle deceptions of their threatened dignity; she saw with dismay and silent protest Austin's youth and insouciance vanish. She saw the irreparable injury to pride and personality set their desperate seal on his step, his look, his speech. He had failed as a man, a lover, a husband. He had been unable to make Celia happy.

Before Christmas he took his mother south again, saw her established in a rented villa at Orlando, and remained with her through the holidays.

Millicent gave a supper dance to which Martha was invited, but though she was grateful to Millicent for wanting her, she did not go. She could not see herself among those youngsters, in years as old as she but still spinning around inside the bright world of their youth, with the veneer of sophistication bright and brittle upon them. But they were not invulnerable.

Christmas morning she knelt with Rob in St. Paul's as the tall altar boy went with his taper from tall candle to tall candle. In spite of the green fragrance of evergreen, the scarlet flame of massed poinsettias, and the immemorial Christmas hymns, she seemed to see Celia standing at the foot of the aisle in her white satin gown, wearing her look of innocence. Instead, when she looked up she saw on the smooth young face of each choirboy, above surplice and collar and satin bow, that same look immaculate of thought.

There was a new rector at St. Paul's that year. The Reverend Mr. Fales no longer faced the congregation with the light glinting amiably on his eyeglasses, his smooth ruddy cheeks and round bald forehead. Mr. Phillips was young and tall, with narrow shoulders and a long bony face, and a moving, eloquent voice.

He spoke of gifts . . . "What have you given, what are you prepared to give, to God . . . to your fellow man . . . to Life itself?" His voice gathered depth and resonance, his pale eyes burned and his words fell like a lonely echo in the winter desert of her heart. If there was a secret core of tragedy it was this: that life could be diminished to a constant withholding of ardor, that the gift was unclaimed . . .

On a snowy Sunday afternoon she walked with Rob out of town and up the hill, along Raynold Road past the deserted stillness of the two houses she had loved, and came to the Glen where, fringed with ice, the stream ran in the depth below the bridge.

"Let's go down," she said. It was so long since she had stood in that solitude of sound and stillness.

"Probably break your neck," he said.

The steep banks were covered with snow, the footpath hidden. Rob went first, catching a handhold from tree to tree. Martha followed, but when she was almost down she felt her step lengthen into a slide on the packed snow of his footprints and gave a cry of warning. Rob turned, held out his arms, and took the impact with his broad back against a tree as she came skidding helplessly and not too gently into his embrace. In the next instant her laughter was smothered on her lips by his long hard kiss. She felt a deep tremor in the arms which held her. The snowflakes fell, dark and slow, from the gray skies, touching her cheeks and lashes like gentler kisses; she heard the still murmur of the stream among the black rocks; and her heart responded with pity and surprise: "Rob!"

When he raised his head, the crest of bright hair upon which the snowflakes were clinging in fragile beauty burned like a torch above the pallor of his face. Still holding her, he said quickly, "Martha, I love you so. Marry me. I'll be good to you forever."

"Oh, Rob . . ." She turned her eyes away from his deep look.

The moment lengthened unbearably. At last he put up his hand and touched the hair curling outside her cap, and her cool cheek, before he took her again, swiftly, and laid his face to hers so that they need not look at each other.

"You still—care for him, don't you?"

"Always," she whispered unsteadily. For a breath of time she had been tempted. Rob was dependable and fine; she would have his love and in return could loose the floodgates of tenderness . . . It would not be necessary to live out her days arid and unfruitful. Without warning the thought of Mademoiselle fell across the moment, and she knew that she was not yet so impoverished that she need betray Rob and herself for security. She had her love for Austin, a real and honest possession.

Rob's voice cut across her musing. "I'm not giving up, you know. I'll ask you again—"

The snare lay in the fact that, for a while, she could give to Rob what she was not able to give to Austin: broken dams pour out their floods regardless of channels. She knew, too, that she *could* love Rob; the pity of that was that she would always love someone else more.

In the days which followed, she wondered whether she were not, after all, making a mistake. Life moved about her with a tantalizing new vividness; an old spring of eagerness welled up in her again, as if she had been sleepwalking and Rob's touch had wakened her. Ordinary things acquired a preciousness as if she were seeing with restored sight after blindness. The cramped parlor of the house was too small to hold her. Her mother sat quietly sewing, evening after evening, a spurious picture of content. Are her thoughts and her emotions in ferment under that bland exterior, Martha wondered. Her father read, unless he forgot and stared into space. He had given up cigarettes as too expensive and unearthed a small neat pipe with a curved stem, relic of his student days. At times he held it clamped between his teeth, so tightly that the muscles of his cheeks were rigid.

She walked to the library as many evenings as she could without giving them the impression that she was escaping from their company. The quiet streets were dark lanes holding a small clear pool of light at each corner through which she passed quickly. The air was hard and cold, the taste of it keen upon her lips and sharp in her nostrils. The crisp sound of her solitary footsteps, the mysterious night sound of a car vanishing in a red point of light far down the street, all filled her with a strange, sad exultation.

The main street was a river of light. The marquee of the theater glittered at the center of it, candy shops and drugstores were open, and the suave simpering mannequins smiled and postured in the lighted windows of the largest department store.

It was eight o'clock by the illuminated hands of the black clock on the town hall tower as she pushed open the heavy swinging glass door of the library building. The warm, book-scented air of the long bright room enclosed her. Light flowed over the varnished reading tables, the long varicolored rows of books in the shelves, the smooth gray coiffure of the elderly librarian. The little assistant was trundling her rubber-tired cart noiselessly up and down the aisles; at one table a group of high-school girls—all of one pattern in their skirts and sweaters, their gleaming bobs, ankle socks, and saddle shoes—was deep in a stack of reference works. Her indulgent glance passed over them. Such a little time had passed, separating her from that blissful unawareness.

Guiltily she thought, I should be following some kind of disciplined program, something to take the place of Wellesley. I should be educated, she told herself; I shall probably never marry.

Out in the night again, with her books under her arm and the exhilarating chill against her face, she found thoughts of Rob and the house in the country (the orchard, the brook, the dogs, the long winter evenings with the good supper laid on the table before the fire, the sleet against the pane) encroaching in spite of her resolve. A sound life and a good one were it not for the thought of Austin sitting in his study, growing thinner and quieter, without love or companionship, or the sweet sound of storm hemming peace—with nothing save his broken memories. She tried not to think of him as bitter. Her errant thought had played with the alternative (for herself), but she could not abandon Austin to joylessness; Austin, who had led her into all she knew of the joy of living: of firm hands cleaving cold waters, of wind flowing past one's face in the easy motion of a horse's canter, of the swift, birdlike flight over ice, of the dreams in a symphony and the ecstasy in a waltz. Even now in his detachment, he never failed to give her the friendliest of greetings when they met in the office. They had stopped riding home together. After Celia's departure he stayed later and later at the plant, explaining to Martha that it was getting more and more difficult to keep afloat. With Roosevelt's election many new programs were being initiated which required a great deal of paperwork . . . She received a modest raise which covered her train fare, and, simultaneously, a few restrained words of praise from Cathy. She had been an employee of Fairlies and Cutting for one year.

She walked on and on, her feet taking her the whole familiar way home, but the crossings and the turnings made no imprint on her consciousness. She felt her body filled with the awareness of life, and thought: January 1934. That is the date to remember: the month and the year when I made the final choice. Once more she was oppressed by the sense of the waste of love: hers, Austin's, and Rob's. We could give and give, she thought, but for each of us the pattern is twisted.

There was, as Celia had said, an ecstasy of art and an ecstasy of love, and she knew well enough that in the course she had set for herself, though there might be, eventually, a kind of peace, ecstasy was not to be found.

She shifted into second gear for the hill; there was the tall peak of the roof above the trees, then the drive opening before her, then the green stretch of lawns and the Hall, gray and white, with its awninged porches away to the left and, at last, the flagged porch bright with small moving figures. A transitory sadness shadowed her expectation for a brief moment. She drove around to the back of the building and parked the car. A little way from her, three girls got languidly and gracefully out of the blue seat of a blond roadster and sauntered by her. New faces. For the first couple of years you can keep up with the new grads: they are the little girls you knew in the Lower School, grown up; after that the infiltration of new faces and new names becomes bewildering.

She watched the three slender figures disappear around the corner on the pointed grace of their high heels, and a remembrance of Celia flicked her sharply. Her heart contracted with a quick longing which she banished as it came. She opened her bag, took out her white gloves and drew them on carefully.

Then she started, alone, around the corner.

She had not reached the steps when the taxi stopped and Celia alighted in front of her.

Celia's laugh, her outstretched hands, her glad, guiltless cry, "Martie!"—these flashed upon her in the moment drained empty by surprise and she was defenseless against them. Assailed by a piercing joy and a blind despair, she took Celia into her arms, feeling her fragility with a startled, physical remembrance. At a glance she had seen everything: the clear, bright look of happiness, the soft unwaved hair drawn back into its heavy twist, the dark hat in her hand, the plain black coat over the black and white print, the shabby slippers. "Black is smart, anytime, anywhere," said the fashion pages reassuringly in the year of the bank holiday. They were mistaken: it was not smart on a stone porch among fifty light frocks and hats and pairs of white shoes on a warm June day. Nor was black ever kind to Celia's lusterless brown hair and the colorless ivory skin which went with her topaz-yellow eyes.

Celia's glance swept the assembled group but did not falter. She took off her coat and hung it over her arm and together they went in to luncheon.

Celia Galland, said the place card. On her left hand, touching her forks into a neat pattern beside her plate as she talked, Martha saw the plain gold band which had replaced Austin's circlet of platinum with diamonds.

"We've a house in the country. Near Dalton."

Dalton was a mill town constantly in the papers during those troubled years. A place of strikes and picket lines, of flung stones and bricks and overturned cars. A man had been killed there a few months past in a struggle at the gates, and several others injured. A mill executive had been taken out of town, severely beaten, and left to find his own way home.

"Thierry's doing a strike novel. When it's published we're going to Paris. I want to study there, and Thierry is going to do a Parisian book. He—"

"And Turetsky?" asked Martha.

Again that quick, innocent smile. "He's disgusted with me. He wouldn't take me back."

Afterward, "I'll drive you home," Martha said, when it was all over and the cars began to leave.

"No; it's too far out of your way. Take me to the station, instead. I have a return ticket for Dalton."

On the way to the station Celia talked freely, without embarrassment, of Galland, of his mission, of his early life, of his work.

"Oh, Martie, he has so much passion, so much *feeling*—he's going to be heard! His is a *ringing* voice—" She did not mention her own work.

It had crossed her mind that perhaps Celia did not want her to see where and how they were living, but at the station she took Martha's hand in a quick hard grasp and said, with her tacit, first admission of estrangement:

"You will come someday, Martie, won't you? I'll be waiting."

The train pulled out of the station and Celia's face behind the sooty pane vanished in a moving blur as it gathered speed. Martha went slowly back to the car, her footsteps heavy with thought.

Thierry Galland had no job and no money. He was writing a "strike novel" and for months there had been a spate of strike novels. However little one knew of the business of publishing, one still knew that any vein, however rich, would eventually peter out; that in this business public taste and preference must exercise the demand, and that by the time Galland's long book was finished, interest in the subject would possibly long since have been satisfied.

They were living in a little house on the outskirts of that notoriously troubled, shabby town fifty miles from New York. Celia had given up her classes with Turetsky, but she must be painting or she would never have worn that look of content. It was also probable that she could not afford to resume her lessons, even if he had been willing to overlook her defection— and the cost of commuting daily to the city was out of her reach. Without a doubt she was supporting herself and Galland with the income from her mother's small legacy. Something over a hundred dollars a month in good times, it must have shrunk to a fraction of that by this time.

The print dress she had worn was three years old. Martha had been with her the day she bought it at Arnold Constable's, signing her name with a careless flourish on the charge slip: "Celia Cutting." Now even her grace was unable to redeem its fading style, the faint but noticeable awkwardness of a past season in skirt and sleeve.

She had promised to visit Celia and she would go; but Austin must never know. Since his mother's return and the opening of their house in April she had been seeing them frequently. Because of her failing health, Mrs. Cutting was now almost completely denied any social life, and Martha knew that her visits were a pleasant break in the sameness of days.

Celia and Thierry Galland stayed in the little house in the country until the autumn of 1935. Of the several times Martha visited them there, only two are sharply and indelibly etched in her memory. The place was only twenty miles northwest of Glen Fells, but she could not get away until mid-September. Rob and she were close that summer, in spite of, or perhaps because of what had passed between them that January Sunday. She took him often to the Cuttings'; he and Austin liked each other, for which she was grateful, but he was another reason why she wanted to keep her visits to Celia a secret. The only bitterness she had ever seen in Rob showed when they spoke of her. He had a positive and unrelenting dislike for her.

"She's not like you," he had said once, scowling. "She's one of those women born for trouble."

The September day was rich and warm with lingering summer. There had been no frost. The gardens were brilliant with color, the trees still thick and green along the hilly horizon. She drove swiftly, certain of the road, following Celia's written directions:

"Turn off the highway and follow the road around the lake . . ." The water lay blue and smiling and empty. "In town, turn right down the long street past the mills and keep on going

[150]

out into the country again." The silent mills, long rows of windowed brick buildings, were dusty with silence, and in the street men gathered, with dark, sullen, waiting faces. The long picket line before the gates moved endlessly and sinuously, turning back upon its length. ". . . And after you pass the store and the gas station and the farm with the gray barn, quite a little way down, on the left, there is a long lane running along the cornfield . . ."

(The corn had been tall and strong, a forest with a sweet voice in the wind all summer, hemming the little house on two sides, hiding it from the road.) Now the stalks were dry and yellowing, waiting to be sheaved. It was a small clapboard house of one story. Once, it had been painted yellow with white around the windows, but that was long ago and in the intervening years it had darkened to a drab mustard shade, and would have been hideous had it not been so small. In summer the vigorous green absorbed it. In winter it would huddle and shrink, piteous in the immensity of the bare countryside at the end of the long lane. On that late summer day the grass was still green up to the very stone which served as a step before the door. An elm overhung the roof, a gnarled pear tree stood in the yard and a grapevine, purple with fruit, hung upon a rotting, blackened arbor at its boundary. Near the house in a long row were sunflowers turning their wide faces to the sun.

She stopped the car where the lane dwindled into two faint wheelmarks in the grass. Thierry Galland lay in a weathered canvas chair under the pear tree, his arm over his eyes. He did not move at the sound of the car.

Celia stood in the open doorway looking like herself in a yellow smock. They met and kissed and went into the house arm in arm.

The place looked plain and bare with Celia's studio furniture spread over three sizable rooms. The largest room, into which they came directly, was the studio. A large window had been cut into the farther wall and was still framed by unpainted new wood. Celia's easel stood near it.

"Mike did that for me," she said, following Martha's glance to the window. She drew aside the cloth covering the easel. "I'm doing his portrait."

Martha saw an unfinished painting of a stocky, swarthy man just under forty; a face strong in structure and color, with fiery brown eyes.

"He's Thierry's friend," said Celia, replacing the cloth, "and our landlord. He lived here with his mother until she died last year. Mike is president of the union at the mills. He spends a lot of time at the union offices in New York, too, and that's where Thierry met him. He helps put out a paper."

Garlich. That was the name. It came to her out of some dim recess where the brain stores its odds and ends of accumulated information. "Mike Garlich, obdurate leader of the strikers . . ."

A wooden table in the middle of the kitchen was covered with a checked cotton cloth, and Celia's copper bowl, filled with dahlias, stood in the center of it. The black iron stove shone with polish, the sink and the bare wooden floor were scrubbed clean. Something other than the bareness and cleanliness was in the room . . . She looked at Celia's hands. They had lost their white look and had a lean strength that was more beautiful.

They went back through the studio room and into the bedroom. Here, too, the floor was bare. The wide bed took up most of the room and was pushed close to the open window beyond which the withering corn rose like a wall to the blue sky. Martha saw the secret look which took possession of Celia's face as they stood in the little room, and her mind was filled at once with a complete knowledge of summer nights when moonlight lay across the sill, and the field of corn was silvered like a wide sea, and had spoken to them in a harsh, rustling voice that died with the breeze to a silken whisper . . . She turned away from Celia for a moment, her throat tight with a secret anguish.

In front of the other window stood a table with Galland's typewriter, and under it a wooden box holding paper and manuscript.

Their glances met and clung in the old intimacy.

"Well?" asked Celia, smiling.

"Is it enough, Celia? . . . Are you happy?" She could ask it of this Celia whose look was warm and took her in.

"I never knew it took so little to be completely happy!" Celia replied simply. "Just life—stripped to its essentials. Food, sleep, work, love—and a little beauty."

She put plates and cups on the table in the kitchen; Thierry came in and they ate radishes and bread and cheese, and drank strong, hot coffee. He was dark and silent, and, Martha thought, uneasy in her presence because she belonged to that part of Celia's life which he had not shared. Celia carried the conversation, bridging their awkwardness with her clear voice.

"We're going to stay the winter and next summer we'll have a garden. Thierry despises the city."

As Martha drove away, Celia stood leaning against the frame of the door, her chin raised, the line of her throat a yearning loveliness in the eye of the beholder.

She did not go again until March. In November that terrible winter began which reached its climax in the first days of February with great drifts of snow and temperatures which, in that region, fell to an unprecedented twenty degrees below zero. The thought of them, living their life stripped to its essentials in that shell of a house, haunted her through the winter nights as she lay huddled under blankets in the furnace-heated house on Grove Street.

But for Mike Garlich they would have died. The pump froze in the dug-out cellar under the kitchen, and Thierry was up nights building fires around it. For a week at a time they were isolated. The house was bitterly cold in spite of two stoves roaring red, one in the kitchen and the other in the studio. Sleeping in the bedroom, which was too small for a stove, was agony. Finally, they moved the bed out into the big room. Their money gave out, Celia's check was late, Thierry sickened with the flu, and the coal was gone.

Mike Garlich saw to it that they had coal and food through the rest of the quarter, but Thierry narrowly escaped pneumonia and was dangerously ill for weeks. Too ill to work, although they could have used a few dollars from the articles and stories he might have written. These things Celia wrote to Martha in brief unemotional notes at long intervals through the winter, in response to her own letters.

By the first of March the snow was gone but it was still so cold that it seemed fantastic that spring would ever soften the iron earth. She drove out, finally, on a sunless Saturday. In the back of the car was a box of groceries: canned soups and beans, cocoa, eggs, bread and sweet buns, jam, butter, and milk. She could not be certain that what she was doing would be acceptable; she shrank from the doing, but these were times unlike those from which her former feelings and sensibilities had derived. Put more simply, Celia was her beloved friend and in need; she wanted to help . . . But all her rationalizing could not dispel her fear of Galland's dark glance. She knew that he would never accept her coming in the same spirit as he had taken Mike Garlich's assistance. Momentarily, she had forgotten that she was no longer an idle daughter of well-to-do parents. She was now a working woman.

The lane was hard and rutted. The car jolted slowly its length. The house lay small and pathetic under the leaden sky in the angle of the cornfield rough with frozen stubble. Galland opened the door to her knock and stood looking down at her. She saw for the first time that his dark eyes were a clear green, the irides beautifully rayed. He wore a faded flannel bathrobe and a thick white cloth was bound around his throat.

"Celia's not here," he said tersely, before she could speak. His voice was ungracious and difficult.

"I'll come in and wait," she said; and without a word he stepped aside.

She took off her hat and coat and sat down on the divan. Galland stood at the window facing the distant road, not speaking. She saw his back, and a little of the side of his face, with a hard muscle knotted at the jawbone, the cheek lean and tight. His hands were thrust hard and deep into the pockets of the old red robe, dragging it into conformity with the shape of his body. He was of middle height, neat and muscular, with broad shoulders and slim hips. He had neither Austin's grace nor Rob's solidity, but a peculiar, feline strength which made her sharply aware of him in the silent room. She thought, If Celia had never known Austin, I would still have disliked him in this obscure way.

She leafed idly through two old magazines which lay on the table at her elbow. The room was less neat and orderly than she remembered. There was a dribble of ashes down the front of the stove and on the floor before it; a pail of coal stood nearby. There was a riffle in the rug, shoved up by a chair which had been jerked out of place; and a pile of carelessly folded newspapers on the end of the divan.

When she could sit still no longer, she quietly rose and began to set things in order. Going into the kitchen for the dustpan and brush, she found the remnants of a hasty meal upon the table among the unwashed dishes.

In the studio she took Celia's smock from a nail behind her easel and put it on. As she knelt to sweep up the ashes, Galland turned, giving her an arrogant, inquiring stare.

She met it with a question. "When do you expect Celia? You didn't tell me where she had gone."

"Into town," he said shortly, saving his throat. "Usually comes back on the one o'clock bus."

She felt his eyes following her about the room as she worked; turned once, and caught his look fixed upon her neat shoes and the hem of her soft woolen skirt which hung below the smock. When she had finished she went into the kitchen. She heated water in a large kettle on the stove which Mike Garlich's mother must have used; cleared the table, washed the dishes, swept the floor. Then she made tea, found a fresh cloth in a drawer, and laid the table again.

Before she did any of these things, however, she stood looking long at the table.

At one place was a coffee cup, empty to its dregs, and a slice of bread crumbled minutely on the plate beside it. Opposite, a cup half full of cold brown liquid stood askew in a swimming saucer, and a great stain spread over the cloth under it. The chairs stood away from the table in startled asymmetry . . . A meal begun with tension and ended in an abrupt passion of anger.

There was no food in the cupboards except a few slices of store bread in a wax wrapper, stale; and a bit of jam in a small jar. She thought of the box in the car and her look strayed to the window as she wondered whether she dared bring it in under Galland's inimical watchfulness.

Then through the curtainless window she saw Celia in the lane a few feet from the house. She was wearing the sealskin coat Austin had given her their first Christmas—the one she had worn that icy night three years ago while they waited for her to come home, when she had forgotten Austin's birthday. She was carrying a great, bulging bag of foodstuffs in her arms, and her steps were faltering with weariness and cold in the rutted road.

Martha heard the outer door open and close; heard the crackle of stiff paper as he took the bag from her, and Celia's voice, as she knew it, husky with weariness:

"My coat, please, Thierry . . ."

There was a moment of silence; then, in a torn voice between a sob and a groan, he cried: "God damn it! Even the clothes that warm you were bought by another man!"

"My feet are so cold, Thierry."

The water bubbled in the little pan on the stove, rattling the lid. She poured it into the earthenware pot, set it on the table, and went to the door of the other room. Once before she had been an unwilling eavesdropper, and had turned and fled;

but now she stood rooted until the tableau in the studio, clear to its smallest detail, had burned itself into her heart and her brain.

Celia was sitting on the divan and Galland knelt before her, his face lifted to hers. She held his head between her hands, the fingers spread and delicate against the dark hair, and her mouth was laid on his in an oblivion so deep that it could only have been the bridge over some dark abyss opened between them. Their faces were as smooth as the faces of the dead, in a tenuous immobility swept clean of all but purest feeling. On the rug near them, Celia's frail shoes lay, fallen on their sides.

The blood which had receded from her heart returned with a suddenness which left her trembling in every limb. With a great effort she moved back into the kitchen and leaned against the wall, her face hidden in her hands, thinking, They have passed the high tide of peace: it is gone like the summer that saw it, and this is a newer urgency.

She knew then that Celia had never loved Austin like this. But this was how Martha loved him and how she would never be able to love anyone else.

The moment was filled with a bitter sentience, like molten liquid poured precariously into a thin vessel. We, she thought, raising her head and seeing a vast anonymous company of unclaimed women, are not unknowing. Like the blind, we possess a heightened awareness. Celia, Galland, Rob, Austin, Isabella Cutting, even Mademoiselle . . . each separate love was complete and poignant for that instant in her own heart.

She stood erect, walked to the stove and deliberately dropped the tin lid of the kettle with a sharp clatter. Then she went back to the doorway.

Thierry was still kneeling, Celia's stockinged feet between his hands. He turned his head quickly, and his eyes accused her; but she had seen his suffering and all enmity was gone from her.

"I've made tea," she said, and turned back to the kitchen.

Now, so much had been made clear to her. Galland had not taken Celia from Austin; more probably he had resisted angrily the feelings which overtook them. Nor had Austin failed her in any way. Celia, herself, had been the motivator. She was a traveler; she could pause in her traveling, making her own environment, thus seeming to be at home. But she was not settled—she was always on her way to another place, another time, another climate. For her, life was ever beckoning, ever retreating with an invitation which it was not in her nature to resist.

"The end is nothing, the road is all," say the French.

For Celia, Glen Fells had become an end, and she could not accept it. She had struggled to move away from that environment through her work, her classes with Turetsky, her companionship with others who were striving to express life in terms of art and art in terms of a crusade.

In other times, Austin's love, the gentleness and order of his environment, her own love of beauty, might have been sufficient to satisfy her yearnings. There can be no doubt that her feeling for Galland was an overwhelming force—but love is so many things: the flesh, the spirit, the mind—even, perhaps, the conscience. Who can say what force, or combination of forces, like the blow of a hammer at one stroke invalidated her feeling for Austin and struck dead her conscience where he was concerned?

Martha thought again of the evenings at the studio, remembering one of their conversations on the way home, with Celia sitting silent between them on the front seat of the car, and the late-at-night emptiness of the towns through which they drove.

"They can make you feel as if you should be more excited, as if you should be doing something," she had said, thinking back over the evening. "You feel ashamed of living as well as you are able, of little joys and the small circle of contentment which is your life, in the midst of such great griefs and deprivations . . . I come away every time, covered with guilt because I have so much and can do so little."

"One shouldn't be forced to feel shame for what is normal.

That is an indication of the abnormality of our time," said Austin. "You have to take a wide view, Martha, you've got to see yourself as only part of the whole because you are certainly not alone in your wish to do something about these things. Government is concerned, business is working to find its own acceptable solution. Mistakes will be made, plans will be tried and found wanting, but we'll work out of it. In its negative way, this thing is as big and as important as the Industrial Revolution, and the decisions which come about because of it may very well affect our way of life for the next hundred years—for good *or* ill!"

"Business, business!" exclaimed Celia in a tone which she tried to make rueful but through which the razor-edge of acerbity could be felt. "And what of *life*—what of art? What of humanity? While you are making your plans and finding them wanting?"

Austin was silent and unsmiling as he drove swiftly through the deserted streets. Lights from the overhead street lights came and went over their faces, his stern and withdrawn, Celia's pale and weary, wearing her faint smile.

To Martha it seemed that Austin's conduct of business and his concern with life and humanity at this time had a touch of artistry quite extraordinary. It would have been quite easy for him to leave many of the problems and much of the administration at Fairlies and Cutting in the hands of those older men who had worked with his father and grandfather instead of, as Celia had once complained, being at the factory "morning, noon, and night," shut in his study with his work, or traveling in other states to secure enough work to keep the plant in operation. She found Celia's expressed contempt for his business activities disturbing; as he accorded her interests a signal respect, so should she have given him the dignity of hers.

There had been no wage cuts at the plant. Contracts were hard to find and the men went on part-time work, at times, but no one had been discharged and all drew paychecks. Working within the walls Martha heard from Miss Cathcart, whose admiration for Austin had grown steadily, that he had accepted a good many contracts on which they barely broke even, others on which they exceeded the percentage of possible recovery, so that the actual profit on better jobs was completely absorbed.

Only once had he tried to explain these things at the studio, not by way of justification or apology, but as one contributing information on another aspect of the problem under discussion. Martha remembered the shocked circle of faces and her feeling of walls that could not be breached, walls that had stood for hundreds of years between those who hired and those who were hired.

Thierry Galland, whose name was not yet known to them, whose childhood had been spent in the shadow of brick mill buildings, who had, as a youth, seen those mills emptied as the owners moved the town's livelihood away to places where workers could and would work for less—Galland broke the silence.

"You think you're God Almighty because you can hand out a few jobs!" he said contemptuously. "The workers should be hiring *you,* if you have anything valuable to give them, if you're as smart as you think you are!"

Austin grew white and was silent. Nor did he ever again venture to speak in that company.

In view of these things, the desperation and violence of the times, it was not difficult for Martha to imagine that Celia's conscience refused, finally, to allow her to remain passive in the Cutting environment when her imagination had been seduced by alien ideologies. And, although she herself was apolitical, and inasmuch as, together with her sacrifice of honor and reputation and Austin's love (which she must have known was real), she had also sacrificed her own work, her progress, her chance with Turetsky—did she not feel that her particular talent was a slight and precious thing, that if she could not produce work which would alter the course of human destiny, she could serve this cause best by acting as handmaiden to Galland's talent, which she considered more relevant than her own?

Martha felt that her task lay now in bringing Austin, somehow, to a realization of these things, of removing the stigma of failure as a lover and a husband which he had accepted as his dark burden. But how, she asked herself; how in the world could she accomplish this without opening old wounds and inflicting pain greater than any assurance she could bring to him?

Summer came, and she went out to Mike's house a few more times. The portrait of Mike had been finished, a new one started. It was a reversion to her old idiosyncrasy—a square of window, with a child, a young boy, in silhouette. She had no model, she was working from her imagination. But Martha saw Galland in the sturdy figure with the averted face, the Celtic head.

He was writing behind the closed door of the bedroom. Between long pauses came bursts of typewriting, violent and rapid as machine-gun fire. When he came out, he gave her, without greeting, his dark suspicious look. It came to her suddenly one day that he was afraid of her; afraid that she would lure Celia away from the privations of their life together, back to Austin and that other life she had known.

One day toward the end of summer she found Celia packing.

"We're going back to New York," she said. "We can't go through another winter here." There was a thin shadow of remembered horror on her face.

They found a three-room apartment not far from the river and the George Washington Bridge. It was pleasantly situated on a comparatively quiet street, and the sun came into the largest room all through the autumn afternoons. The rent was moderate and left a little of Celia's income for their other expenses. It seemed as if, at last, they might have some degree of comfort and security.

That was the autumn of 1935.

That same autumn Martha and Austin began to ride together again. They got their horses from the local riding stables, and for some part of Saturday or Sunday, as weather permitted, they took to the high country where they had spent so many hours during their earlier years. She had expressed a longing for this, to entice him backward into a happier time, trusting that the associations would trigger memories less painful than those with which he lived in the present.

Within its limits, her life was satisfying; she had none of those things she had once dreamed of having, but she had a precious salvage of friendship. She was twenty-three and Austin's next birthday would be his thirtieth. She tried to believe that by now he had finally accepted her as a woman; that she was no longer the child he had grown up with, affectionately bullied and teased.

The lines edging his mouth had never gone away; they were deepening instead. An ever-present control had chiseled all the lines of his face a little finer. When he was not looking at one his expression was remote and cool and unexpectant. Sometimes, studying his thin profile, Martha thought, He will look like that for years; his hair will change almost imperceptibly to silver but it will make very little difference. She could see him down the years: tall, slender, and fraily old in his immaculate and well-fitting clothes, listening to his music, handling his books, walking in his garden, spending a part of each day at Fairlies and Cutting . . . In one of those moments she realized, also, that his mother would die, someday, and he would be utterly alone. Her heart broke as she imagined the sterility of a life which had, in its early years, had so much vitality.

He never spoke of Celia.

Mrs. Cutting spoke of her—once.

They were sitting together, she and Martha, in the quiet interval before dinner. Austin had not yet come in. His mother was crocheting and Martha, taking up the fad for knitted suits and dresses, had revived the art taught her by her Grandmother MacLean in a long-gone summer.

"If she were a bad woman," said Mrs. Cutting in a low voice, "I could hate her. But even that comfort is denied me." She closed her eyes for a moment, then opened them and spoke again in a younger, stronger voice. "An old woman's confusion, Martha dear; there *is* no comfort in hatred. Remember that."

She was increasingly given to reminiscence, Martha noticed.

On a bright day in October, while it was still warm enough to sit on the porch, Mrs. Cutting let her work fall into her lap and allowed her gaze to wander over the grounds and gardens. "I have spent forty years of my life in this lovely place," she said. "I was an October bride. We had an automobile quite soon after they became available—sometime around '98 or '99, I think, but we arrived here in a surrey. Shining black, with yellow wheels and a yellow fringe." She smiled at Martha. "I was exactly your age—twenty-three."

"How old were you when you came from England?" asked Martha. She had never known any exact dates; it was remarkable to think of Austin's mother as a girl—a bride—of twenty-three, driving up to this very porch in a horse-drawn vehicle. She thought of her being handed down from the carriage by Austin's father (young and successful, so that he had been able to maintain this house for his bride), wearing one of the imposing hats of the period and skirts sweeping the ground . . .

"I was eleven. My father came over to introduce his invention, and my brother and sister and I came with him. It was to be a summer's holiday. Our mother had died the year before, you see, and he was trying to compensate us for her loss by keeping us very close to him."

She was silent for an interval, having picked up her work again. "Well, one thing led to another and we never went back to England—to live, that is. We lived in Connecticut."

"Did you go to Niagara Falls for your honeymoon?"

Mrs. Cutting smiled. "No; it was too late in the year. Rather chilly, as I recall. We went south instead; to Charleston, South Carolina, by way of Washington and Richmond. I had been fascinated by stories of the Civil War. I was born seven years after the War ended and President Lincoln's assassination. In school, in England, of course, only the slightest mention of these events was included in our history lessons—we had hundreds and hundreds of years of English history to assimilate, with all those kings and queens and the successions, to say nothing of the invasions and conquests—the Anglos and Saxons, Norsemen, the Normans and Celts—and so on.

"When we went to school here in the United States—I was sent to a young ladies' academy in Farmington—I must confess that I was not too interested in the American Revolution. For one thing, the British and American versions did not correspond, which created some difficulty for me. And it seemed such a pathetic little affair which, perhaps, need never have happened at all if a bit more clear-sighted intelligence had prevailed . . .

"But the Civil War with its great, passionate human drama, its air of chivalry, the lofty purpose of the North to abolish slavery, the South's tragic defense of a whole way of life which vanished almost like a modern Pompeii in the ashes of a cataclysm—this captivated my imagination. And over it all, the great brooding sadness of the President, grieving for *all* his children—and paying the ultimate price, himself, in the end!"

Martha was quiet for a moment, contemplating the fact that Austin's mother (who by no means gave the impression of being an old lady in spite of her fragility) could reach back—almost—and touch the most colorful epoch in American history.

"I wish you had taught history at Severn," she said, at length. Miss Prescott had never made anything live so vividly.

They dismounted in a wood and sat on a log in the still sunshine. The yellow leaves were falling thinly with the slow, drifting peace she loved. She drew off her gloves and laid them on her knee, spreading her hands in the sunlight. A leaf, falling, caught in her hair. She held the moment carefully, lightly, as if it had been a blown-glass bubble.

"Penny," said Austin.

She looked up and found his eyes, grave and kind, upon her.

"Oh—I wasn't thinking—anything!" she stammered.

He smiled and her heart turned over slowly to see his eyes unshadowed and clear. His look grew long. "You have a very beatific smile when you are not thinking—'anything.'" He made a few holes in the earth at their feet with the end of his crop. The horses moved restlessly, shuffling the leaves.

"Rob is a steady fellow," he said presently.

"Yes," she said.

"One of these days he's going to ask you to be Mrs. Rob Farr, I think."

"He already has. Over a year ago."

He looked at her quickly with a slanting glance. "And you?"

She shook her head. "I'm afraid not." His waiting look drew the words out of her. "I—I fell in love a long time ago —with someone else. It didn't work out and—well, I guess I'm just a one-man woman . . ."

Then for the first time in those long three years she heard him laugh; saw him throw back his head and laugh his old laughter of delight. She cherished the memory of that laughter a long time, but it lay with sadness on her heart, for with it she learned that not even now did he consider her a woman, capable of a woman's heartbreak. She was still, for him, the kid next door.

Late in November she received a special-delivery letter from Celia. It had been delivered just before she came home from work. Without taking off her coat and hat, she crossed quickly to the lamp and tore open the envelope.

Martie,

Thierry is ill again. Imperative that I see you Friday. I will expect you.

Celia.

The writing was angular with haste and something else. The urgent pressure of the pen had scored the paper so that she could feel the imprint of it on the back. The next day was Friday. She would call the office in the morning and plead personal business as her reason for taking the day off, and go directly to the apartment. She read the note again before going to bed. She knew Celia too well to suppose that she needed a convenient shoulder to cry on. No; although mystified as to Celia's possible need, she knew that it would be something definite and effective.

The morning was pale, cold, and sunless. In the central room of the apartment the curtains were drawn back from the tall windows and the light lay uncompromisingly upon every object in it with the same cold impartiality. Celia was at her easel. She opened the door to Martha and returned immediately to work. Her face was colorless and a little drawn in that cold light; her figure had a strange, defiant tension, her hand and brush a quick, seemingly thoughtless facility.

Martha stood uncertainly in the center of the room. Here were none of the things she had expected; no doctor, no nurse. She heard no sound from the bedroom beyond, nor was there any hint of that depressing medicinal odor which accompanies illness at home. The door was open; she saw the light clean athwart the white wall.

The last thing she had expected to find was Celia at work. She could not, from where she stood, see what she was working at, but her pale mouth had a ruthless line that was strange. She glanced up briefly.

"Sit down. I'll be through in a minute."

In perhaps fifteen minutes she laid down her brushes and

stepped back, rubbing her middle finger in the habitual gesture she had used at Severn as she laid down her pen—a small, disarming reminder of love. A flicker of expression, ironic, and scarcely a smile, touched her eyes and her lips.

"All right. Want to look?"

Martha went around. A gold-rimmed plate of tomato soup, rich and steaming, on a lace doily, flanked by a neat silver service and a tall water goblet . . .

"There are, thank God, four others," said Celia, counting on her fingers: "Vegetable beef, chicken gumbo, cream of mushroom, and clam chowder. Fifty dollars apiece!" She dropped into a chair, closed her eyes and pressed her fingertips to her temples. "I've been a fool. I should have done this long ago. Lilian offered to put me on to it last winter, but Thierry felt so strongly about it—'prostituting' my art, and that stuff . . ." She opened her eyes. "Thierry's in the hospital. He hemorrhaged Tuesday. They say it's T.B."

"Oh, Celia!"

"It could be worse. He has a good chance. About three weeks, the doctor says, and then he'll be able to be moved. To the mountains. I must have money, you see." Her eyes were quiet, her voice level.

Martha thought: It's all in her mind, complete. And I am part of it. She is as sure of me as of her own brain. She waited.

"I am sending him to the Poconos. There's a place near where we stayed that summer . . . just a farm, but the woman is a nurse. It will be cheap; he'll have everything he'd have at a sanatorium: sleep, and rest, and mountain air." Her face quivered. She got up quickly and went to the window. "The doctor says a year. Maybe longer. To get well."

There was another, longer pause. Celia turned slowly and looked at her. She did not lean, she stood lightly poised and erect, with the bright glare of sunless daylight outlining her figure; only her face, to Martha's eyes, half-blinded by that light, was shadowed.

"Martha, I want you to go to Austin and borrow a thousand dollars for me."

She felt her cheeks go cold, as if she had been struck a stunning blow. To go to Austin, to tear open that old wound and destroy the peace that was at best only a negation . . . Was *this* the thing Celia had been so certain she would do?

"I cannot!" she gasped.

Celia took a step and dropped to her knees beside the chair, taking both Martha's hands in a quiet, hard grasp as if she were a person ill or mentally unsettled.

"Listen to me, Martha: This is Thierry's *life*. I can support myself, I can perhaps pay the doctor and the hospital . . . but as things are, I must not, *I will not take a chance on his safety*. A thousand dollars will guarantee him his year no matter what happens. I mean to have it. No one else that I know is able to give it to me. Tell him anything you like, or nothing. But if you don't go to him, I shall!"

And she would have.

So Martha faced Austin across his study desk in the somnolence of a winter Sunday afternoon, twisting her fingers tightly together in her lap, listening to the clock whir softly and chime the half hour in the mellow, intimate silence of the familiar room.

She asked him for the loan of a thousand dollars that afternoon, allowing him to believe that it was for herself. Far better to go herself, to present her merciful lie; even to bear on her own heart the burden of wondering, afterward, if she had been believed, but it was a task not without peril. As Celia rendered her defenseless, just so Austin's grave look established in her at once an impulsive candor. To face that look and meet it with subterfuge was the most difficult thing she had ever attempted, and she was only partially successful.

She brought out, too quickly and breathlessly, the stilted phrase she had rehearsed: "It has become necessary for me to have a thousand dollars without anyone knowing of it—" (Her parents, of course.)

He had not taken his eyes from her face since her preliminary words ("I have to talk to you, alone"). Now she saw his look deepen into a sharp intensity. It was almost as if he started, or cried out, although he had not moved or made a sound. His hands held an ivory paper knife delicately suspended above the blotter, motionless as if they, too, were carven.

"Forgive me, Martha—are you in some kind of trouble? Can I help?"

She felt color stain her cheeks and cried swiftly, forestalling further questions she might be tempted to answer, "No, no. It's all right. Truly. I'm all right. But please don't ask me any questions—"

"O.K." His air of relief was so marked that she understood suddenly what he had feared—for her. Around the edges of her thought was a hovering sense of incongruity which she was too disturbed to examine.

He opened the top drawer of the desk and took out his checkbook. For as long as it took him to take up his pen and deliberately write out and carefully blot that momentous slip of green paper, she was secure from his regard. When it was done, she felt a fine, trembling weakness pass over her in a wave. She looked into his downbent face and her heart closed like a hand on its treasure of love.

He laid the check before her, then leaned back as if preoccupied with screwing together his fountain pen while she picked it up, folded it and put it away. She did not look at it. Now that she had secured it, there was room in her mind for Celia and Galland—and the thought burned.

Austin returned his pen to the breast pocket of his neat gray suit and looked at her again, a reflection of light—or a smile—in his eyes. She could not be sure.

"No personal problems?" he said again.

She shook her head. "More of an—investment."

As he stood aside at the door of the study for her to pass, she stopped, and looking a little upward into his face with an impulse of honesty that would not die, said hesitantly,

"I'm not sure if I shall ever be able to pay you back."

He smiled then and touched her shoulder. "Don't think about it now. Best of luck with your—venture." Was there an indefinable sadness behind his smile, or did she imagine it?

She cashed the check so that Celia's name would not appear on it, and gave her the money, ruefully meditating upon the ease with which the arts of deception can be learned.

As she took it, Celia's eyes lighted with relief and the thin mask of anxiety on her face relaxed a little. She held the thick roll of bills in her slender, clenched fist for a moment, looking down at it as if she saw the price of an invaluable future.

After a moment she raised her head. "I'm not likely to forget this, Martie . . ."

They talked, then, of other things: the work Lilian had lined up for Celia, Horty's new play, the last reunion, of Bennett, whose prize-winning piece had been included in a new anthology.

At last Martha rose to go.

"Did you tell him?" asked Celia, at the door.

The cryptic question stood apart from all else that had been said like a single tree in a wide field.

"No," she said shortly. Her mind darkened with the thought that the money was not enough; that it was also important for Celia to know whether Austin's generosity had been for herself or for Martha.

She did not go up again to the apartment until the afternoon of Christmas Eve. Galland had come home a day or two earlier to spend the holiday. He was sitting in a chair near the windows, reading. His thick, dark hair was neatly brushed and he was wearing a brown suit. The color was right for him. She had never seen him dressed before: once in that old flannel robe, other times in baggy tweed trousers with a shirt open at the neck, his unruly hair falling forward on his brow. Even when he used to come to the studio, he dressed in nondescript clothes like a laborer.

He did not look especially ill. His face was too dark for pallor, his lean cheeks no leaner.

He looked up as she came in with her packages under her arm, that familiar, wary glance.

Celia's voice spoke her name from the bedroom beyond. "Come in here while I dress."

But she was dressed; she stood in front of the mirror, her arms uplifted, putting the last pins in her heavy coil of hair. The little lamp shone upward into her face, revealing a faint warm color under her skin, the bright, carefully drawn curve of her mouth, and her eyes, wide, dark gold, and lustrous meeting Martha's in the glass. She turned around and made a little motion with her hand.

Martha closed the door softly behind her.

"How does he seem to you?" Celia asked quickly.

"I'd never suspect that he'd been so ill."

Celia's look searched her face. "You do mean it."

She picked up a thin, faded blue dressing gown which lay across the bed and hung it away in the closet.

"No friends, no parties, no excitement. Doctor's orders. Just this holiday together . . . and then the long year." She closed the closet door gently and stood for a moment with her hands laid, one above the other, on its panels. "He must get well. If anything happened to him, I'd kill myself." Her tone was unvehement, casual, and frightening.

On Thursday, two days after Christmas, they journeyed together up to the Poconos, and Celia came back alone.

Time can be unimaginably long when it is suspended in waiting between fixed points of promise. Galland's letters—irregular, infrequent and dispirited—and Celia's lonely journeys became the two pegs upon which the fabric of their days was hung.

Her winter with Celia was a voluntary exile. Mrs. Cutting was in Florida surrounded by friends, with Mrs. Maxwell to take care of domestic details. Her winters had now taken on an assumed routine as the doctor had forbidden her to risk spending the coldest months in the northern climate. Austin was spending the winter in the city, also. But only her mother and Rob knew that the girl with whom she was sharing an apartment was Celia. Rob's disapproval raised a slight but unmistakable barrier between them; nevertheless, she was tolerant of his disapproval, aware that probably no one would ever understand the inescapable, resilient quality of her feeling for Celia. She did not altogether understand it herself.

She could not trace the change in Celia as it occurred; she had only a memory, an image of eagerness and youth to place beside her present observation of a woman who had, in three years, grown both hard and selfless. Where once Celia had looked upon the whole of life in relation to her own necessity, now she was submerged in her only acknowledged necessity—Galland. To him she had yielded all things: even the last and greatest of all her possessions, her talent, was debased for his sake; but her very yielding was stern with purpose and untouched by regret. Now and then, as when she had wanted the money from Austin, one encountered that relentless purpose beneath her quiet, like the hard edge of rock under a layer of leaves in the wood. As if she were sleepwalking or had lost her way, she seemed to have left behind the brilliance of her dreams. Much that had been bright and vivid in Celia Pence shone forth but rarely now, and then only with the diminished gleam of reflection.

Martha felt poignantly and unavailingly the loss of what had been, but it was the knowledge of what might never be that twisted her heart; almost as if the fever of that ambition had passed into her own soul, she set her will against its final loss. "We shall watch your star ascending," Julia had said to Celia; and they had seen, all that callow immovable gathering of pleasant people, a personal, a prophetic splendor.

It was too late to save the past but it might yet be possible to rescue the future. She remembered, hopefully, that Hubert Pence had done his best work after grief and bereavement and the malicious theft of his love's integrity. If it were true that art roots best and deepest in pain, then these months of waiting should give Celia's work a new impetus. So it was with the humble purpose of seeing that Celia slept, and ate, and had enough money to pay her rent that she begged to be allowed to come.

"It will be like the old days," she said eagerly and thoughtlessly.

Celia gave her a fleeting look. "Not quite . . ."

She was right about that. They were never free, that winter, of Galland; an old pair of slippers stumbled to light from the dark recesses of the closet—an acid comment penciled in the margin of a page he had read—the scent of his soap and his tobacco—the thought of him, alone on the mysterious outer fringe of the winter nights, as she lay beside Celia in the double bed . . .

Celia finished her "soup ads." Others followed: an obscure breakfast food, prunes, dog ration, all less lucrative than the first. She ceased to exercise her caustic wit upon what she was doing and worked at it with a dogged, unflagging industry, but its execution seemed to drain her of vitality so that she had little heart for diversion, the small pleasures which Martha had hoped would balance the work and the waiting and the secret fear.

It happened, a few times, that people dropped in to inquire about Galland; but there were not many whose memories could encompass those three years between the Village and the Bronx or whose curiosity could be stirred by the fact that an obscure writer who three years earlier had eloped with a married woman was fighting T.B. at some remote, unfashionable mountain retreat. So they came and went and did not return. And after they had gone Celia would rise and gather up the glasses they had soiled, the bottles they had brought and emptied, as if she were grateful for the impersonal task.

She was too restless to read; she had begun to smoke, and too much. In the evenings she would sit, remote and withdrawn, narrowing her eyes against the smoke of her cigarette. She had a habit of prolonging the twilight interval before they lighted the lamps. She would sit longer and more quietly within the secrecy of the dusk. Martha's pity and yearning tenderness were eased in the dim quiet as Celia sat between her and the pale square of the window like a subject in one of her own paintings, her head against the back of the chair, showing the lovely curve of her throat, only her hand moving now and then to touch the ash from her cigarette, the lines, the pallor, and the tension of her weariness erased or hidden.

Or she would sit at the little desk over against the wall and write hastily, with many false beginnings, to Thierry, the sound of her pen harsh against the silence of the room.

There was always silence that winter. Even over and around the small mundane necessities of speech, it hovered insidiously. "Martie, are these my stockings or yours, the ones you mended last night?"—"If you go out today, Celia, will you get the things on this list? We're out of oranges."—"Would you like me to get *Lucy Gayheart* or *Vein of Iron* from the library?" None of these words touched the silence enfolding like a great cocoon all the unspoken hopes and fears, the portent of the future.

And Martha, watchful above her book or her mending, would wonder which of the doors along the corridor of the past Celia opened, which rooms she revisited . . . Were her thoughts always of Galland? The first, startled moment, when meeting his brusque and angry gaze, she had known. Had known what? That she would follow him anywhere? That she should never have married Austin, that she did not love him, or did not love him enough? Or merely that the life she had mistakenly chosen —the continuity and security, the four-poster bed and the heirloom spread—was meaningless for her? That the door was wide open to a new dream of an old freedom? Did Galland, for her, replace the life and the love which had died with her father's death? Or was she remembering only the voice of the cornfield, and the bitter winter; a cup overturned in anger at the breakfast table, and her feet held between Galland's hands?

Did she ever remember—no, could she ever forget!—a grave voice, rough and shaken with discovery: "Celia. Celia, darling!" Or a tide of organ music filling St. Paul's, a white veil, and Austin's kiss? (No; only Martha remembered . . .)

Nor would Celia remember Austin's face, gray in the last clear light of a spring evening.

Celia's weariness increased. She was very thin. Two Sundays each month she went up to the mountains. Eight Sundays. Wearing her thin black coat with its strip of fur drawn close under her chin, the brim of her hat slanted over her pale face, her mouth gallant with lipstick and her eyes bright, for a day, with unquenchable hope, she would go out; and Martha, at the window, would watch her move down the street on her slim heels until the wall of the building hid her from view and cleft their day apart.

It was a cold winter. One of those days—a February Sunday—was both cold and snowy; snow that dissolved into wet slush on the city streets, but in the mountains hung soft and heavy on the sagging evergreens and lay deep and trackless all the long mile from the station to the farm. Celia had no overshoes; but Galland did not notice—perhaps, at the moment, she did not notice it herself—for he said to her as she left him, "When you are gone, I'll have the marks of your feet to look at as long as the snow stays." Snow doesn't melt quickly in the Poconos. It was probable that Thierry had her footprints to look at all those ten days that Celia lay ill.

In March it rained and she borrowed Martha's umbrella. Perhaps, to her pride, there was some subtle distinction between borrowing overshoes and borrowing an umbrella.

Then it was spring. The days lengthened and the evening light over the roofs had a lucent clarity; the wind was suddenly gentle, elusively sweet; the sun came out in the midst of a shower, splintering the rain with silver, and flowers appeared in the corner markets. Thierry's letters acquired a new, vigorous note of impatience that month. "Get hold of the doctor and tell him I'm perfectly able to work. It's not going to kill me to scribble a few lines in a notebook. This old fellow up here is driving me nuts—" He was, he wrote, "sick of being chained in idleness!"

She went up that last time on a brilliant April day. The doctor who had taken care of him in November had told her that while he had had no recent contact with the patient, and while he was averse to interfering where another doctor was in attendance, it was his considered opinion that Thierry would do himself less harm by "scribbling" than by his present mood of frustration and impatience, and that the fact might be insinuated tactfully in her conversation with the "old fellow."

She wore that day a pongee suit of natural beige, four years old, made in Paris; and a small brown hat with a wisp of veiling. The little hat was a year old; she had bought it with Thierry one afternoon when the mail brought a small flurry of checks for articles and stories. Martha had never seen him merry, but she wanted to imagine his impetuous, "This calls for a celebration!" and his sharp satisfaction in being able to buy something for Celia.

Brown was her color. She paused in the doorway, smiled, and went out; and, unaccountably, Martha was reminded of an autumn day flown with time, when Celia had stood, wistful, like some dreaming nymph, in the Glen, her face enchanted and her hands held palm upward to the slow drift of falling leaves, russet and gold and scarlet and brown . . .

Two days later, in the evening, the telegram came. It was delivered just as Martha came in from the office. She had not yet had time to remove her coat when the buzzer sounded; the boy must have followed her into the building.

She came out of the bedroom and saw Celia holding the yellow envelope in a shaking hand. Her face was drained of color, her eyes dark and wide with a dreadful, intuitive knowledge. Her lips moved; no sound came but a dread echo of the unspoken words hung upon the silence of the room. She tore

[176]

open the envelope and read, and the yellow sheet went fluttering from her nerveless fingers. For a moment heavy as stone, she stood, and it is probable that she never knew she swayed like a reed in the wind, then raised her hands to her face and cried sharply, in a rending voice,

"No! . . . Oh, *God,* no!"

After that she made no sound. She neither spoke nor wept as Martha touched her, only suffered herself presently to be led, unresisting, into the other room, undressed, and put to bed. But from the cup of hot milk which Martha brought, she turned her head away.

In the night she began to tremble deeply and uncontrollably, and Martha, turning, gathered her into a close embrace. Still she made no sound, suffering the wordless manifestation of her grief until, after a while, she slept and was still. Toward daylight Martha, raising herself on her elbow, discovered that she was again awake. She asked gently: "Is there anything you want? Something hot? . . ."

Celia moved her head briefly in negation. Her face was hidden in the pillow and Martha, leaning above her, thought how effectually we are secluded by sorrow. Her own throat was painful with unshed tears; but they were for Celia, not for Galland. Something hot, something warm . . . A substituted embrace, an unheeded tenderness . . . These were the offerings one gave to the bereaved to ease one's own unendurable pain of sympathy.

When it was light, she got up and telephoned the doctor. Celia slept all day under the influence of the sedative he gave her.

Thierry Galland had died Tuesday at dawn. While they still slept, his life ebbed in a bright unstemmed tide. As the sky over the mountains began to pale slowly and the stars fled before the new day, the doctor and the priest came hurrying along the dark road from opposite ends of the village.

Daylight had vanquished candlelight in the little room before the young priest came back, alone, through the dark corridor and saw that the sun was rising. In the outer room he was met by a middle-aged woman of whom he asked a question, wrote a name in a notebook taken from his pocket, and went out into the young April day. At the station in the village he went in and dictated a brief message to be sent to an address in New York City, and signed it with his name.

Friday of that week, toward evening of a day gray with rain, Galland was buried in a little country churchyard in the mountains where he had known a brief summer's transcendent happiness. To their last tryst, Celia insisted that she go alone.

In the days that followed, all the fears Martha ever had known paled before the dread significance of those remembered words, "If anything happened to him I'd kill myself." Miss Cathcart had given her a week's early vacation when she explained that a close friend had been tragically widowed and needed her presence. But the time came when she could no longer delay returning to work. She hurried home in the evenings, climbing the stairs day after day with the same dark dread; and day after day she opened the door to find Celia lying motionless on the divan, her face turned to the window where the pale gold wash of sunset was fading in the April sky. The days were lovely that spring with the unbearable impress of beauty upon a heart laid bare to grief.

She had no way of knowing how Celia spent those days. One evening she said gently, "You should go out a little during the day; the air will do you good."

Celia gave her an oblique glance. "I'd step off the curb in front of a truck, if I did."

Her voice was quiet but a new realization flared for an instant in Martha's consciousness. That unmistakable note of bitterness . . . somewhere, somehow her sorrow had taken a new direction. Might not bitterness be more salutary than the numbed stupor of those first days?

Celia rose from her chair and went to the window, grasping a handful of the curtain in her locked fist. Her own reflection faced her on the dark mirror of the night, jeweled over with the small glittering lights of the city. Her whole figure was rigid with a defiant, bitter sadness. Time passed in the soundless room with the heavy throbbing beat of a labored pulse. Martha got up and went to her.

"Celia. Celia, dear—" (Old, old echo of a gentler grief than this.) At the touch of her hand Celia turned and drew away from her. Her eyes were dark, and brilliant, and unhappy.

"You needn't torture yourself for words of comfort, Martha: there are none. I have been repudiated, so I imagine I have no right to comfort anyway. The last thing Thierry did on earth was to deny our love and our marriage. They called a priest—" Her voice quickened, almost angrily, as Martha said nothing. "He had done with all that—superstition, he called it—years and years ago. But to enter heaven he had to deny me!"

"You can't know that," Martha faltered. "The nurse, the woman where he stayed, must have thought she was doing the right thing for him. And perhaps he never knew—"

"I was a divorced woman. Must I tell you what that means? And at the cemetery, the priest put his hand on my shoulder and said to me, 'Be at peace, my daughter; he died in a state of grace.' "

The disillusion in her eyes was like the flash of a bright and terrible blade; Martha's glance wavered and fell before it, and the words she would have summoned retreated, secret and unsaid. That moment bore the seed of the end, but this was not apparent to her then.

The days followed each other slowly, burdened and apprehensive. Then one night she was wide awake in a startled instant. She put out her hand: the pillow beside her own was empty. She sat up and swung her feet hastily out of bed, groping for her slippers. A thread of light showed under the bathroom door. Without pausing to knock, she turned the knob and the door opened under her hand. Celia was standing in front of the medicine cabinet, a glass in her raised hand. Martha's blood drained away from her heart in a chill of paralyzing fear. She took a long step forward and quickly thrust up her arm; the glass flew from Celia's hand and shattered on the rim of the basin.

Celia sat down suddenly on the edge of the bathtub. She wore her dressing gown over her pajamas. Her hair was loose on her shoulders, her eyelids dark with the shadow of pain.

"Aspirin," she said drily. She pushed back her hair, got up, and left the room without a backward glance.

After a moment Martha went into the kitchen for dustpan and brush, swept up the slivered glass and disposed of it. She shook two more aspirins from the bottle into her hand, filled a second glass and carried it into the bedroom. The light was burning. Celia lay with her eyes closed. Speechless with chagrin and a rebellion she could not define, Martha stood beside the bed looking down at her. After a minute or two Celia opened her eyes; they held a depth of scorn. Silently, Martha held out the glass and the white tablets, and, as silently, Celia raised herself on one elbow and took them.

Then she set the glass carefully on the night table and, still leaning on her elbow, spoke distinctly in the light, brittle voice she had turned on Austin.

"If my freedom is to be the price of your eternal vigilance, Martha, I refuse to pay it. I am weary of your interference; it has gone on too long. For years you have been trying to tidy my life as you once tidied my house . . . Again and again you have presumed where you had no right. What on earth possessed you to drag Austin in to the studio that day? What did you accomplish? What did you hope to accomplish?"

Thus suddenly do the unimagined specters of resentment rise up and confront us. It seemed unimportant to deny that she had taken Austin to the Village that terrible day. She began to speak, to think aloud, in a soft, measured tone warmed faintly by surprise.

"The impossible. I know that now. You were finished. He couldn't believe it, nor could I, but it was true. As you had written, there was no possibility that you would change your mind. All the way, you have taken from those who loved you, not too much, but too little—only the part you *wanted,* and left the rest. You speak of price: two men loved you, Celia, and each of them paid a price for loving you. But even from Thierry you will not accept the whole . . . How can anyone repudiate what has been, any more than he can repudiate what he is? Everything you have done, every joy, every grief you have known is a part of you forever. That is why Austin goes on paying, living with the bitterness of his unclaimed love, shut in with the past."

Still, her heart falters as she recalls the dark, deepening look of new intelligence which Celia gave her.

"You hate me!" she said at last, softly, in a tone of wonder. *"You* wanted him; and because I took him, always, after that, you have hated me. Facing me, day after day, year after year— how *could* I have been so simple as to imagine that there was not a bone of deceit in you . . . when there was this!"

The soft, steady glow of light from the lamp on the table lay warmly across the bed, on the sheet and the faded blanket, and on Celia's bare arm which lay outside it. The light illumined the left side of her face and was absorbed into whiteness by the lusterless smooth fall of her hair, curling slightly at the ends. There was no rancor in her voice or eyes, only a seclusive wonder. The clock on the dresser had stopped; but it was as if an inevitable hour had struck for the charting of all the crosscurrents, secret and formidable, beneath the surface of their relationship.

"I could not hate you," said Martha with difficulty. She was aware of the futility of those words against that crystalline certainty of Celia's; but they demanded utterance. She thought, with a pain so great that it had no edge, only a blunt depth, This is the end. In the moment of its severing, the lyric memories of her long friendship—her love—for Celia settled upon her heart as suddenly as a flock of birds in a tall tree at evening.

"But you have never forgiven me!" cried Celia, swiftly and clearly. "No woman ever forgives another for taking the love she thought was hers!"

"I could have." The words went on, halting, inexorable, as if possessed of a separate intelligence. "What I could not lightly forgive was the destruction of the thing I would have cherished . . . But even then—"

It was said at last.

When she first lost Austin to Celia her heart had broken, truly, and the egoism of her young grief was like shattered crystal, thin and sharp and shining. Later, when Celia left him she suffered a darker anguish, but neither of these had had the finality and poignance of her parting from Celia on a bright June morning in that stripped room chaotic with luggage and packing cases. Her heart was heavy with the knowledge that unless Celia sought her out, they would not meet again: they were now naked to each other and even the benignity of time could not heal the wounds they had dealt each other.

Yet, at the last, she hesitated.

Celia stood checking a list in her hand. She stood straight and proud and implacable, with her few household gods and the tools of her trade piled about her. Martha saw the shape of her mouth in her thin face, the inimitable precision of that lightly held pencil, remembering both the hope that had welcomed and the annihilation which had overtaken her there in that place.

"Celia. What are you going to do?" Now she was bruising herself against that impersonality of Celia's.

Celia lifted her head. Her look went beyond Martha to the bare wall garish with sunlight, a look filled with stillness and devoid of serenity.

"Nothing that I ever dreamed." And while Martha hesitated, still, the last sands ran out, the last silence of that room held them and then was broken as Celia said, in a different voice:

"Your taxi is waiting, I believe," turning half away in what Martha recognized as the complete gesture of her dismissal.

Somewhere in the long narrow stairway between the bare, light room and the busy sun-warmed street, she acquired the numbness, the emotional apathy which was a protection until it became a prison. As if a thick wall of glass had come down between her and the rest of the world, her brain had a strange lucidity, but she was untouched by what she saw: the corner, where so many times she had watched Celia out of sight, the little market run by the Italian matriarch where they had done their shopping, the Danish pastry shop where they had occasionally stopped for a cup of chocolate, recalling for a brief half hour the careless ease of girlhood . . . All the bustle and movement of the city, the clamor, the blue sky above the river and the gulls riding its green swells, were sharp and unreal. She stood on the top deck of the ferry, and she did not look back.

A week later she went up to Severn. Bennett was there, and Lois, and Virginia. But Celia's place, between hers and Bennett's, was vacant, the chair standing in close to the table, the silver unvisited by her fingers, the rim of the water glass untouched by her lips. The white place card stood tilted against it: Celia Galland.

Bennett's dark eyes flicked it with a glance. She leaned slightly across the intervening space. "How did she take it? You've seen her since, I imagine."

The customary expectant hush which fell upon the room as Julia rose to speak spared her the necessity of reply.

Life fell into its old pattern. Her heart was but faintly stirred by the loveliness of that burgeoning summer; grateful, as the heat grew more intense, for the privilege of leaving the city behind her at the end of day. The months passed as in a dream. She was very tired; she seemed never to feel really rested, although she slept rather more than usual.

She lay in a long chair in the narrow side yard of the Grove

Street house, behind the tall privet hedge. The book she was reading fell often into her lap, and she found herself looking into space, her mind empty of coherent thought, drifting, in a vague suspension of time. When Austin rang up and asked her to dinner or to go driving, or Rob invited himself out for the weekend, she put them off, pleading unfinished work ("sewing something to wear at the office" or "this heat has me so tired, I'm going to bed early and rest up for Monday").

Then summer was gone, and the ripening, genial autumn days. The air and the light were sharpening with the imminence of November; then it was November.

It had rained all week, but Sunday morning the wind fell, the rain ceased, and toward midafternoon a white sun stood palely in the vaporous sky, shedding a distant clear light along the wooded hills. The wind-driven rain had stripped the last of the leaves, but here and there the golden torch of a hardy maple burned along a hillside. Rob parked the car and they got out to walk.

Crossing a high field still green, they saw a low-lying rim of hills purple with shadow, and nearer, a cluster of houses lying in a cold pool of light. Westward the river ran toward the town: light—colorless and opaque as the sheen of metal—on its surface. Below the hill they could hear the occasional swift flight of a car along the highway.

She leaned against the rail fence whose ribbed gray wood was still sodden under her hand and Austin's old laughter rang in her memory. She remembered, then, the wealth of joy, the rich surge of feeling filling her young heart in one of those springtimes: a joy born of nothing more than a cloudy sky and a soft wind and some mysterious promise stirring her blood.

We can remember but not recall, she thought, the ardor we knew; our joys stand like trees along the avenue of youth: we look back but cannot summon them, they are rooted there. Even our pain and its futile gestures fade in the memory, unenduring as the color of smoke.

"Probably be colder after this rain," said Rob, filling his pipe with blunt, careful fingers.

So many things—high places, like this, the intimately fashioned, gently wooded countryside to which her eye was accustomed, narrow roads, and winding rivers, and small deep valleys, smoke rising, and the sound of rain traveling with the wind —had had power to waken that strange heartache called ecstasy. But the ecstasy that dies in the heart and is preserved in the brain is like rose leaves, withered, brown and without fragrance. The hope and terror of this life lies in the truth that all things will pass . . . nothing here is eternal.

At Rob's suggestion, they had driven out to the Log House that afternoon. The place was unchanged: dark, low and raftered, with little amber-shaded lamps on the tables and flames leaping in the great fieldstone fireplace at the end of the dining room. Sunday diners had made it popular in recent years. The large room was animated by a low murmurous sound of conversation and laughter. The waitresses moved with a waltzing step between the tables. There was a flare of matches and lighters in the warm haze redolent of wood smoke and tobacco. At a table near the center of the room, a fair girl wearing a dramatic velvet beret leaned forward to light her cigarette; the quick flame was not more ardent than her laughing, upward glance.

Martha's brain, but not her heart, remembered that once some years ago in that room she had been transcendently happy.

Leaning upon the fence in that high field she saw the last cold light vanish in a folded rift of cloud and the gray winter dusk come swiftly down upon the valley. The year was dying. She was almost twenty-five and the bright peril, the blithe hazard of life that was to have been hers had eluded her.

What are you going to do? Nothing that I ever dreamed.

Ah, Celia! You have lived all of it—comfort and privation, decorum and its peace, madness and its consequence, love, received, given, and rejected, the flare of ambition and the lamp of sacrifice, and, finally, that forced surrender, the yielding to death; and with it the discovery of a bitterness greater than loss. This, then, was the dark direction; this, the quality of your haste long years ago in the silent summer night; this, the strangeness of your fear and that cry, clairvoyant with the impatience of youth: "Life is so short . . . Everything is going to happen within the next ten years!"

As some people are stirred by a physical touch, so was she wakened to realization that, at last, her mind had crossed a pathway taken by Celia's.

"Rob," she said suddenly, laying her hand on his arm, "I want you to do something for me; find out where Celia is, if she's all right."

He knocked out his pipe against the fence post and put it into the pocket of his jacket before replying. His eyes, when he spoke, were cold and steady with the expression he reserved for Celia.

"Haven't you had enough, *yet?*"

She averted her face, feeling the line of her jaw grow taut and stubborn. "I must know. I thought I would never again— be concerned. But I must know how she is." Without pride she acknowledged silently, She is my mainspring; it has been too long a commitment for such an ending.

After a long silence, he spoke.

"Martha," he said, "I'll do this for you, if I can, in return for a straight answer to an honest question."

A cold little wind blew over the hilltop and the long grass rustled faintly. There was still a little light.

"Go ahead."

"Would you, if it were possible, marry him, still?"

"It isn't possible—"

"A straight answer."

"Yes." She could afford to give Rob an honest answer. He knew all the rest and his question was asked out of kindness, not curiosity, she knew.

He moved his shoulders and looked away down the darkening valley.

"If it were one or the other!" he said, and his voice was rough, but not with anger. "But together they've crowded you out of your own heart."

He moved suddenly and took her in his arms. She accepted the swift, hard pressure of his kiss, laying her hand for a moment along his cheek, then leaned back to look into his eyes.

"Dear Robin . . ." If there were such a thing as platonic love, she and Rob shared it, she thought. Warm, strong, sustaining. Tears came into her eyes; she could not deny him the comfort of physical manifestations of that love, neither could she avoid a sense of guilt lest he interpret them as leading to a future which did not exist. But, she told herself, this was not playing games as with Carroll; it was, she admitted to herself, so real that had it not been for the thought of Austin, immersed in his work, growing ever quieter and more withdrawn . . .

"Martha, marry me. Forget it all and marry me."

She shook her head. "It wouldn't be fair to you, Rob. Every time you held me, I would be thinking of his arms—"

"And if you could marry him, each time he held you, you would be thinking of *her* in his arms before you. Marry me, Martha, and I'll *make* you forget them both, I swear it!"

She moved a little way and rested her arms on the fence. There was the problem: she didn't want to forget Austin.

"There is a kind of content in wanting what you have, especially if you can't have everything you want."

Rob laughed shortly and wryly. "Is this gem of wisdom intended for yourself or me—or for both of us?"

She held out her hand. "Let's not be sad, Rob. Let's just —like being together. It's getting dark; perhaps we should go home."

It was after seven when they reached the house, and dark. Her mother came into the hall at the sound of the door. Before she spoke Martha met her grave glance, and her thought flew to the Cuttings.

"Austin called about four o'clock. Mrs. Cutting had a mild heart attack this morning. She's all right now, I think."

[187]

Without speaking, she went to the telephone. She gave the number automatically, her whole heart and mind tense with an inarticulate prayer: Oh, God, don't let this happen to him, too!

"Austin Cutting," said a quiet voice at her ear, and for an instant she was unable to reply.

"Austin—it's Martha. Mother just told me . . ."

"Hello, Martha. Everything is all right now. It was not severe. Dr. Martin didn't think it necessary to hospitalize her. But he says it is fair warning, that we shall have to be more careful . . ."

"Do you want me to come over?"

"Not tonight, thanks. She is resting comfortably. But she's not to do anything at all for a time, so I imagine a visit from you now and then will be a great help in relieving the monotony."

"Good night, then. Austin," her voice broke, "I'm so glad —I was so afraid—"

"It's all right, don't worry. And good night, Martha."

She replaced the receiver and, looking up, met Rob's eyes. They held a sadness and a comprehension which she would have spared him if she could.

Once, she had run lightly up that long curving stairway, Celia's fingers laced within her own.

Now she mounted thoughtfully, alone, her way taking her along the wide carpeted hall past the closed door of the room that had been Celia's. Her thought, obedient to its discipline, did not trespass beyond its narrow walnut paneling.

Beyond, Mrs. Cutting's door stood lightly ajar, and entering a room peopled with the hovering silence and shadows of dusk, she would find its occupant sitting in the wide bay overlooking the gardens—English gardens planted over forty years ago for an English bride—and the wooded western hills.

That first evening she had been frightened by the immobility of that figure in the big chair: quickly—almost but not quite coincident with the sound of her indrawn breath, Mrs. Cutting had spoken.

"I have been enjoying the afterglow. The sky was such a beautiful, depthless green over the hills tonight."

When she touched the lamp on the oval table beside her chair, the room would come to life, restored to its familiar outlines, showing the covers of the bed turned down, the night-dress laid out, the pillow deep and inviting, with the bluish shadow of the heavy embroidered monogram on the smooth linen case, embroidery done by twenty-year-old fingers for a hope chest long years past.

Sometimes for an hour they would sit in darkness as the impenetrable winter night blocked the windows or the young moon sharpened in the cold indigo sky, those accumulated hours leaving upon the shores of memory a highwater line of reminiscences, significant and precious. This winter, Dr. Martin advised against Isabella's sojourn in Florida removed from his surveillance and Austin's presence.

Each woman approaches the thought of her beloved's lost childhood with a peculiar regret, and because, unlike other women, Martha had no expectation of retracing the pattern in the lives of her children and thus appeasing that regret, she treasured the things Mrs. Cutting told her that winter, listening to the unhurried procession of words, the precise voice warmed by laughter and tenderness. And to her own yearning the darkness was kind.

There were always books on the oval table; not leather-bound volumes from the library downstairs, but new books which Austin brought, smooth, secret and alluring in their paper jackets, presenting the adventure of uncut pages and unfamiliar minds.

"Father used to say, it is necessary only twice in a lifetime to read the classics: before seventeen and after seventy," Mrs. Cutting said, her gray eyes clear with laughter.

Meanwhile, she leaned her head against the high back of

her chair, turning her serene, attentive profile to Martha as she read aloud. Beyond the silken curtains and the enclosing ring of light from the lamp on the table the wind made a wild sound halfway between a song and a shout of triumph. Sometimes sleet rattled against the pane or snow crept silently, inch by inch, up the walls and steps outside. They read *North to the Orient* and *Lucy Gayheart;* and a slim first novel, taut and defiant as a stretched string—*Adder's Tongue* by Bennett Marsh. Parts of the book were written by a Bennett she had never known, and were rarely, painfully beautiful, like the inner drama of blood and arteries laid bare by the surgeon's knife. The rest . . . Mrs. Cutting's eyelids fluttered as she listened; and once she said, in a voice deep with amusement:

"A strange marriage—Hemingway and Austen. But she'll even out; the usual adjectives are all appropriate. Unusual. Promising. Arresting."

Sometimes when Mrs. Maxwell came in at nine, Mrs. Cutting would plead like a child for the end of the chapter, and the rigid little Scotswoman who had become nurse and companion as well as maid, would sit down, folding her spare hands in her lap, to listen to a fragment of the story whose beginning she had not heard and whose ending she would, in all probability, never learn.

There were evenings when Austin came unobtrusively into the room as Martha read, taking his place a little outside the circle of light, and on these evenings there was a tendency to close the book earlier, to draw him into the warmth of that circle by comment and question. As the sunflower turns . . . With a sad little flicker of humor, Martha perceived this instinctive response to the magnetism of his presence, the quickening of new life in the intimacy of the room.

When they took their leave of her, Mrs. Cutting's lips were soft against her cheek, but her slender hand held Martha's in a firm, unrelinquishing grasp as Austin bent above her on the other side, imprisoning her, an unwilling witness, to that long look which passed between them, freighted with the knowledge that one of these good-nights might be their last.

Memory forced her into the admission that it is often the seemingly inconsequential which claims our attention, while the precise color and flavor of a portentous incident—even the incident itself—may pass beyond recall.

Thinking of that winter, she sees first in her mind's eye Mrs. Cutting's listening profile, fair against the patterned fabric of her tall-backed chair, and second, an hour out of a January evening. She remembers coming down the wide stairway, and the broad band of light from the study which lay across the darkened hall; and Austin's quick upward glance as she stood in the doorway. He was standing before his desk and his hands, moving with the precision she loved, were taking the contents of his briefcase and disposing them over the top of his desk in orderly piles of paper. The light from the desk lamp shone upon his hands, leaving his face in a softer, shadowed illumination. Her thought turned back to the boy of twenty-one who had fallen in love with Celia.

Bereaved of his father, vested with new responsibility and authority, he had entered soberly and sweetly into the new world of love with Celia, bringing to it all the tenderness, awe, and dedication of his young manhood. And she, long alone, unaccustomed to being so cared for, succumbed to this new idea and this new life, to the purity of his intention and his fineness, believing it was all the love she could ever know.

Then, because he had, briefly, held quicksilver in his hand, Austin accepted, as Martha had, a life without expectancy; had quietly and firmly closed the door on his personal life. All his emotions were safely put away behind that closed door . . . This showed now in the stern, reserved expression which controlled his features: the flat plane of his cheeks tapering to the firm line of his lips. Yet it was not a bleak face. He smiled, he spoke, the corners of his mouth moved humorously; but he permitted himself only the surface. The depths were not stirred.

She thought she knew his mind as completely as she knew this familiar house wherein dwelt so much of her security and content. It was not merely the clairvoyance of love. Deeply as she loved Celia, Celia's mind had ever been a mystery, like the colorful quick flash of an unidentified bird in flight.

Austin placed a paperweight on his pile of papers.

"Is Mother still awake? I was detained and just got in."

"Mrs. Maxwell is preparing her for bed now, but she planned to wait until you came in before going to sleep. I was just about to leave."

"Have you looked at the weather in the last couple of hours? It's snowing hard. I'm going upstairs. Wait for me, I won't be long. I may be able to drive you home."

There was no sound in the house and none in the room except for the sweet, measured tick of an old clock. She sat at Austin's desk. She could hear the rising moan of wind in the trees outside. It held her attention, counteractive to the mellow peace within, until restlessness drew her to her feet. She snapped off the desk lamp and went to the window and opened the draperies. When her eyes became accustomed to the darkness, she saw that the outer air was white with a remittent swirl of snow. On the drive under the window, the tracks Austin's car had made less than half an hour ago were no longer visible. The infrequent street lights along Raynold Road were luminous nebulae in the thickened air. Across "the valley" she could see the faint radiance of lighted windows in her old home. It had finally been sold. She knew nothing of the buyers and tried to imagine strangers in the familiar rooms, but in her mind's eye it was still furnished with their rugs and sofa and chairs, her mother's piano.

Lost in reflection, she still was aware that Austin had come into the room before he spoke.

"On second thought, you'd better call home, Martha, and tell them you're staying over. It was all I could do to make the hill."

For a moment she did not reply. Austin came and stood behind her at the window and together they watched the storm in silence. A lonely car struggled slowly by, heading toward town. She was so aware of his closeness that it seemed as if she were trembling inside her body. What would happen, she wondered, if I turned and put my arms around his neck, drew his face down . . . *told* him . . . She thought of his reserved face as he had arranged the papers on his desk, and shook herself free of fantasy. If he rebuffed her, ever so gently, quietly removing her arms, placing them at her sides, stepping away, putting a space between them, she would lose it all—her tenuous love which lived, like an air plant, on his friendship, comfortable for him because he did not suspect. And there was the shared love for Austin which existed, unspoken, between her and his mother, irradiating their hours together; the gracious refuge of this house, a happy vestige of her growing-up years in a world grown grim and strange and frightening. (Millicent's family had relatives in Germany from whom or about whom they had had no word in over a year.)

She brought her thoughts back to the reality of the present. The weather was infinitely more besieging here on the height than downtown, laying emphasis on the security within.

She would breakfast with Austin in the morning . . . If the roads were impassable, they could be marooned here in the country for an unexpected holiday.

"You couldn't get the car out again if you had to," she observed, still gazing, fascinated by the onslaught. A dark thought fell across her mind after she had spoken, and she knew its shadow touched his, for he said quickly: "It's not bad enough to bring the wires down."

"It was snowing a little when I walked up, about six-thirty, but it didn't look as if it would amount to anything."

"That reminds me," he said, switching on the lamp, "Mrs. Maxwell's bringing a tray; you'll join me for a snack, I hope? There was no time for dinner in the city, I just had time to catch my train. When I got to Glen Fells, they were shoveling the cars out of the drifts on the station drive."

"Sounds lovely. We have such an early dinner nowadays." That was so the kitchen work could be done early, also, and leave some evening for companionship. Her mother never stopped trying to break through her father's reserve. Startled, she thought, like Austin he has also retreated from what he considers *his* failure!

They did not draw the curtains again. The card table was set up before the window, their chairs drawn close. Mrs. Maxwell's tray brought coffee in a silver pot, and chicken sandwiches. The snow was swift as a flight of silver arrows within the boundary of light from the window, disrupted at intervals by swirling eddies as the wind tore at the eaves in gusts.

"Remember when you broke your collarbone, skiing?" he asked.

"And how I finally screwed up my courage to try Hollings' Hill and that night it rained and there wasn't another decent snow that year?"

There were so many things she might never have done had it not been for Austin going fearlessly before, taking her courage for granted. Looking back, she saw her girlhood marching like an army behind the bright flag of his leadership.

"If they can't open the roads, we might go skiing tomorrow," she suggested.

"It must be seven or eight years since I was last on skis," said Austin.

They fell silent then and all their common memories invaded the stillness of the familiar room, a gay and gentle troop untouched by the worm and wisdom of those later years. Turning her glance, at last, from the window to his face, she met his look and her surprised heart stood still for an immeasurable instant of bright communion. It was an intent look, long and thoughtful, and she felt a physical lassitude, as if he had touched her. Her look fell away and when she looked back, he was staring out of the window, his profile once more young and stern.

Afterward she would look back to this moment.

In the morning when Mrs. Maxwell came in to waken her the snow had stopped falling, the sun was red at the horizon, and Raynold Road was plowed wide and smooth under the dark arch of the elms all the way in to town.

A week or two later she had lunch with Rob one day and he told her about Celia. It was not a long story; it occupied only a moment, brief, bitter, and unbelievable.

Celia was working and living with Mike Garlich.

She could not remember—cannot, even now—what it was she had expected when Rob, facing her across the narrow table and their heavy metal trays, said:

"You asked me about Celia."

There was no warning, or none that she heeded. She was accustomed to the gray look of disapproval in Rob's eyes when he spoke of Celia; and a greater tact than his would have found it difficult to reduce the impact of that information upon her sensibilities.

"Nothing that I ever dreamed," she had said. Was this what she meant, that she would begin a bitter journey taking her from the arms of one man to another, and another, in a kind of revenge? Her thought stumbled—as she had revenged herself with Carroll Owen?

She saw above the heads of the hurrying crowd in the busy cafeteria the huge electric clock facing her from the white wall; and wondered how long she had sat still and bewildered by that sidesweep of dismay. She picked up her fork but did not eat. The salad, rolls, and tea on her tray might have been chosen by any stranger in the room. She laid her fork down again and, lifting the cup, touched her lips to the tea. It was as bitter as experience to her inhospitable taste.

Afterward she reproached herself for not having understood, but at the moment she could only assume that she understood and weep inwardly for the loss of what had been bright and beautiful, that strong selfless passion for Galland, even though she had left Austin because of it.

Before they rose from the table, Rob said, angrily and inaccurately and irrelevantly, "I've been waiting ten years for you to grow up, Martha, and I am still waiting!"

She saw the years, seven of them, actually, laid out like the shards of a broken mirror which someone had been trying to fit together; only, because of certain infinitesimal pieces that were missing, the design would never approximate the shape of the original . . . And all at once she saw that Rob was jealous, not of Austin, but of Celia, who, in breaking her marriage to Austin, had rendered ambiguous the design of all their lives.

To say that she knew him immediately would not be the exact truth, but it is near enough. There was enough of intuition blended with rapid elimination in her mind to tell her who the man was when she opened the door to his knock one night in May of that same year. No man of her acquaintance had that stature, small and stalwart; nor that voice, rich with kindness and personal dignity. There are people who are born to the use of a foreign tongue and speak a flawless English; but the elimination of accent cannot change the national cadences of a voice. Mike Garlich's was one of these.

He held his hat in his two hands, and the porch light illuminated the thick, dark, upward-springing hair and the strong planes of his Slavic face.

"I want to speak to Miss MacLean—Martha MacLean," he said firmly, as if he expected to be denied.

"I am Miss MacLean," she said, and saw his look deepen with relief as if he sighed and delivered into her hands something too valuable for his peace of mind.

The car was small and shabby and filled with the incessant rumble of its own progress. Rain fell: fine and soundless, and unremitting as a mist of tears. There was no windshield wiper on her side; trees, buildings, and other cars loomed up quickly, dark and distorted by the blurred glass, an annoyance inconceivably linked with the dull pain in her breast. They passed through a town. It was late, and the gleam of wet rails led straight through the black, deserted street. At intervals, in the brief, wan light of a corner lamp she saw Mike Garlich's face, the square cheek beneath his hat brim pockmarked by the shadow of raindrops on the window.

The question she dared not ask trembled in silence on her lips. Her spirit fled ahead of the plodding car, so eager for the rendezvous that she could scarcely bear the slow miles between. Yet, suddenly, there was a smooth roadway under the wheels after miles of jolting car tracks, a decorous group of buildings fell away and they drove into the vast, asphalted parking yard, gleaming wet, and lonely with a dozen cars.

Out of the car, she stood still in the drizzle, hatless as she had come away, unheeding and oblivious of the rain on her face. For, looking up at the looming graystone hulk of the hospital main building with those significant, solitary windows lighted here and there along its darkened face, her heart failed her. Somewhere in that labyrinth of suffering, Celia lay nameless and soulless . . . a case, no less apart from the hope of the living than Thierry Galland in his lonely grave.

"Please," said Mike Garlich. He touched her arm and they moved forward.

They spoke through a round hole in a glass partition to a dark-haired girl with a diamond brilliant as a teardrop on her finger.

"Stairs at the left. The elevator does not run after nine o'clock." Her smile and her light voice belonged to a world where there is no death.

Their footsteps made the merest whisper on the stone stairs, a whisper immediately lost in the lofty silence of the stairwell. As they came out into the wide corridor on the third floor the doors of an elevator directly opposite moved back and two nurses maneuvered a wheeled stretcher into the hall. Neither they nor the third nurse who walked beside the stretcher with its long sheeted burden took the slightest notice of Martha and the man with her. And although they were forced to wait its passage, she was unable to discern whether life or death had passed them by. While still they stood hesitant, the equipage turned a right angle in the corridor and was silently gone like some strange and ominous dream at dawn.

Midway in the whispering wilderness of the empty hallway was the brightly lighted oasis of the nurses' station. The flawlessly manicured floor nurse examined their cards.

"Three-oh-nine. Left."

A paneled screen was curved around the opening of the door, and on it was hung a starkly lettered notice, NO VISITORS. As they passed within, permitted to disregard its arbitrary command, the faint, lingering hope she had cherished flickered and went out.

In one of the two high white beds, under an oxygen tent, Celia lay motionless . . . The other was white and smooth and empty.

An elderly nurse was sitting in the armchair in the corner of the room. She rose and indicated the chair for Martha's use, pushing a bit of crochetwork into her pocket as she did so. Martha hesitated, glancing toward the bed.

"She can't hear you. She's unconscious," said the nurse in a flat, matter-of-fact voice. She sat down again on one of the straight chairs in the room. Mike had already taken the other.

The room had a brown floor, buff-colored walls, and two windows, tall and gaunt, facing east. There were also a dresser, a long cabinet with double doors, and a bedside table with a sterile look of utility. She had five hours or so in which to note these things.

From time to time the nurse approached the bed and bent over her patient. Presently a doctor and another nurse came into the room . . .

At the end of the fifth hour, a red stain of light appeared on the wall above the bed with the partially drawn curtain. A few minutes later, leveling, it touched the white shoulder of the doctor's tunic and, as if in answer to a summons, he straightened. Movement spread through the room, furtive and relieved. The tall elderly nurse removed her pince-nez and rubbed her eyes with a curiously living gesture; the short dark nurse stood on tiptoe, stretching her corseted body, and drew the curtain closed around the bed.

The doctor turned toward them. He was young, with a dark mustache and a vertical line in either cheek.

"I am very sorry," he said. His words came back to her a long time afterward like a lost echo; but in that moment it was as if he had not spoken, as if no sound or voice could penetrate the vacuum of her grief.

His thin brows twitched and contracted above his narrow nose. His expression may have been either pity or impatience.

"You understand there was nothing to be done. It was an utterly hopeless case. No miracle . . ." He moved his hands in an odd, effacing gesture.

It was no longer raining. As they came out on the broad steps the newly risen sun was spilling its red gold on the buildings, the white walks, and the trim city shrubbery. On a small rectangle of grass a young tree stood shaking its silver leaves in the light morning air, like a young girl trembling with delight.

One instant she saw these things before the bright world reeled and tilted before her eyes, her foot sought the step and missed it, and Mike Garlich's strong hand under her arm bore her up in a moment of darkness. This, then, was the final sorrow of all her sorrows for Celia, the deepest and the cleanest—that the world should be fair and she unknowing.

She walked ahead of Mike through the door he held open for her, straight ahead through the sounds and the numbness which enclosed her.

"Coffee," said Garlich to the heavy-eyed girl in a crumpled pink uniform.

As if a shutter had clicked open in her brain, she saw the gray-tiled floor, the bare tables, the men clinging to their stools at the long counter; smelled the strong, rich, heartening coffee; heard the hot sizzle of ham and eggs on the grill, the drone of voices, the clash of heavy china and cheap tableware, the slam of a door or a lid. Sharp, acute, real . . . *alive.*

She had no purse, no handkerchief. The palms of her hands were wet with tears that fell faster than she could wipe them away. She saw one of the men glance at her over his shoulder and turn carelessly away. The girl came, wearing her air of weary disdain, and put before them two thick cups of black coffee and two thimblefuls of milk. She made a brief scrawl on a slip of paper, laid it down at Mike's elbow, and went away without having looked at them, absorbed in some private distaste for life.

"Drink it hot," said Mike quietly.

Some of the coffee was spilled in the saucer; the bottom of the cup dripped of it as she lifted it between her unsteady hands. It was scalding hot, but the pain of it going down her throat was only half as formidable as that other.

All that she remembered of that long ride home was the brilliant morning sunlight and Mike Garlich's warm, rich voice telling her a story she was never to forget. Later there were the long intervals of pity, of remembering and remorse; but that day there was nothing but the simplicity of the man who had befriended Celia at the end.

"She came to me in December. She had no money and she had not been able to work. I saw at once that she was ill; she had that look. I was broke, too, but my partner got married at Thanksgiving, and his room was there. She came and stayed in it . . .

"When she was a little better sometimes she would come down to the office and I would give her things to do. There wasn't much, the paper wasn't doing well. She wanted to earn her way, but you never thought of the things you did for her: it was like having a fine picture to take care of, you were repaid by having her there. Everything was different when she was there.

[200]

"Sometimes she was very quiet, just sitting there with her head back and not talking, and you felt as if all her sorrows were marching through the room. You wanted to say something to her to break that look, but you couldn't get past it. When she talked at all it was only about two people . . . you and him. She didn't really talk *about* you—she would smile a little and say, 'as Martha would say'—and things like that.

"But she talked a lot about him . . . It was the time of year he was away, you remember. She talked about the things they meant to do, and the chance he should have had, and how good he was that last time she saw him. That, to her, was the worst: he seemed to be getting along fine, and then—But it wasn't as if she was talking to you, and you kept still so that she wouldn't remember you and stop; because it was better for her to talk about it than sit there silent with it eating into her mind. She had some things he had written and she would hold them in her hands, the way you see old women holding the things their babies wore, and with that look on her face.

"You wanted to know if she did any painting. One day when I came in she had her things set up by the window and she was busy mixing colors, but it began to get dark and she had not touched the canvas, and when she spoke of this, I said, 'Tomorrow is another day.' She was still a moment and then she said one of those things you keep remembering: 'There are so many tomorrows, Mike. And I am so tired.'

"But she had got an idea about that painting and she kept on with it for a while. Sometimes for several days she would not touch it, and then while you were talking to her she would get up and cross the room and take the cloth away from it and stand and look at it.

"There was quite a lot of it done that day . . . enough so that I could see your face, enough so that I recognized you by it there on the porch last night.

"You or I would not have known the difference. But she wanted something else . . . When I came in she was standing before it and there were tears on her face, and then she looked at me and I saw in her eyes a kind of anger. 'I can't do it,' she cried, 'but no one could! The hand on your arm, the voice in your ear—Mike, who can paint his own conscience?' And then she took up the knife and drew it through the canvas so that the strips fell out and hung down.

"It was only a few days after that—three, I think—that I heard her and went in to her. It was not quite daylight. She was leaning on her elbow with her face buried in the sheet and her long hair hiding everything. I turned on the light and spoke to her, and she lifted her head and saw the stain on the sheet. She stared at it a minute, not frightened, but with a bright look that was like a smile. Then she lay back and closed her eyes. I think it was the first time she realized what was the matter with her, because while I was changing the sheet, without opening her eyes, she said, 'This makes it all so simple, Mike.'

"That was in March. She got better. They do, you know. It seemed her mind was more tranquil after that. She thought once that she should go away somewhere, for my sake, but where would she have gone, even if I had let her go? She wouldn't go to a doctor—said she couldn't bear it if they shut her up somewhere . . .

"It was a beautiful day that day she went out. No one could have foreseen the rain and the hail, or that she would walk so far—she was drenched and shivering when she got home. She changed her clothes right away, and I made her drink some whiskey, but it was too late. By morning she couldn't breathe. I got the ambulance. Toward evening the doctor said to me, 'If there are relatives you'd better get in touch with them. It's pneumonia, and with her lungs—'

"I knew she had a sister. I found the address among her things, but when I went there they told me she was traveling abroad with her husband. And then I remembered you; and that you were her friend."

The funeral chapel suggested a small private theater. A little before two-thirty of that spring day people began filing in out of the sunlight, singly and in pairs, taking their places quietly in the upholstered chairs. Their feet made no sound in the heavily carpeted aisle but at intervals a discreet cough sounded in the half-darkness.

The flower-banked casket stood on a dais before the velvet curtain.

This was not the shape of her special dread for this day: she had envisioned herself and the man, Mike Garlich, alone in some bare room cold with the grief of finality; but that grief was blunted, as perhaps it was meant to be, by the flowers, the muted organ music, the invisible lighting, and the unimpassioned promises delivered in the urbane voice of the strange minister.

"Do you want me to come with you?" Rob had asked.

"I don't think so," she replied with honesty. "You never liked her very well."

"For your sake," he amended.

"Thanks, no. Mike is meeting me at the train. It's to be in New York . . ."

The momentous reality was lost in the calculated perfection and impersonality. For all this had nothing to do with the blithe, eager spirit of Celia Pence, which had been deathless and ageless. Nor had its flawless luxury (arranged according to cabled instructions from Lilian Pence, now the wife of a wealthy man) any relation to the life and death and sorrows of Celia Galland, which had been stripped to their barest essentials. Here, one could almost forget the thin, parchment-colored face on the hospital pillow, wearing its gleam of imminent death; the sunken eyelids, the parched lips parted for difficult breath, and the long night during which the withdrawn intelligence never returned.

Instead, this body upon which the skill of human artifice had been expended for the last time was the shell of Celia Cutting! Like the photograph in the papers the day before, taken during the first autumn of her marriage to Austin, this was a gentle deception, the revival of a serenity that had had its death a long while before. And there were few present to know that this face, in which the color of life had been delicately laid on cheek and lip, was not thus finely chiseled by death alone, but by the strong and irresistible carving of life as well.

Not the unknown hairdresser whose hand had copied, yesterday, an arrangement original with Antoine of Fifth Avenue, in a world removed. Not the person who had laid those calm hands in repose on the quiet breast, noting only the plain gold of the cheap wedding ring, never having seen those fingers sentient with skill, or white as butterflies on the black sleeve of Austin's coat, or spread with tenderness against the dark of Galland's head.

None of these other people who were strangers to her, an intrusive alien presence in this final hour; friends and acquaintances of Lilian Pence, who, because the fastest ship would take seven days to reach New York, could not be present. Not Horty, wearing a sheer black dress and a wide black hat on her golden head, and a tender, spurious air of bereavement.

Only Julia Severn and Helena Gracie, sitting together, their unlike profiles delicately rigid. Only Alicia Whittaker, her arms folded across her chest, her dark head bent. And perhaps Bennett, upon whom a curious immobility had descended, quenching the fires of avidity; perhaps, too, Lois who had touched her shoulder in passing, whose uneven breath made a ragged sound in the silence between two phrases of the minister's reading.

Mike Garlich.

And Austin. Of whose presence she had not known, and with whom she came face to face in the bright light of the doorway at the conclusion of the service.

Wordlessly, as if he had been waiting for her, he took her arm.

The cemetery was some distance out on Long Island. The cortege which moved through the city traffic was small. A diminished group stood by the open grave in a far-reaching wilderness of granite markers. The strangers, their courtesies rendered, had disappeared into the anonymity whence they had come. The sunlight was clear and shimmering, the sky high-arched and flawless. The ground sloped upward imperceptibly, showing the grass green and tended between the close-set stones.

She stood between Mike and Austin.

Langham, Slater, Wiss, Morrison, Beckner, Carey . . . A company of Beloved Wives, Mothers, and Sisters receiving in silence the aloof, alien presence of one who was no longer wife or daughter, who had never been a sister or a mother, whose tenuous tie with the living had no name and now was ended.

Or was it?

At Severn, Julia had occasionally embarrassed them with intimations of a mysticism which violated their youthful prag-matism and the temper of their times. Thus, she kept before them the spirit of her father by appropriate ceremonies on Founder's Day (the date of his death) and his birthday—his *first* birthday, she called it. The day he died, she told them, was his second—his "passing into light."

They had all heard the story of the Porters; "one of Julia's ghost stories," they called it, looking at each other uneasily.

The Porter girls had been students at Severn before the war. The three sisters were all in their teens, and there were also a smaller brother and sister. When Kate, the eldest, was a junior, their mother died of an incurable illness which had kept her an invalid for over a year. Before the end, she gathered her family around her and charged the older girls with care of the younger children. Kate would be the head of the family. (Their father had died five years earlier.)

"I am going to join Daddy," said Mrs. Porter, "but I shall be with you always. I shall never leave you—remember that."

One winter's night, a year later, lying in her bed Kate heard her mother's voice speaking to her in tones of extreme urgency. (It was past midnight and she was unable, afterward, to recall whether she had been asleep or awake.)

"Get up, *quickly,* and take all the children out of the house at once!"

Without hesitation, Kate sprang out of bed, calling her sisters. They rushed to the back of the house and roused the younger children, snatching up blankets to wrap them in. In minutes after they had left the house and stood shivering on the front lawn, the faulty boiler exploded in the basement, was blown upward through the back of the house, and the structure was in flames . . .

"There is," Julia told them, with her luminous glance, "only the thinnest of veils between this life and its extension."

They could not assimilate this; few if any of them had suffered loss. Modern children were not taken to funerals. Until she looked upon Celia's quiet face, Martha had never seen death. She had been left behind in New York with friends when her parents went to Ohio to attend her grandmother's funeral.

Standing by Celia's casket, the inadvertent thought had come, "the shell of Celia Cutting." It was true. A shell, no more. The bright spirit had escaped. To nothingness? She glanced up involuntarily at the bright air, at the faint quiver of a breeze moving the foliage. Life's extension, Julia called this death.

She looked down again.

"Ashes to ashes," intoned the minister, "and dust to dust." The sound of earth falling on the casket shocked her although she had read of this and knew it was coming. Her slight start communicated itself to Austin, who took her hand in his.

As they turned away, Mike touched her arm.

"May I speak to you alone a minute before you leave?" He nodded to Austin. "If you will excuse me?"

When Austin had left them, pacing slowly down the graveled path toward the car, Mike took from his pocket a small thick book held together by a heavy rubber band.

"I guess I ought to keep her things—like clothes and her painting things and a few books—for her sister. But this"—he looked at her uncertainly—"it's a diary. All her handwriting. Something so personal—I think you will know what to do with it. I don't think she would want just anyone to read it. She said you'd grown up together, that you were more like a sister than that Mrs. Upshaw . . ."

Martha took the small thick volume in her hand. It had a smooth, scuffed suede cover and she had seen it a number of times at Severn but never after that. Not during Celia's years as Austin's wife, nor in the apartment after Thierry had gone.

Opening her bag, she dropped it inside. She looked down the slope to where Austin waited by the car. She and Mike shook hands gravely before they parted. She looked at him wordlessly, and he made a dismissing gesture with his other hand as if to forestall the gratitude she was trying to convey and, turning, walked quickly away.

The afternoon was ending.

The rattle of traffic on the bricked avenue, streetcars, buses, taxis, came up to her as she walked toward the car, the sound of the living hastening along their several ways, she thought, to meet these dead.

She wondered if Austin would talk on the long drive home, break the silence they had maintained for so long. I can't bear it, she thought, if he makes "ordinary" conversation; it would be intolerable while our hearts and minds are filled with memories and regret, regret for her sorrows and the lost star which never ascended, for all the unspent delight . . . Seven years; three with Austin and three with Thierry, and one alone, except for Mike. She was only twenty-six, she thought. Again, the waste of life! She had been in such a hurry to live; had she had a premonition of the short span of years which was her portion? Do we, each of us, respond to an inner clock which regulates our pace of living? Is this why some live more urgently, more voraciously, than others? She thought of Galland, his seemingly constant anger; was he aware, somehow, that he would be thwarted in all he hoped to accomplish?

[207]

Austin looked sideways at her face and laid his hand on hers.

"Talk, if it helps . . ."

She swallowed. "Will it bother you—to talk?"

"I'd rather listen. But no; no more. One lives long enough, finally, to acquire—" The word must have eluded him; he did not finish the sentence.

"I was thinking of her—how odd, in that strange place among strangers; and—Thierry—on a mountain in Pennsylvania, and her parents somewhere in France. All of them so far from the places they started from . . ."

His face was still. They were passing through the city streets, threading the labyrinth, crossing town from the East River to the Hudson. She fell silent. Presently they were on the bridge above the river. She saw the gulls wheeling in the high air . . .

"It wasn't at all what she wanted," she said, suddenly reminded.

He was startled. "Did she discuss it with you? She knew—?"

"Oh, no! It was when she came back from Pennsylvania. After he died." She was remembering Celia's voice in the dark one night, *That awful, dark wet hole in the ground! I hope no one ever puts me there, away from the light. I'd want my ashes scattered from some high place in the light and air—*

"I think she wanted—she spoke of wanting her ashes scattered from some high place in the light and air . . ."

His hand sought hers again. "Never mind; I don't believe it matters now." He drove without speaking for a long time. Then, in an altered voice, "I'm sure there is both light and free space—there."

Later that night she again wondered how he had known when and where to come. But that was a question she would never ask him.

She had forgotten the diary until she opened her bag to transfer its contents to a lighter one for the next day. She

[208]

slipped off the rubber band and opened it at the beginning. Mike had wanted her to have it, no doubt, as a memento of their school years together. Something of Celia's that had a meaning for her. She was well into the first entry before she realized that this was not at all that kind of diary, but she read it through to the end before she closed the book.

There was no salutation and no date, but this was a letter . . . Having read it, she sat holding the book in her hands, and the tears on her face were for an older bereavement, which had occurred in a distant time and place, and for the young heart which had suffered it.

I must continue this writing. For although I can no longer see your smile or hear your voice—who knows—perhaps somewhere you are still aware of me. It would seem that there should be some slight advantage to compensate for the separation. I had never given these matters much thought until you left me. As a good (unchurched) English-American Protestant, I accepted—without question, it seems to me now—the conventional French Catholic theology which was a part of my convent education.

However, one seems never to know how useful anything is until one attempts to use it. So it is that I cannot square what I feel with what I was taught to believe. In the first place, I cannot accept the fact that you are forever gone. *I cannot see you, it is true, but you refuse to depart from me.*

Dead. Such an ugly dull word. It falls like a clod of earth—I know it is not you in that long black BOX. *This I* feel *and can therefore believe. Nor can I imagine you in purgatory. (Of what should you be purged?) The Sisters said it over and over again, no one who is not perfect shall enter Heaven.*

What is perfection? Who is perfect? In this life you were the dearest of fathers, good friend, warm companion. How was it Philippe's mistress (the little one who wrote poetry) said it once, "the man with the hospitable heart."

I am here. The longest journey is the one we take from the past to the present. My past is a book that has been closed. After we took

the long black box to that little town in the south of France and placed
it beside the grave of my mother under the ilex tree (that interminable
train journey, the black dress they put on me, the black veil they hung
in front of my face through which to view the lovely world that day!
—How you would have hated the entire business!)—afterward, they
put me on a ship. Do you know what a bad joke you played on my half
sister by appointing her my guardian? Lilian, the soignée, sophisticated
New York career girl with her entourage of eligible men. A little girl
she would have placed in the care of a governess and kissed good night
as she went out for the evening, swathed *in furs. (By the way, she does*
not resemble you in the least. She must look like her mother.) But a
young girl of such an awkward age—She cannot refer to me as "my
little ward," which would make her a very interesting woman indeed.
Perhaps even somewhat mysterious—

There was only one thing to do with me. So here I am at a place
in the country called Hammondville, quite a pleasant place with a small
mountain and a valley with a river. The school is called Severn and
sits on a hill. I shall spend the next two or three years here, I imagine.
With nothing to remind me. But, dearest friend, I shall not soon forget,
I promise you. Good night.

After a long time (her tears had dried on her cheeks)
she fluttered the pages from front to back. They were
closely covered with Celia's writing and, again, there were
no dates and no demarcation between the separate entries.
Apparently, when she had thoughts which she could not or
chose not to express to anyone, she had written them into
this book. There were blank pages near the back. When had
she stopped writing? After Galland came into her life?
Could she confide in him, then, and so had no further need
of the book?

A thought came to her: In this book was probably recorded
the entire story of her marriage to Austin: the tremulous, day-
by-day discovery of herself and him in the changing relationship of marriage, the demands met and demands refused, the
joys and apparent failures, all building toward the final climax

. . . Here, too, could lie the answer to whether, if Galland had not existed or had not happened to come into her life at that time, she would have had more patience to put into her marriage.

Quickly Martha slipped the elastic band around the book and returned it to the black purse, which she put at the back of her closet shelf behind her hatbox. Someday soon, as soon as she had figured out a way, she would dispose of it. No one must read what Celia had written from the depths of her secret heart. That was what Mike intended. He, too, had recognized the special significance of this book and had entrusted her with its secrets.

IV

"T here's something I want to talk to you about," said Rob, shutting off the motor and coasting to a standstill at the side of the road.

All about them the countryside was opulent with the richness of late summer. The year had reached its peak of perfection, the fruits of summer were ripe and waiting to be gathered, the harvest was in the making. On far hillsides the grain had been cut and they were golden in the sun. Serenity had returned to her, as it eventually will, after one has felt too much for too long and emotion is spent.

"It's now or never, Martha, for you and me. I have asked for a transfer to the Chicago area and it's coming through. Now I want to know—are you coming with me or am I going alone? There comes a time when drifting must end."

She was silent for a moment, thinking of Rob as a person, her thought touching lightly all the years of their friendship, tracing his growth to maturity, contrasting his firmness and steadiness with the undirected boyish exuberance she had first known. Undeniably, her days would have been lonelier, her loneliness more grim without his love. Strangely, he had been the one person able to help her. His knowledge of her love for Austin and Celia and its strange entanglement had created their feeling for each other, however much he may have resented it. Truly all things were relative; if she had never known the white candle flame of her love for Austin, her feeling for Rob, compounded of respect, dependence, and affection, would have

[215]

been as near to love as anything she ever would have known, as near as many people come to a love which sustains them for a lifetime. And always it had been tender with pity and shadowed by a kind of guilt because she could not and would not allow it to grow into the love which his devotion had earned.

She would miss him.

His face was a little pale and set with a firmness of purpose. Yes, she thought, this is the time. She had no right to hold him any longer, to depend on his strength and loyalty.

"Rob," she said, "I can't go with you. I can't leave him. He'll be alone someday, and then . . . what will be left? For whatever it's worth, I am a part of his life, as it is now or as it could be, I can't tell. If it is never anything more than it is now . . . that will have to be enough. But I can't leave him," she repeated.

He knotted his fist upon the wheel. "You're going to settle for half a loaf."

She laid her hand over his. "Rob, please be happy for me. Don't you see: I have finally resolved it in my own mind. For me, anything at all is a whole loaf. We don't all walk the same road . . . And for you, no half loaf, either. You'll see. I want to say something very appropriate to you, something poetic and prophetic because you loved me and I so nearly loved you. But I would make such a mess of it."

He gave her a brief smile. "Consider it said. If you feel that this decision is right for you, I'm happy—with reservations, of course. I guess I've always known how it would be . . ." He hesitated, looked away and then back at her. "Tell me, unless you don't want to: Do you think he'll consider marrying again—now that she's gone?"

At his mention of Celia's death she winced. The hurt was not that far in the past, yet.

"I don't know," she said slowly. "Something seems to have changed. He came to the funeral, you know. I don't know how he knew. After Mike came and got me—and I came home again—I thought about calling him. But it was all in the past,

I decided, and he had never talked about her . . . not once. So I let it be. I can't think where he learned what had happened unless it was in the papers. Not just an obituary, which he wouldn't have seen; but a story. Perhaps her sister wired the papers, because of Hubert Pence; she was really quite proud of being his daughter. I know Mike didn't have anything to do with it—"

"I called him," said Rob, staring straight ahead, and when she didn't speak he continued, "I figured you wouldn't. I know how your mind works by now—but I thought it would be—that it would close that chapter, finally. I didn't know whether he would go there, but I knew you would need him afterward. If you want to know what I think, I'd say he went because of you . . . not for anything that was over and done with a long time ago."

"Dear Rob—" She turned her head away, unable to continue.

"For God's sake, don't cry! Just—work things out . . . will you? Don't just go on, from year to year, after I leave—"

She sat in a stillness, remembering a lot of little things— a snowy night on Raynold Road, a look, the consoling touch of Austin's hand on hers, shared moments of warmth and love as they sat in his mother's room. And, as Rob said, the fact that he had come to Celia's funeral.

"I can be patient," she said quietly.

He started the car with an abrupt movement. "Don't be too patient," he said roughly.

Rob was leaving for Chicago around the twenty-fifth to start his new job after Labor Day. Mrs. Cutting invited them for dinner on Sunday evening and, despite protests from Austin, Mrs. Maxwell and Martha, insisted on coming downstairs to preside.

" 'T'will be too much exairtion—"

"Mother, you know you're supposed to be careful—"

"Dr. Martin said I could do anything within reason; that

I will very soon recognize a 'stop' signal if I have gone too far."

"Seems as if 't'would be too late to mop up the spilled milk by then," commented Mrs. Maxwell dourly, impatience and anxiety in her voice.

"Let us say no more about it, please. It is certainly within reason to sit at my own dinner table and bid Godspeed to an old friend. You know I don't come down often, but that is because I do not enjoy dining alone when Austin is so seldom home for dinner. In my room I can read as I dine, which is considered rude at the table," she finished complacently.

So she came slowly down the stairs on Austin's arm and sat at the head of the table in a lovely gown that was not quite blue and not quite lavender, with lace around her neck and her gray eyes alight.

"We shall miss you," she told Rob after he had outlined his opportunity for their benefit. "I trust all your expectations will be fulfilled and that you will be too busy to be lonely, so far from all your friends."

"Rob's home is really in Chicago," said Martha. "He came East to college and never went back."

"Well, my mother was widowed while I was in school, and did a lot of traveling for a while. So nobody was home most of the time. She's remarried now, to a man with two daughters, so I have a couple of 'stepsisters' I've never met."

"Oh?" said Mrs. Cutting with a rising inflection.

"Of course, I'm shy with girls so it may not be easy to get acquainted—"

Even Austin hooted at that.

Rob sobered suddenly. "Kidding aside, I am going to miss you, all of you." He let his glance travel over the charmingly appointed table, the crystal and china, flowers and candles. "It seems as if I have a good deal of your hospitality to remember and be grateful for. Hospitality that balanced out the furnished-room years. And you may tell Mrs. Maxwell that I don't expect to find the equal of her cooking soon again."

"Ah," said Mrs. Cutting banteringly, " 'the way to a man's heart.' "

There was a short pause, during which Mrs. Maxwell came in and changed the plates. Her cooking and her service were flawless, but she had been so long a member of the household that she felt free to contribute to any conversation which interested her unless the occasion were formal or strictly business.

Now she bent a severe but softened look upon Rob which indicated that she had overheard his compliment.

"It seems as if ye're old enough to be having your ain hus wi' a wife to keep ye out o' the restaurants. Ye'll come to na guid end eating all that fried food—"

Rob looked up, his expression all innocence.

"Well, I did ask Martha to go with me," he said plaintively, "but she turned me down—again. Said she had some unfinished business to take care of here."

She hoped her gasp of surprise had not been audible. Having said his piece, he avoided her eye. It had not been an inadvertent remark, of that she was certain. Turning her glance away from him, she met Austin's sharp, inquiring regard and had an impression that he was disturbed by Rob's light remark.

She could think of no reason; long ago she told him that Rob had asked her to marry him and that she had refused him; that he, furthermore, had promised to go on asking her, over and over again. A slight flush warmed her cheeks as she recalled, also, that on that occasion she had confessed to being in love with someone else and Austin had laughed.

"Do you expect to find your dream place in Illinois?" she asked Rob to bridge a silence that was growing too long. She turned to Mrs. Cutting. "Rob told us once that he wanted a house by a brook in an apple orchard with a fireplace for winter evenings, and a couple of big dogs—" That was going even farther back in memory, dangerously far.

Mrs. Cutting rescued them. "Shall you be right in the city? Or is your new position in a suburb?"

"It's a suburban town, about fifty thousand population, I'd say. Not exactly a suburb in the sense that Glen Fells is a suburb, though. More of a business and industrial town. Midwest bustle and progress, you know—out of Tarkington, Sinclair Lewis, and Bromfield." He looked at Martha. "I might just look around for that brook and orchard as a weekend retreat, maybe, to start with."

She sensed his underlying eagerness to take up the new job, a new life. Man's love—how did it go?—is of his life a thing apart; something like that. He was not, she thought thankfully, inconsolable. But, of course, she had never, from the beginning, led him to believe . . . Yet they *had* drifted in so pleasant and comfortable a relationship that hope would not, perhaps, entirely die. She, too, had been guilty from time to time of an unspoken ambivalence. If times had been better, this drifting would no doubt have been less prolonged, but it had been a time of long engagements and tacit "understandings" for many couples.

Rob was twenty-eight. It was not too late for him, and meanwhile, the awkward, impetuous young clown had attained an attractive maturity.

"Are you going by train or by bus?" asked Austin.

"Neither," laughed Rob. "I'm driving out. In my new 1937 Ford Tudor. I get delivery Wednesday. Light gray." He became serious, although the smile lingered behind his eyes. "I'll need a car out there; distances are larger than here and a good many of my prospects will be living miles out of town as my territory includes more than just the town itself. I had a jalopy in high school, but this is the first new car I've ever owned." He turned to Austin. "It's got a lot of extras—comes with a heater, for instance—streamlined . . . You can't beat a Ford for economy, and they last! Look at all the Model Ts you still see around. It'll probably be the best seven hundred I'll ever invest!"

The talk strayed then into matters concerned with industry and production, the wave of labor unrest in the past year which had culminated in an epidemic of sit-down strikes. Austin asked Rob if he had read a recent *Atlantic Monthly* article by William Allen White, "The Challenge to the Middle Class," which dealt with labor solidarity in the last election, among other things.

Presently Mrs. Cutting said, "This has been so nice, Robin. I want to thank you for taking time out during your final preparations for 'transplanting' to spend the evening with us. You must remember that any time you are in the East, we shall expect you to visit us. And do keep us informed of your progress." She turned to Martha. "I have asked Mrs. Maxwell to serve your coffee in the living room and beg you to do the honors. Coffee is a pleasure I must forgo these days, so Austin, if you will see me to my room, I'll say my good-nights now to all of you."

They all stood as Austin drew out her chair. Belatedly, Martha had an anxious thought about the long staircase. Coming down on Austin's arm had not required much effort, but now a faint shadow of weariness lay on Mrs. Cutting's features.

Rob and Martha turned toward the living room as she proceeded toward the stairs. At the foot of the stairs Austin, without hesitation, lifted her in his arms and carried her up around the bend. They heard the light sound of her laughter.

In the living room they looked at each other wordlessly. There was no need for words; they shared the same thought that when Rob left this house tonight, it might be for the last time while Isabella Cutting lived.

After a moment he said in a low voice, "I think it would mean a lot if she knew he was settled—"

Tears clustered suddenly on her lashes. "Rob, let up on me a little. Stop being too good to be true, will you?" He was making it more and more difficult to say good-bye. Can a woman love two men equally and at the same time? she wondered.

Mrs. Maxwell, with the tray, and Austin came into the room at the same time and the moment was dissipated. A little later Rob announced that he had a train to catch.

"You're going back tonight, then. Can I drive you to the station?" asked Austin.

"I have the car," said Martha quickly. "I'll drop him off."

Rob looked at his watch. "I can make the nine-fifty-five."

The long commuter platform was deserted. No one was taking "the ten o'clock" out of Glen Fells that Sunday night except Rob. They sauntered, waiting for the train, in and out of pools of light cast by the overhead fixtures spaced at intervals. The station waiting room was locked and dark. The night was soft and windless. They heard the train rounding the bend west of town, saw its great eye bearing down on them out of the night; then it drew into the station with a rush and a sigh of brakes. This was no huffing, chuffing steam monster; the Glen Fells branch was electrified. There was a low, pulsating sound from the engine; of four cars only one coach was lighted, the others dark. Two pullmans and a baggage car.

"Well," said Rob. "This is it."

He held her tightly for a minute, gave her one of his quick, hard kisses, and released her.

" 'Board," called the conductor on a rising note, swinging himself up the steps. Rob swung on after him, waving.

She raised her hand as the train sighed again, moved, gathered speed and its lights diminished rapidly into the distance. She had been unable to think of anything more to say, could not have spoken for the lump in her throat, if she had.

This is it. The finality of it.

Her eyes were misted with tears. She had lost—relinquished—her anchor.

"Damn!" she said, aloud, beginning to walk toward the old Packard, obscurely angry at the untidy, "almost" quality of life. If she had to entertain a hopeless passion for a man whose heart belonged to someone else, whose unchanging conception of her was one of the friendly kid next door who never grew up, why did she also . . . ?

Alone in the night, with Rob figuratively receding westward each passing minute, she was not as confident as she had led him to believe, not at all certain that she would be able to move any closer to a life with Austin than she was at this moment.

And if not? What then? Fairlies and Cutting for the rest of her life, just to be near Austin? Or an exodus, a new life somewhere else—north, south, west? Another town instead of the familiar, elm-arched, maple-shaded roads of Glen Fells? Another office, another set of file cabinets, another desk and typewriter, another view of a brick wall out of another row of windows? A furnished room, a small apartment instead of her parents' home and their companionship, sustained by her mother, protective toward her father. He had begun to emerge, finally, from his private and personal depression; the dark moods were less frequent. He had, this summer, consented to go picnicking and boating at Long Lake, had played golf again (for the first time since Les Patterson died), and was sleeping better. He was sharing her mother's room again.

They had been house hunting. Somewhere, they decided, there must be a simple, inexpensive house in an edge-of-town setting with a country view. All three shared a vision of the horizon bounded by woods resplendent with autumn's colors, and the etching of wintry distances in the months ahead. But without her additional income it would not be possible.

Rob could break out of a situation which had become—not exactly intolerable, that was too strong a word—but stultifying. He would probably seek, and find, a mate. Like her, he was not a casual person; his needs and desires would have to be met by a secure and exclusive devotion, a one-to-one continuing relationship—marriage. (She wondered, with curiosity, if the girl he would finally choose would resemble her, or be entirely different.)

Some could go, and some could not. Twice bound, by duty and futility, she would stay. Her lack of talent (she could not break the mold in a grand gesture and become a singer, a dancer, a movie star—or a writer or painter . . .), her lack of advanced academic accomplishment, precluded teaching or research (which she was too restless to embrace). Her Depression training, her acquired office skills were all she had to offer. She was limited in building a "new life" to a duplication of the old. But by sticking, she could help her parents one step back to the kind of life they had enjoyed.

Perhaps there was such a thing as predestination, after all.

Her family moved that autumn to a house on the Littlefield Road three miles beyond the country club in the kind of high, lightly wooded countryside where she had spent the freest hours of childhood; but this was a world removed from suburbia. The house was a farmhouse, perhaps eighty years old, to which modest improvements had been added from time to time: a bath, kitchen cabinets, a sun porch on one side, a recessed porch had been screened at the back. (Her mother called it a "pea-shelling porch" because country women in Ohio sat on porches like this one and prepared vegetables and fruits for canning.) There were old-fashioned shrubs in the yard: lilac, rose of Sharon, mock orange, syringa, and hollyhocks in a row by the fence. Around an old disused pump in the yard were lilies of the valley in a luxuriant spreading bed of green leaves —a promise for spring. There was a gnarled pear tree and two venerable apple trees and a blackened, rotting arbor covered by a huge twisted grapevine.

The house was shabby inside and needed painting outside. The owner, out of work for five years, had finally been offered a job as a WPA supervisor in another state, and was happy to sign a three-year lease.

"We've let it run down," he said apologetically, "but we couldn't have held on to it at all except that my mother had the mortgage. My wife worked as a sewing and cooking teacher at Middlefield High so we managed taxes and interest. If you want to paint or anything, it's O.K."

She had come home. The faded walls on which the squares of absent pictures glared, the scuffed floors, the worn linoleum, and the water-stained wall above the sink made no difference.

There are certain psychological climates in which we live and breathe; others where we wither.

Grove Street was behind her; the slam of its screen doors, the creak of its rockers, the passing echo of footsteps along its flagged walks had long been a minor accompaniment to the invisible life she lived; a life dissociated from all that was Grove Street, in its beginnings, its manifestations, and its conclusions.

She tried to decide what condition it is that alters the proportion of a life so that, like an iceberg cruising an empty ocean, the submerged part is the greater. Is it the passage of the years, or the temper of experience, or the particular suppressions and repressions of circumstance which diminish the importance of the outward, visible life?

Willingly or unwillingly, much of life is concerned with externals: the comings and goings, the mechanics of getting and spending, the support of the visible structure of life. And none of this touches, or is important to what we mean by Life . . . the knowledge, the wisdom, the well-being that comes from an acceptance of the only reality that matters: the thing we live by, the need we fill, the ideal we cherish, the love we cannot withhold.

She no longer rode to work with Austin. She did not want him to come out to the new place to pick her up and they were now too far out for walking. Instead, her mother drove her to the station and her father adjusted his hours, leaving home an hour earlier in order to take the same train. Her mother had the car all day for errands and met them at the evening train, unless it was a day she planned to spend at home or it was stormy, in which case they parked the Packard at the station. And so the fabric of living was stretched a little here, tucked in a bit there, to fit the new routine, the new circumstances.

Life, she thought, might be a desert with nothing more substantial than mirages to mark its distances, but living was *now,* and each day was filled. There was her job, of course, and all the job-related chores: shoes to the cobbler, dresses to the cleaner, collars and hose to wash, slips to mend.

They painted inside the house, varnished floors, laid new linoleum in the kitchen. The farmhouse had more rooms than Grove Street. The hired girl's room off the kitchen made a small but comfortable study. The sun porch became a music room. The rest of the books and the piano came out of storage and there was music in the evenings. The thirty-foot Persian rug was sold to a New York dealer.

She went once a week regularly to the Cuttings' for dinner; sometimes Friday or Saturday evening, more often on Sunday. After the going-away dinner for Rob in August, Mrs. Cutting began to come down for these dinners, and even, as long as the weather was mild, to sit on the porch, reclining on a chaise in the warm afternoons. They had talked of installing a chair elevator, but there was a technical difficulty because of the bend in the stairway. However, when Austin was there to carry her upstairs, she could leave her room at intervals. She seemed quite well and in excellent spirits. She laughed frequently, light-heartedly, like a girl. But she had an increasingly transparent look, and the doctor had said, unequivocally, "No stairs."

There had been no further attacks, only fleeting twinges of pain. She was suffering, he said, from a "tired heart." If she avoided any sudden strain or undue effort, she might never have another attack; it could well be fatal if she did, however. As things were at present, he said, the probability was that when the time came—"in a year, or two, or ten, who can tell?"—she would pass away in her sleep.

She confided to Martha, with amusement, that the doctor was evasive.

"Poor man! He doesn't want to tell me my 'days are numbered.' But aren't all our days numbered, from our very first one? And all our heartbeats? I happen to know that I have used a large portion of each—my past is greater than my future, which is quite normal at sixty-six. So I am grateful for each new day that dawns and try to enjoy it to the fullest. It's very restful. I no longer need trouble myself with all those details of living—the machinery I set in motion years and years ago continues to operate quite efficiently with Mrs. Maxwell to give a nudge here and there. One likes to believe that one has been useful, even indispensable in one's little sphere. To relinquish that idea is difficult, the most difficult, perhaps, of the decisions that come with diminishing capability. But, eventually, it becomes apparent that numerous causes and committees go on and flourish like the green bay tree, even though we are forced to abandon them."

Another time, letting her gaze wander over the tranquil lawns dappled with sun and shade and brilliant with the last passionate blooming of the flowers before frost, she said,

"How lovely it is to be able to enjoy this quiet time in one's life—a time to remember and be grateful to one's Creator for the gift of life and all the gifts added thereto. I was thinking this week of Mr. Parkins and Mr. Huber—so many years younger than I, and deprived of this time."

In the past year, the two Glen Fells men in their forties had collapsed and died suddenly; Parkins while running for his train and Huber one evening as he rose from the dinner table.

Representatives of the "causes and committees," particularly Mrs. Cutting's contemporaries, like old Madame de Vary (no one ever said "old Mrs. Cutting"), who had had the conservative means to remain in Glen Fells despite market collapses and bank failures, stopped by from time to time, but she seemed to enjoy most of all her hours spent reminiscing with Martha.

So the year proceeded toward its close. The frosts came and the flowers, all except the hardy chrysanthemums, faded. Austin made a business trip and asked her to stay in the house while he was away. He was gone a week.

He bought a new Buick coupe, a business coupe, they called it. The color was "maroon"—a deep wine-red. Since his mother no longer went out, the 1928 Cadillac was used but little. Williams' duties were more concerned with general maintenance around the property, his driving confined mainly to a series of errands about town, executed with an impeccable dignity. He was getting on, a landmark in his own right.

There were new people moving into Glen Fells, buying the houses from the banks which had foreclosed them, at a fraction of the prices originally paid in the halcyon years before the Crash. The character of certain avenues changed subtly. The large homes appealed to families with several children. Where there had been sports roadsters on the drives, bicycles clustered about the porches and some lawns had bare spots marking the bases of impromptu baseball.

One Sunday in November they went for a long drive in the new car. They came to a riverside picnic park where the weathered tables had an abandoned and lonely look among the trees. It was late afternoon and had been a sunny day, but now the long shadows were stretching themselves over the leaf-carpeted aisles between the bare trees, and the sun's rays were horizontal.

Austin pulled off the road suddenly and shut off the motor. "I want to talk to you, Martha."

Something stern and accusatory underlay the plain statement and she saw as she glanced at him in surprise that the look on his face matched the tone of his voice. She rolled down the window and let in the sound of the river hurrying over its stones together with a damp leafy smell from the wood.

"What are you going to do with your life?" Now, after the long pause, the question was casual, almost light.

She looked at him again. He was looking directly at her now, but his expression had changed; it was completely bland and told her nothing. A half-dozen replies went through her mind in an instant:

What are you going to do with *yours?*

Nothing that I ever dreamed (which was literally true).

Get up in the morning and go to bed at night.

Take over Miss Cathcart's job when she retires.

Once she had said firmly to Rob, to justify another rejected proposal, "We have a future together. I'll make him see it—if I have to do the asking myself." Brave words. She tried to remember: Had she actually believed them or were they spoken for Rob's consolation, to prove the validity of her feeling for Austin?

This was the age of the emancipated woman. You didn't have to wait to be asked anymore. You could say, "Let's go" and the male would say, "O.K., let's." To some men you might even say, "Hey! Tell you what—let's get married!" And they would say, "Sure—why not?"

Austin wasn't that kind of man.

And she wasn't that kind of woman.

Or—wait. She could have said it to Rob, knowing what his answer would be. Next question: Could she have said it to Rob, *not* knowing what his answer would be?

Yes, she thought, picturing his face.

Austin touched her arm. "Where'd you go off to? You were miles away."

"Well, ask me profound questions and you start me thinking in profound circles." (So it was going to be the old sibling-type flippancy, after all.)

"How long have you been in the office? Four years?"

"Five."

(Time slips away—a song?—a poem? Or only a thought in her own head? A ring of the familiar, anyway.)

After a year she had taken Cathy's advice and enrolled for a six-month night course in typing and shorthand. Her shorthand never quite came up to Cathy's standards, but after another year someone of the eleven departmental executives decided that machines were more efficient; a girl could be at her desk transcribing the morning dictation while her boss worked at the afternoon mail, instead of sitting with her pad on her knee wasting time while he coped with interruptions by telephone and otherwise. With the advent of the machines she had become a kind of secretary shared by three men, as well as supervisor of the file room, responsible for the commissions and omissions of two eighteen-year-old clerks. Oh, she was well on the way to filling Cathy's shoes! Cathy had—how many?—seven years to retirement. Now the girls called her "Mart"; from there on she would be Miss MacLean, or, behind her back, "Mac.")

"Five years! Somehow, I can't believe it."

"You've been around, too, you know," she said lightly.

He wasn't smiling. "I saw Rob when I went out west last month. Had dinner with him."

"Oh?" (Rob, you *didn't,* you couldn't have said anything. Or could you?) "How was he?"

"Just great. Busy and successful, I take it. Wanted 'all the news from home,' of course."

"That made an exciting story. What changes in Glen Fells in three months?"

"He asked me if you were wearing an engagement ring yet." He had not taken his eyes off her face. "I understand you turned him down because there is someone else . . ."

She interrupted him quickly. "That's all over now," she said firmly. "And neither you nor Rob have any right—"

"My concern for you gives me the right," he said quietly. "You didn't tell Rob the truth, did you? There isn't anyone else —now—is there? But I remember something you told me *years ago,* when you were practically a kid—"

(And you laughed, of course.) The corners of her mouth lifted as she recalled that refreshing laughter which had renewed her even as it irritated her.

"Don't smile, Martha. You may have made a serious mistake . . . perhaps are still making it. No one can live forever in the past or in the what-might-have-been. All we have is *now,* and tomorrow may never come. Or, at least, the tomorrow we have imagined. You aren't the kind of person who can shut herself away and deny life forever, Martha. I've been watching you try to do that for a long time. It probably seems like a nice safe kind of existence; no danger of getting hurt, you tell yourself. But that's all it is—an existence. It's not living."

She stared at him. This retreat from life of which he was accusing her—she had seen it happening to him. When, in all this time, had he become reconciled to "living" again?

"Martha—you are capable of great love and loyalty, one of the warmest people I know. You are twenty-five years old—"

"Your arithmetic is perfect," she said with an edge of irritation. "And that makes you thirty-one; thirty-two, come January, my friend!"

"Forgive my intrusion," he went on more gently. "I haven't forgotten a word of what you told me, but you were much younger then, too young to make an irrevocable decision. But just young enough to idealize a first love, perhaps, and enshrine it . . . It's only that I doubt whether Carroll Owen was worth such a—renunciation."

"*Carroll Owen!*" she cried, shocked into vehemence. There was a long pause in which the memories of old follies and frustrations collided. "You couldn't have *forgotten*—you never *knew.*"

"Knew what, Martha?" he asked sharply.

She looked at him.

"Austin," she said in a voice taut with impatience, "I have loved you all my life!"

He had not known. Until now. She saw it in his quick, incredulous look; but even as she was thinking regretfully how little he knew her, after all, she remembered how unfairly she had used Carroll to get through that first desperate year of Austin's marriage.

He leaned forward and took her hands. She saw the smile growing deep in his look.

"I guess you'll have to marry me, then," he told her cheerfully, "before we both get too old."

"You're absurd!" she said, laughing, disarmed as she always had been by his raillery.

He kissed her then, and she was startled to realize that it was the first time in all their life together; that just as her age and propinquity might have propelled them to a greater intimacy, Celia came into their lives and everything was changed . . .

[231]

"Will you, Martha?" He was serious now, his face almost stern, the lines beside his mouth noticeable.

"Will I what?" she asked innocently. She was beginning to tremble.

"Marry me."

"Of course," she said, lightly and breathlessly. "You're my last best hope . . ."

The confidence which, as a child, she had learned from him took possession of her now. She felt at once fearless and joyous. She held her love in her arms, at last; and there were no more forebodings. She had, suddenly, the key to all the mysteries, all their loves: Austin's, Rob's, her own, Celia's . . . The love they had given and received from each other. Love exists, she thought, to fill the need of the beloved. But the needs are never identical. There is no constant.

Her instincts had not betrayed her: in love as in music, it is important to know when to play melody and when to play harmony. It is in these sensitive adjustments that marriage can falter, she thought, understanding the effects of Celia's implacable course, at last. From Austin, who wanted to give her the world and everything in it—his love, his respect for her genius, the opportunity and serenity to pursue her dream, and a place at his side as an equal and partaker in his own endeavors—from him she wanted, finally, nothing. Even before Galland became her total obsession, she had begun to destroy Austin, little by little, with her rejections.

One could only guess how bitterly Galland, burning with the passion of creativity himself, had resented the necessity for her to "prostitute" her art, as she had offhandedly remarked. But Celia had been obdurately sacrificial, apparently insensitive to his anguish . . .

The sun had set. It was growing dark in the woods. She rested in Austin's arms, passive under his touch, yet delicately alive and responsive with every nerve in her body.

"Not in St. Paul's," she thought. There was a little wooden church in Hammondville where Severn girls had their baccalaureate. And up in Maine was an old house where she had spent two summers with her parents when she was thirteen or fourteen. They would travel by car through the little New England towns with their white spires and green commons, partly by day and partly by night, until they came to the low weathered house on the Point. She could remember the smell of the sea, the bare clean kitchen with its wooden cupboards, the stacked kindling in the woodshed, the glow of fire in the polished black stove.

There was a narrow stairway leading to the upper floor, and a wide bed under the sloping eaves. They would light the oil lamp with the curved handle and go through the chilly hall, and as they mounted the stairs, all the shadows would flee before them in that place unreminiscent of any ship, of any English lane, of any French inn . . .

And, after a time, they would come home.

But it wasn't like that, after all. For one thing, Austin wanted to be married almost at once, and it was winter. For another, it was not prudent to leave his mother alone. So they were married in the house Martha had loved for so long, in a deep bay window of the long drawing room. Alicia came out from New York to be her attendant and Austin's cousin from Connecticut was his best man. Her father gave her away, and her mother smiled at her through tears. Isabella Cutting presided, from her chair, over both the ceremony and the collation served to the guests afterward. When they all had gone, Austin carried her upstairs.

"This has been one of the happiest days of my life," she said, smiling at them, holding a hand of each. "Blessings on you, my dear children, and on all the days of your life together."

In love. (How lightly they had tossed the phrase around in their adolescence, in those curious, wondering years!)

In love! Submerged, enveloped, possessed so that no separate existence was possible. *I love, therefore I am.* She held Austin in her arms and was conscious of her strength as a woman to shield and shelter and minister . . . She was virgin, wife, and wanton, newly discovered to herself. The reason no one had told them was that it was too difficult, if not impossible, to perceive where the general and the particular experience became separate and unique.

Celia had married Austin, believing. "There is no death when you are sure." That was what she had believed on her wedding day. The flaw became apparent only later; and then there was Galland. Isabella Cutting had held her blameless, recognizing, in her wisdom, both the risks and the rhapsody of the human relationship.

Time of joy and time of sorrow. In February, Austin's mother died, as the doctor had predicted, quietly and painlessly.

She was sitting in her chair by the window late in the afternoon of the winter's day. When Mrs. Maxwell came in to turn on the lights, she told her to go away and come back later.

"There is such a lovely saffron sunset over the woods, I want to watch it a little longer. I think, though, it means a spell of colder weather; it often does at this time of year."

Mrs. Maxwell went down the hall and busied herself in the linen closet for fifteen minutes or so.

Martha was in the dining room, setting the table for dinner. Austin would be arriving shortly. Somehow, he did not find so many details to detain him late at the office nowadays. When he came in, he would go upstairs for a few minutes; then, after dinner, when Isabella was comfortably settled in bed against her pillows, they would both go up and sit with her until she decided to sleep.

There was an inarticulate sound at the dining-room door. Martha looked up and saw Mrs. Maxwell. At first she thought she had been taken ill; the little woman's face was tightened in a wrinkled grimace as she tottered to a chair and sat down, an act so unprecedented as to be alarming in itself. Martha hurried around the table to her side.

"Mrs. Maxwell, are you ill?"

The Scotswoman shook her head slowly from side to side. "It's the mistress, ma'am—she's gone!"

For an instant Martha misunderstood. Then realization swept over her. While she had been calmly placing knives and forks, and Austin was driving home—She saw the same thought mirrored in Mrs. Maxwell's eyes.

"Will ye tell him, ma'am?" Her voice was a hoarse whisper. "I canna."

Martha captured one of the fluttering hands in her own. It was like the dry cool claw of a bird. "Tell me, please . . ."

". . . and so I went back, and the room was fair dark, then, filled with dusk and shadows it was. And she was sitting as I'd left her. Her head was drooping to one side, like, as if she'd fallen asleep. I turned on that lamp on the table by her chair, and I touched her hand to waken her—" She paused, looking at what Martha could not see. "But I knew, I knew as soon as I entered that room. I just wasn't paying attention to what I was feeling."

Martha stood up, her hands pressed instinctively to the pain in her breast, and moved toward the hall, listening for the sound of the car. She must not let him go bounding upstairs . . . But how, with what words, was she going to tell him this?

She heard Mrs. Maxwell follow her into the hall, heard the car door slam, the sound of footsteps on the porch.

Standing just inside the door, Austin looked at them.

"It's Mother . . . When?"

"Just a few minutes ago."

He kissed her gently as her tears came. "Don't come up. Wait for me."

So for the second time within a year they stood together at a graveside. Their shared grief was real, but there were many consolations. The life that was ended had encompassed much joy and some sorrow, as all lives do. It had embodied dignity, grace, and loving-kindness. A church filled to the doors with

[235]

friends and their children was evidence of the affection that had not diminished with her retirement from the active life of Glen Fells which, for her, had meant her "causes and committees." She had enjoyed her time of rest toward the end. Martha had repeated her conversation to Austin to help him accept the fact that his mother had been aware of the precious quality of every hour—every remembered hour—and unafraid of the last of those hours. If she suspected a gentle letting go of a precarious hold on life, she did not mention it.

"It's going to take us a while to realize that she's no longer here," he said, with an involuntary glance up the stairway, as they reentered the house.

She is here, thought Martha. In the loveliness and serenity of this old house, as bride, wife, and mother. I can close my eyes and see her as she was when I was a child and an adolescent, coming toward me with her welcome and her smile and her air of being a great lady. She will always be here.

"Would you like to go away somewhere for a few days?" asked Austin one evening, looking at her over the book he was not reading.

She paused in her counting of stitches. She had decided some time past to do all the dining room chairs in needlepoint. Mrs. Cutting had been enthusiastic. "How marvelous!" she had said merrily. "I thought of it once, but it takes younger eyes than mine for needlepoint."

"Go away? No, I don't think so—now. Unless you want to? I'd like to go to Maine quite early in the summer, in June, perhaps. There's something I want to show you."

"All right. We'll go to Maine in June."

Time of sorrow, time of joy.

When they went to Maine she was three months pregnant with their Christmas baby.

Felicity was born December 28, 1938.

DECADE
CLASS

JUNE 1939

The flowers droop upon the cloth, the pale smoke of cigarettes hangs motionless below the ceiling; beyond the open
doors the valley, the river, the lawns, and the trees are as still
beneath the effulgence of sunlight as these hundred women
languidly attentive and waiting upon her words. Martha sees
the grace of drooping shoulders in lace and crepe and chiffon;
pale hands, ringed and careless, among the ashtrays, the empty
coffee cups, the candy dishes, the dying flowers; the slant of hat
brims, the carmine and crimson and scarlet of lips beneath them
. . . For an instant she sees their minds faintly and quickly
shadowed by the preoccupations of personal thought as the
surface of a lake is dulled by a passing flutter of wind.

Sensing their withdrawal she unconsciously withdraws
also, so that it seems as if her words are spoken, not for them,
but for the absent one.

". . . and one more there was. In the silent library, as a thin
paper-covered copy of the *Sentinel* from ten years past falls open
in my hand, I see the grace of those delicate drawings with
which she adorned its pages. These are of her, inanimate. But
in that upper corridor, in those windowed classrooms, dwells
the light and life of her. To those of us who were at Severn
when she came, she is a living memory. For a later generation
of Severn girls there are only those carefully preserved copies
of the *Sentinel* and a little framed picture which hangs with
yours and mine upstairs in Senior Hall. Some may ask, 'Why
is she remembered here?' and we echo their question. She

brought no fame to Severn. Those there have been who went forth from here to success and renown, and the unpretentious walls of this place have been mellowed by the shining of their glory afar.

"On the blue cover of one of those earlier *Sentinel*s is her silhouette of Hortense Giles, the same clever Horty whose portrayal of Rite in *Dark Windows* enthralled New York playgoers last year. Here today is Dr. Alicia Whittaker; and sitting beside our dear friend Mrs. Gracie is Ruth Kane, our feminine Liszt; and here, at my left, is Bennett Marsh of this decade class, author of the deft and enigmatic novel, *Cloak in Tatters.*

". . . If any ask, say of Celia Pence that she left something lovely and unforgettable running like a golden thread through the ordinary fabric of our days. That she was made of 'spirit, fire, and dew . . .' "

She sits down and a rustle like a whisper of protest moves swiftly up the length of the table. Now all their faces are turned toward her wearing their expressions of inquisitiveness, thoughtfulness, and faint unease. Alicia Whittaker's is black-browed and still; Lois Dillon's (née Gracie) is striving tremulously for a smile; a little nearer, on the opposite side of the table, Lois' mother is sitting with her fine lips folded, her eyes cast down.

Bennett Marsh leans toward her:

"Perfectly lovely, Martha. 'Tears for Celia.' And what a beautiful job of subordination you did on the rest of us!"

Still the same Bennett, unchanged and unchanging, the mark of success stamped imperiously upon her pale face, visible in the elegance of her black costume and the smart arrogance of the scarlet quill in her hat; possessing, still, her malicious gift for words to wound. An odd little smile grows upon her face as she sits looking at Martha, her chin propped upon her hand.

"You can, of course, afford to be generous," she remarks. Her glance falls to Martha's place card slanted against her water glass. " 'They also serve who only stand . . . and wait,' " she says softly.

Miss Severn rises in her place at the official head of the table and Martha turns attentively. There stands a woman once so beloved and still so deeply respected that only to look upon her is to turn back time and experience, again, in all its ardor and freshness the youth which lived its convictions and aspirations in clear bright colors unmuddied by qualification. There she stands, Julia Severn, looking at them, one by one, all along the table, missing no one, touching each with her glowing smile; straight and slender in her tailored white silk, bearing her years so lightly, so joyously . . .

The dark eyes meet her own; there is a swift exchange.

There is something she remembers about each one of us, Martha thinks; nor has she forgotten those who are not here.

Tears for Celia! Memories which have moved only in her mind catch suddenly at her heart, filling it with an exquisitely merciless, swift succession of pictures. Celia drying her hair in a sunny window . . . Celia dancing with Austin, her cheek against his shoulder . . . Celia standing among the trees, still and entranced by the beauty of falling leaves . . . Celia's eyes and voice acquiring a new, dark intelligence (No; not that one!) . . . Celia lying on a summer hilltop with her face to the sky, saying, "I'm so happy I shall never die!"

Miss Severn has closed her farewell, those very few, very gracious words with which she has dismissed them at each reunion. Now they are all rising from the long table, drifting toward the doors. Talk—soft, mingled with laughter and gathering in volume as restraint ends—eddies about her.

Helena puts out a hand as she comes near.

"Lovely, Martha." Her firm hand gives Martha's fingers a light, quick pressure. "Come and see me very soon, won't you?"

The stream moves through the doors to the porch, overflowing on the drive and the lawn. It has clouded suddenly; the sun is hidden and, belying the still heat of the afternoon, the river and the hills wear a cool look.

Someone says, "It's going to shower."

She stands on the step, watching the light frocks cluster, waver, hesitate and drift apart like blossoms on a wind . . . Cars move up the drive. Behind her a group of four emerges from the building. She steps aside to let them pass and, giving her a glance that is both curious and cursory, they go down from the porch, linked closely, arm in arm.

Theirs are all unfamiliar faces; their self-possession and their arrogant youth make her feel as if she, like Celia, lives on in this place only by virtue of an imperishable memory. They, comes a quick thought, are the usurpers; these are their faces, this their assurance. Unknowing, they tread a way echoing with phantom footsteps. Thus, unaware, does one come upon the crossroads of the unimagined future.

She steps down, following the grassy edge of the drive, smiling a little as she visions the distant day when Felicity, that fair child who might have been Celia's, shall walk this way.

Across the lawn lies the Hall, its wide awninged porches spread like wings under the summer sky. In her car, moving slowly around the wide curve of the drive, she has one last glimpse of the lovely lawns, the high view of the valley and the river in its depth before dropping downhill into town. But now the scene is a little misted, like something seen in an old mirror.

Twelve years lie, warm with life, within her memory.